PERCENTAGES

OF GUILT

To all my friends who supported me during a very difficult time.

———— ◆ ————

ACKNOWLEDGMENTS

———— ◆ ————

THE MEMBERS OF MY "MONDAY MAYHEM" WRITING GROUP, Jenn Ashton, Carole Beers, Sharon Dean, Clive Rosengren and Tim Wohlforth were instrumental in keeping my plot lines plausible, noting the typos and placing the missing commas. I'm indebted to Professor Joachim Meese at the Faculty of Law of the University of Antwerp for explaining the intricacies of the Belgian justice system to me. Any liberties I took in writing this novel are my own responsibility. My friend Alison McMahon read the complete draft and was a fount of useful suggestions that made it a better novel. Finally, thanks to Jennifer McCord at Coffeetown Press for her incisive comments and shepherding this project towards completion.

Chapter One

Just One Sheet

———◆———

THE GRATING BUZZ OF A DOORBELL wormed its way into Valentin Vermeulen's dream. His subconscious tried hard to integrate the sound into the storyline it had conjured. Despite valiant efforts, it didn't succeed. Whatever else was happening, the doorbell just didn't fit in. The night shift part of his brain gave up and let the day shift take over. He opened his eyes. Small fragments of the dream still hung on, not enough to remember anything, but sufficient to make him wonder where he was.

This disorientation wasn't solely caused by the dream. Vermeulen worked as an investigator for the Office of Internal Oversight Services of the United Nations. In that capacity, he often traveled to faraway places, making sure UN funds expended reach their intended recipients rather than disappearing into someone's pocket. Which meant he woke up quite often wondering where he was.

There was another person in his bed, the clearest hint yet that he was at home. Tessa Bishonga, his partner, was blessed with cast iron sleep. She needed multiple alarms to wake her. True to form, she rolled away without acknowledging that he was getting up to deal with the disturbance.

The doorbell buzzed again. It sounded angry, but not as angry as he was. Who the hell rang the doorbell at eight fifteen on a Saturday? It'd better be good. He shuffled to the intercom. Ever since they'd moved into a larger apartment on West 119th Street in New York City, he couldn't just look out the window anymore.

The male voice from the street was crisp and matter of fact. "Global Express delivery for Mr. Vermeulen."

That didn't seem a good enough reason to interrupt his dream, whatever it had been.

"Can't you just leave it in the mailbox?" Vermeulen said.

"Sorry, I need a signature."

Of course, he needed a signature.

"Who is the sender?" he said.

There was a pause.

"Sorry, I don't know how to pronounce the words."

That was it, then. He had to go downstairs. The night was officially over. He slipped on yesterday's clothes and padded down the two stairs to the front door.

Outside stood a courier from a service he'd never seen before. The uniform wasn't brown or purple or yellow. It was some poisonous green. *Global Express* was embroidered on the shirt in yellow thread, right above the man's heart. He stuck a tablet under Vermeulen's nose and pointed to a box at the bottom of the screen. Vermeulen scribbled an approximation of his signature, the courier handed over an envelope and went back to his van.

Even before reading anything, Vermeulen knew the envelope came from abroad. It wasn't the right size for something American, "A4" rather than "letter" or "legal." He looked at the sender label. It said, "*Rechtbank Van Eerste Aanleg, Gerechtgebouw, Bolivarplaats, Antwerpen.*" He'd never heard of the street. As far as he remembered, the Justice Building was on Britselei. Even so, why would he get mail from the Court of First Instance? The handwritten name above the address was illegible. He looked after the green van disappearing on Amsterdam Avenue.

Talk about a blast from the past. Before he started his job at the UN, he worked in the prosecutor's office in Antwerp. The Court of First Instance was his bailiwick. He didn't know that it had moved and couldn't imagine why he'd get mail from it.

He walked back up to the apartment. The envelope wasn't very heavy. Not a stack of papers, just one, maybe two sheets. That seemed like a good sign, until he remembered that the stack of papers usually arrives with the follow-up mail, providing the details necessary to back up the initial message.

It could only be bad news. Good news wouldn't require expensive Global Express delivery on a Saturday morning. The people in Antwerp had no reason to contact him. He'd been gone too long to get some certificate for meritorious service. And once he quit that job and moved on to the United Nations, he might as well have moved to Mars. Contact with former colleagues, even those he got on with well, died off quickly. Besides, just saying, "Hi, long time no see," didn't require Global Express.

In the kitchen, he looked at the envelope.

Coffee first?

Whatever it was, a cup of coffee would certainly fortify him. But then, how bad could it be? It'd been thirteen years.

So, no coffee.

He grabbed a knife from the magnetic holder by the stove and sliced open the envelope. One sheet—just as he'd guessed. It was important. He could tell even without reading. Important enough to require four paragraphs, leaving barely enough space for the signature.

He started reading.

A curt greeting followed by what read like a court decision—two paragraphs summarizing the facts he remembered better than he'd hoped. It had been his last case in Antwerp, before he got the job with the United Nations. The third paragraph also didn't tell him anything new. Yes, he'd been seconded to the investigation because of his expertise in financial crimes.

It was the fourth paragraph that ruined his morning for good. A review of the case had revealed serious irregularities. There was convincing evidence of malfeasance in the prosecutor's office, warranting a thorough investigation. The demand was straightforward: *Per §14 of the civil service employment act, you are hereby required to appear in Antwerp and explain your actions in this case. Please present yourself no later than Wednesday, October 15, 2015.*

* * *

Unbelievable. That was the first word he could think of.

Coffee was the second. He felt a bit nauseous. Caffeine would straighten out his stomach. It always did. He hit the button on the grinder and its raucous noise filled the kitchen. He put filter paper into the coffeemaker and waited for the grinding to stop.

Caught up in his own private anger, he flinched at a sudden touch. Tessa stood behind him and put her arms around him.

"You're making quite the racket for a Saturday morning," she said.

He turned around. Her short, graying hair was still flattened by sleep, the cinnamon skin on her arm showed the imprint of the pillow case seam, because she slept on her belly with one arm stuck under the pillow.

They'd met five years ago during his investigation in Darfur. A native of Zambia, she'd been a top freelancer, producing features and commentary for many international news outlets. For a while—due to their unpredictable schedules—their relationship was more off than on. It would have been easy to let it fade away. But their harrowing experiences in Mozambique a few years before pushed them towards each other as only danger could. They moved in together in New York City and Tessa became the co-editor for a curated investigative news website.

Her eyes were soft as she said, "Is it that bad?"

He pointed to the letter that lay on the counter next to the Global Express envelope. She picked it up and looked at it. "Your former employer?"

He nodded.

"I can't read Flemish. Tell me what it says."

"It's about my last case. Something's cropped up. They want me to come."

She looked at the signature and the seal. "Are you going?"

"I don't have a choice. They invoked §14. It means that I have to make myself available if any case in which I participated is being revisited. If I don't come, I'll be in violation of my contract. That could mean an arrest warrant and an Interpol Red Notice. Next thing you know, the cops'll be knocking at our door."

"What do they want?"

"I have no idea. The letter couldn't be vaguer. Supposedly, there are irregularities and convincing evidence of malfeasance in the prosecutor's office. What does that even mean?"

"Well, you worked on the case. Remember anything?"

"It's been thirteen years, and I need coffee."

He spooned the grounds into the filter cone and filled the reservoir with water. Once the machine started sputtering, he sat down at the kitchen table.

Tessa shook her head.

"How strange," she said. "Bureaucracies are loath to spend money, so it must be something major. They wouldn't pay for your ticket otherwise."

"Well, that's also part of §14. The *quid pro quo*. The employee's association wouldn't have agreed to it otherwise."

"And you really don't know what they want? What was the case about?"

The coffee wasn't finished brewing yet, but he got up and stole a cup anyway. He blew across the surface of the hot liquid and sipped it carefully. Being upset was no reason to burn his tongue. He sat down again.

"Cocaine. Masses of it," he said.

"What did you have to do with drugs? I thought you were the money man."

"Yes, that's why I was brought in. To find out how all that money got back to South America. We figured that arresting dealers was like emptying the North Sea with a spoon. There'd be two new ones for every arrest. But if we could turn off the money flow, it'd make the cartels in Colombia sit up and maybe they'd skip Antwerp."

"Honestly," Tessa said. "That sounds a bit naive to me."

He slapped his palm against his forehead. "Oh, how stupid of us. Where were you when we needed you?"

His sarcasm made Tessa frown.

"You sound just like my boss did back then," he said. "And you're wrong, Antwerp is the largest European port for the Latin American drug trade, so cutting off the return flow of cash would have had an impact."

"Okay, okay. I get it. Why would they arrest you if you don't show up?"

He shrugged. "Because they can? But, I think they are on a fishing expedition."

"And you have no idea what malfeasance they could be speaking about?"

Vermeulen shrugged.

"No laws broken, or suspects roughed up?" she said.

Vermeulen rolled his eyes. "Really? You know me better than that."

"I do, but you received that letter."

She got up and poured herself a cup of coffee. "You want more?" He nodded and she topped off his cup. After getting milk from the refrigerator she sat down again.

"Well, someone must have done something."

"You know how it goes. Everybody is up to their eyeballs into the case. You have to cut corners at some point. We never did anything illegal. I made sure of that, because I knew there's nothing worse than to jeopardize a case that way."

"Relax, love. I believe you. I'm on your side. I just don't think they'd call you back over improper paperwork. I'd like to know what awaits you when you arrive in Antwerp."

"That makes two of us."

"Do you know if it's going to be a deposition, or just an interview?"

"It could be anything from a friendly chat to going before the judge."

"Wait, why is a judge involved. Aren't they investigating first?"

"The Belgian judicial system is based on the Napoleonic Code. A presiding judge and a public prosecutor handle the investigation of a case."

"That's too weird. Do you want me to come?"

Vermeulen shook his head.

"No, this is my thing. I don't see why you should come along."

"It's no bother. I can do my work from anywhere as long as I have internet access. They do have that in Antwerp, right?"

"Yes, they do, but no, I don't think it's a good idea for you to come. For all I know I'll be done in a day and then you'll have taken a long trip for nothing."

He was pretty certain it would take longer than that. Maybe a lot longer.

"We could stay on and you could show me where you grew up."

"We can do that some other time. Really, it's best if I go alone and take care of this. Better to keep a low profile about all of this right now."

"Will you see Marieke?" she said.

Finally, the cat was out of the bag. Marieke was his ex-wife, the mother of his daughter Gaby. It was their divorce that had made him flee Antwerp and take the job with the UN. Tessa had met Marieke once in Vienna. It wasn't a happy occasion. Funny thing was, his ex-wife was the last thing Tessa had to worry about. The rest was an entirely different story.

CHAPTER TWO

A SMALL ENVELOPE

———— ◆ ————

THE THALYS BULLET TRAIN PULLED INTO Antwerp's Centraal Station and glided to a halt. A female voice announced the arrival in three languages. If it hadn't been for that voice, Vermeulen would've dozed right through the stop and ended up in Brussels or Paris. He grabbed his briefcase, his bag and hurried to the exit. He'd managed to book a flight to Amsterdam, then took a train that got him to Antwerp on Wednesday, barely in time for his first appointment.

He was sleepy because he'd spent the six-hour flight between JFK and Amsterdam's Schiphol Airport in the last row of the plane. Between wandering passengers bumping him, the toilet's noisy evacuations, and the audio of his neighbor's action movie bleeding from his headphones, the flight had been sheer misery. He'd wisely abstained from alcohol, so the inevitable headache was just a dull pain without the angry pulsing of a hangover.

The Thalys whisked away with a whoosh and left him standing on the platform. For a moment, he thought he'd gotten off at the wrong stop. He remembered an airy arched roof, not an underground platform. The station must have gone through an expansion to accommodate the express train. An escalator carried him up a level and there he found himself in the Centraal Station he remembered. It was even brighter and airier. The renovations must have been thorough. The steel girders were painted a bright red and the glass panes between them were clear and let in the sunlight.

He left the platform and entered the station proper. It too looked like it had just been scrubbed. Muted pastels, like a tasteful wedding cake, recalled the station's past glory days. They definitely hadn't skimped. A bench looked inviting, but he needed to get to his hotel, take a shower and get an hour of sleep before his first meeting at the prosecutor's office.

The square outside the station was bustling with locals and tourists alike. The sun was surprising. October in Antwerp was the month that brought the first winter rains with steel gray clouds. Instead, fluffy cumuli drifted across the blue sky from the North Sea and headed toward Germany. Maybe the weather was a good omen. He hailed a taxi and settled into the back seat for the ride to the hotel where he had reserved a room.

Antwerp. Vermeulen had lived in the city for over two decades. He'd arrived as a teenager when his parents lost their small farm by the North Sea and moved the family to the city. His father ended up selling insurance for a living and died not too long afterwards. He never got really sick, just lost the will to live. Vermeulen never knew if it was the shame of having lost the farm, or having to cajole people into buying policies they really didn't need. Vermeulen had finished high school here, and, after his mandatory military service, gone to law school. His degree in his pocket, he'd taken the job at the Prosecutor's office.

In a way, Antwerp reminded him of Manhattan. The city was just as densely built, compact, and the Schelde River defined one of its boundaries. That's where the similarities ended. There were no high-rises since buildings couldn't be taller than the cathedral. The streetscape was dominated by four or five story buildings, often with shops at street level and housing above. Each structure had its own character, their individualism more important than any sense of uniform look. And there was no grid. The streets followed a logic long since forgotten. *Going around the block* wasn't even a figure of speech here. And there were cyclists everywhere.

The hotel wasn't far from the Schelde River. It was of the budget variety. His room was functional, clean and sparse. The Scandinavian decor made the lack of amenities feel stylish. He dropped the suitcase, took off his shoes and texted Tessa that he'd arrived safely. Exhausted, he fell onto the bed. The shower could wait.

* * *

THERE MUST HAVE BEEN A RUSTLE, but it hadn't been loud enough to disturb his sleep. When his alarm did wake him up—an hour later and with barely enough time to get showered and make the meeting—a small white envelope lay there on the carpet.

There was nothing special about it. He picked it up. His name was scrawled on the front. Odd. The office had his phone number and the name of the hotel. They would have messengered any documents or called if it was urgent. Nobody else knew he was coming and where he was staying. He hadn't even told his ex-wife, Marieke.

He opened the envelope. There was no letter or note. Nothing written at all. Just a photo. And a bad one at that, printed with a cheap printer on regular paper. The white streaks told him that the printhead needed serious cleaning. The photo showed a man walking past a building with beige stucco walls. The man was carrying an A4-sized envelope. Nothing interesting to see. Except, there was something familiar about the figure. Vermeulen had seen that coat before. It looked very much like a coat he once owned. A second look confirmed his suspicion. He was the man in the picture. His hair was longer then, and he sported a mustache, which may have been the final straw that broke his marriage.

The absence of any visual cues made it impossible to tell where he was walking. It had to be Antwerp because he'd gotten rid of the mustache before moving to New York City. But where in Antwerp? And what was in the envelope?

His phone dinged. Damn, the meeting. But it wasn't a calendar reminder, it was a text message from an unknown sender. All it said was, *nummer een.*

Who would send this photo? Who even had his US phone number. If this was number one, would there be more? He had no recollection of walking on a street holding an envelope. Obviously, he must have done so multiple times. But the stucco wall in the photo didn't trigger any memory.

His phone buzzed with a reminder for the meeting. Better get in the shower fast. The photo and the strange text kept him from enjoying the warm water. A call came in as he was toweling off. This time it was the office telling him that someone was on his way to pick him up. That improved his mood a lot. So far, they had treated him as if he were the dodgy uncle that had to be invited to the family reunion, even though nobody wanted him. No sense that he'd been a successful prosecutor, who'd worked there for almost a decade. Sending a car was the first decent gesture since he'd gotten the express delivery in New York.

He finished in the bathroom and got dressed. The photo and envelope lay on the bed. He decided to leave them in the room. Without knowing what was behind it, it'd be better to wait before showing it to his former colleagues. He put the photo back in the envelope and stashed it in his suitcase.

Outside the hotel, a gray Renault stood in the no-parking zone. Its driver side door opened as Vermeulen stepped onto the sidewalk. Jan Smits had come to pick him up. Smits was a short, pudgy man with a round face and a rumpled suit. He'd been at the periphery of the investigation thirteen years ago. Vermeulen hadn't dealt much with him but remembered him as a pleasant man. Smits had a big smile on his face.

"*Goedemiddag,* Valentin. It's been too long."

They shook hands.

"Hey Jan. It has been. For sure. Thanks for coming to pick me up. How are things at the office?"

"Same old. Trying to stay ahead of the bad guys and barely making it. The terrorism thing has made everything else more difficult. Since Molenbeek, everyone is on high alert."

Vermeulen had followed the news about the terrorist cell in Molenbeek that was responsible for the attacks in Paris and Brussels. But it hadn't occurred to him that it would impact the prosecutor's office in Antwerp. "I can only imagine," he said. "Are you involved in terror cases?"

"Not at the moment. As a matter of fact, my front burner item is you."

They got into the car.

"Can you fill me in on what's going on?" Vermeulen said. "The information I got from the office was vague at best."

"It's total bullshit. I remember that case. You went by the book."

"Thanks. I'm glad you think so. Why is the office even pursuing this?"

"Well, they haven't told me."

"How come, if I'm on your front burner?"

"They're keeping their cards close to their chests. All I know is there's been a complaint. No word as to who's complained. The office is on the hook for damages. Unfortunately, it landed on the desk of a judge who's on a mission to 'clean up the department, root out corruption,' you know the spiel. And its easiest to make an example of an ex-prosecutor. He's going to get credit for cleaning up past messes without ruffling the feathers of the current staff. Like I said, total bullshit."

Vermeulen's collar suddenly felt too tight. This sounded dangerously different from the letter. Instead of helping solve a problem, it sounded as if Vermeulen *was* the problem, and, even worse, the sacrificial lamb to make the prosecutor's office look better? No wonder they didn't bother to tell him what he was accused of. Having someone run into a buzz saw works best if they don't see it.

"This judge, do I know him?" he said.

"Martijn Mesman? Nah, he came after you left. Young, ambitious, with the right connections. And I mean 'right' in the political sense. Ever since the *Nieuw-Vlaamse Alliantie* got to be the largest party in parliament, they are throwing their weight around. The judge is one of them."

Vermeulen knew about the New Flemish Alliance. Another of those pseudo-populist movements that whipped up anger against the elites, to enact policies that benefitted the very same. He despised what they stood for.

CHAPTER THREE

GROWTH INDUSTRY

———◆———

TRAFFIC SEEMED WORSE THAN HE REMEMBERED. Although it was past the main tourist season, the sidewalks were busy. And cyclists darted in and out of traffic is if they wore invisible armor. The city also seemed greener. Maybe that was just the sun highlighting the leaves of the trees. Despite the dread he felt after Smits' account of the investigation, the familiarity of the city lifted his spirits.

When they reached Bolivarplaats, Vermeulen whistled with surprise. The new justice palace was a stunning edifice with sharp angled roof structures resembling sails. Six of them towered over the building. The rest were shallower. They all faced the Schelde to the west as if to catch the wind coming from the North Sea some fifty miles away.

"That wasn't here when you left, was it?" Smits said.

"No. I remember talk about a new building, but construction hadn't started yet."

"They call it the 'butterfly palace.' Some famous British architect designed it. It looks nice enough, and the lighting is good, what with all the glass. Most criminal justice offices are here now. They use the old justice palace only for the Assize Court sessions. That's supposed to be renovated eventually."

"Looks like justice is a growth industry," Vermeulen said.

"Tell me about it."

A wide staircase rose from the street level to the entrance, but Smits didn't head for it. He turned right and navigated to a parking area for employees. They used a side entrance instead.

Inside, the building was as bright as Smits had promised. The sail-like roof structures let in a lot of natural light. Quite unlike the dark office on Britselei, where Vermeulen had spent most of his work time. They took the stairs up two levels and entered the prosecutor's headquarters. The wooden floors were a pleasant medium brown and interspersed glass sections allowed light to reach the floors below.

Smits took him to his office. The air was cool. A hint of river aroma added a pleasant tang. This was good; the new building, the new offices. No memories, good or bad, to trigger any flashbacks. The past wasn't just past, it had happened elsewhere. He couldn't have asked for more. He took a deep breath and let the air out. The anxiety that had been building since Smits picked him up eased a little.

The office itself was as modern as the building—wood, brushed metal and glass. There were two desks, facing each other. One was clearly used, the other neat and ordered.

"No office mate?" Vermeulen said.

"He's on vacation at the moment. Just as well. He's such a neat freak. Drives me nuts."

Smits's desk was messy enough for two.

"So, what's the plan?" Vermeulen said.

"We have a meeting with Mesman in a little while. No big deal, just saying hello. Tomorrow morning the deposition begins. Alas, I'm not conducting that."

"Do I need a lawyer?"

"You've been in the US too long. We're still in the investigative phase. No accusations are being made. They're just gathering information and putting it in the file. If the judge decides that the file warrants a trial, you'd probably need a lawyer. But don't worry. It will never go that far."

Vermeulen didn't share his colleague's sunny assessment. If anything, the years at the UN had taught him to be optimistic without harboring illusions. He hadn't done anything wrong and part of him knew there wouldn't be a trial. But he also knew that, given the right circumstances, the facts didn't matter. He had to be wary.

The politics of the case worried him. A magistrate wanting to make a name for himself by clearing past misdeeds of the judiciary fit right into the current climate. He remembered reading about a survey taken a couple of years after he left. The results indicated that the majority of Belgians didn't think they'd get a fair trial in court. Their opinion of lawyers was terrible. He didn't know if public opinion had changed in the years since. Some of what had gone on in the past wouldn't have inspired confidence in the judiciary. Worries about terrorism might have changed that.

"Let's go," Smits said. "We don't want to be late for the magistrate."

* * *

Martijn Mesman, the magistrate, looked impossibly young. *Does he even shave?* Vermeulen couldn't tell. He had a longish pale face with hollow cheeks and narrow gray eyes. His hair was cut very short and showed signs of early baldness. The rest of him was standard issue bureaucrat—white shirt, light blue tie and dark gray suit, the jacket of which was hung over the back rest of his chair.

"*Welkom terug*, Mr. Vermeulen," Mesman said. "Have a seat. Glad you could make it on such short notice."

He didn't really have a choice, but he said, "Thank you, *Magistraat* Mesman."

"You must think this is a lot of ado about an old case. It certainly would appear that way from the outside. But a complaint has been filed, a very serious complaint, claiming that this office is responsible for the death of a man. The complainant is demanding compensation. The reputation of this office is at stake."

"I don't understand why this requires my presence here. I'm sure that could have been handled by phone or mail."

"The complaint holds you responsible for the death in question."

Vermeulen's mouth went dry. *Responsible for a death?*

"That's preposterous," he said. He struggled to keep his bland expression, almost succeeded. "Who's making this accusation?"

Mesman flipped through a couple of pages. "One Theo Vinke. Do you know this man?"

Vermeulen's palms felt damp. Theo was the son of a smalltime gangster. But he'd been the exact opposite of his father. He'd finished school and taken a regular job afterwards. Vermeulen had thought the son wouldn't follow in his father's footsteps. Maybe he had after all.

"I know who he is," he said. "But I don't recall ever meeting him. It's a ludicrous accusation. I focused on the money laundering aspect of the investigation. I spent most of my time in the office, looking at numbers and company invoices. Who's the corpse anyway?"

"His father, Frans Vinke." Mesman was curiously detached. "Theo Vinke is accusing you of coercing his father to spy on the syndicate you were investigating and, later, of leaking the identity of his father to the syndicate. Vinke senior was murdered as a result of that leak."

Vermeulen's blood was pulsing in his ears now. Frans Vinke had been a conniving little toady. Not worth a bucket of warm spit. He was the kind of man who'd throw people under the bus if it served him, but sucked up to the bosses whenever they were around. When Vermeulen got the news of his death, all he thought was, *good riddance.* Impossible that this toad should come back from the dead, as it were, to haunt him. "That's utter baloney," he said a little too loud. "And you know it."

Mesman reacted predictably. He puffed himself up and leaned forward.

"I don't know that. We can't ignore this complaint, and especially not the liability."

Vermeulen dialed back his volume. "Why is this happening now, thirteen years later?"

"Theo Vinke only now received this information as part of a cache of documents he inherited after the death of his father-in-law, a well-known figure in the criminal underworld."

Vermeulen's skin tightened. Theo's father-in-law was Jordi Vanderfeld, a lawyer and mob fixer. Whenever his name came up, trouble followed. Hell, he lived up to his reputation even after his death.

"And why isn't the person who murdered the informant being held responsible?" Vermeulen said, hoping to cover his agitation.

"The suspect in that killing was himself murdered shortly after Vinke's death."

Vermeulen knew that, of course. But it didn't hurt to plead ignorance.

"We will investigate this matter thoroughly," Mesman said. "Then I'll decide if charges should be filed. I promise you, Mr. Vermeulen, that I will conduct this matter fairly and expeditiously. No need to keep you here longer than necessary. Your deposition starts tomorrow morning at nine. Don't be late."

With that Vermeulen and Smits were excused.

"Pompous ass," Smits said after he'd closed the door. "He's half my age and pretends to have the gravitas of King Leopold."

And his politics too, Vermeulen thought. His ribcage seemed too small to contain his racing heart. His worst expectations were coming true. He needed a plan.

Back in Smits's office, he asked to see the case file. Smits shook his head. "I wish I could, but I don't have it."

"How can I defend myself if I don't know what accusations are leveled against me?"

"Come on Valentin, you know how this goes. First comes the investigation, then comes the trial. The file is kept by the judge in charge."

"And what should I do in the meantime? Sit tight and twiddle my thumbs? I do have a job and I can't hang about forever. I've got a week. Then I have to get back to New York."

"I think in a week this will all be over and done with. Just tell them what happened. That should set the record straight and show that a random document in the estate of a bent lawyer isn't evidence that a crime was committed."

Vermeulen nodded, but Smits's assurance sounded hollow.

"Has Theo stayed above board. What's he doing today?" Vermeulen said.

"He owns a chain of *frietkots*."

"What? He manages a bunch of shops selling fries? I thought he'd made a break from crime. You know that *frietkots* are used to launder money, don't you?"

"Of course, it's the first thing we checked." Smits shrugged. "He's clean."

"What's the name of the chain?"

"Each *frietkot* has a different name—it's all about history, authenticity and all that—but he's the owner."

"And he's really clean? No trouble with the law?"

"Well, he got in trouble for hiring employees off the books. There were some troubles with suppliers and late payments. Not your clean-cut neighborhood entrepreneur, for sure. But we didn't see any criminal associations. And definitely no connections to organized crime or drugs."

Vermeulen shook his head. Frans Vinke. After all these years. Risen from the dead, so to speak. The headache was back, pulsing in his temples and his jacket was too hot. He'd be lucky if he got back home in one piece.

And to think that it was Jan Smits's call thirteen years ago that had started the whole messy affair.

Chapter Four

Correspondence Course

————— ♦ —————

"THIS BETTER BE GOOD," VERMEULEN SAID, as he entered Jan Smits's office. It was June 2002 and he'd been with the task force for less than a week. Things weren't going so well. Everyone was focused on stopping the flow of cocaine coming in, as if they could seize everything. Nobody was paying attention to all the money involved. Sure, the money part was why he was asked to join, but he expected the basics to be in place. There was nothing. Vermeulen had to start from zero. Then Smits called and told him to come over and talk to this guy who might have information. Vermeulen had too much on his plate to stop everything and talk to some small time criminal.

"I think it will be worth it," Smits said after Vermeulen came to his office. "Meet Franz Vinke. He was picked up for possession of stolen goods. Not the first time, either. He refused to talk to the cops. After a day in the slammer, he asked to speak to a prosecutor about confidential matters. That's how he ended up here."

Vinke was at that fuzzy middle-aged range. He could have been in his forties or his fifties. Right then, he looked like he was pushing that upper limit. A day in jail will do that for you. He had that unkempt, unwashed look and the pallor of not having seen sunlight.

"What's he fencing?" Vermeulen said.

"Twenty stolen cars with forged titles. We're talking top models, Beemers, Audis and Benzes. He's getting them ready for export to Venezuela."

"That's not true," Vinke said in a whiny voice. "I didn't know these titles were forged. I bought the cars in good faith."

"He has no receipts and won't tell me who the sellers were," Smits said.

"That's not public information," Vinke said. He sat up a little straighter. "You know, like trade secrets. You can't make me give that up. It's my competitive advantage."

"Where'd you learn those big words?" Smits said. "Take a correspondence course from some online college in Turkmenistan?"

"Why am I listening to this? I've better things to do," Vermeulen said. This small-time crook couldn't help him with the flow of money.

"I know a few things," Vinke said. "About how money is moved."

"He also threw out some big names," Smits said. "Do Bastiaan Beukes or Jordi Vanderfeld mean anything to you?"

Vermeulen's impatience evaporated like a drop of water on a hotplate. Beukes was said to run the largest drug syndicate and Vanderfeld was the legal brain that kept the authorities at bay.

"I thought so," Smits said.

"Can we step outside for a moment?"

After closing the door, Vermeulen said, "How strong is the case against him?"

Smits shrugged. "We got the cars and can prove that the titles are forged."

"But if he claims he bought them in good faith, it's his word against the prosecutors?"

"Pretty much. Especially if he makes up some fake sellers. The signatures are illegible. We can confiscate the cars, but we have little on him."

Vermeulen was quiet for a moment.

"How many priors?" he said.

"At least six or seven. Nothing violent, all property crimes. He's the poster child of the repeat offenders."

Vermeulen nodded. "Let me have some time alone with him."

Smits gave his okay.

Back in the room, the door closed again, Vermeulen fixed Vinke with a stare.

"Tell me more about the money."

"They have several ways to move it," Vinke said.

"Tell me something I don't know."

"They use couriers."

Vermeulen shook his head. "I said something I don't know. How do you know Beukes and Vanderfeld?"

"Well, I'm a man of the world. I get around, know people."

"Nonsense. You are a bottom feeder. How do you know them?"

"Professionally and personally." Vinke had a smug smile on his face.

"Double nonsense. The likes of Beukes and Vanderfeld wouldn't come near the sewer where you live."

Vinke sulked. "That's not true."

"What? The sewer part?"

"Everything. I'm a small businessman and have dealings with other businessmen."

"So Beukes set up the export deal for your stolen cars?"

"I'm perfectly capable of arranging these sales myself."

"Oh yeah? Where'd you apply for the export license?"

Vinke's pretense fell apart immediately. He didn't even try to make up some story. "Beukes and Vanderfeld are family," he said. "They help out here and there."

Vermeulen made a quick calculation. If Vinke wasn't lying, this was the best news he's had since joining the task force.

"Ever heard of the Habitual Criminal Statute? It was passed a few years back. Its sole purpose is taking lowlifes out of circulation. Congratulations, you've accumulated enough convictions to qualify for the prize, extended incarceration. Once we nail you for the current charge, you are looking at five, most likely ten years in prison."

Vinke grumbled. "I didn't do anything wrong. How could I know those cars were stolen? The paperwork looked correct."

"The paperwork is so lousy a blind man could have seen that it was forged. Besides, what do you know about selling cars to Venezuela? Hell, you couldn't find Venezuela on a map with an arrow pointing to it. You've been a tool all your life, but it turns out you have one redeeming quality."

Vinke was all ears.

"Wait here," he said and steps into the corridor. Smits was standing there, waiting.

"I have to make a call," Vermeulen said and walked away from Smits. He found an empty office and called Alex Timmerman, the lead detective on the task force.

"Hey Alex, I'm talking to a small-time crook, Frans Vinke, who claims that Beukes and Vanderfeld are family. Is he making this up?"

"Who? Vinke? Never heard of him. I bet he's blowing smoke. But I'll check. Call you right back."

The ten minutes that passed before the return call felt like a day. Could this be a crucial break in their investigation?

Timmerman called back. "You won't believe this, but he's right. His wife is Beukes's sister and his son is engaged to Vanderfeld's daughter. Where'd you find him?"

"He's being held on possession of stolen goods. What's our play here?"

"You interrogate the hell out of him," Timmerman said.

"He isn't playing along, so I put the squeeze on him. Made up some statute and claimed he'd be in prison for the next few years," Vermeulen said.

"Made up a statute? You kidding me? Listen, man, I'm game for almost anything, but that's crossing the line."

"I just wanted to get him good and scared. I think I can push him into becoming an informant."

"On the basis of a made-up law and an empty threat? I don't think so."

Vermeulen thought it was. "What's the worst that could happen? He says, 'No.'"

"Worst case is that he sues us for extortion."

"Come on." Vermeulen was adamant. "He won't. He's got a string of priors. If this blows up, I can always claim that he misunderstood. Remember, he's a small-time crook. He even tried to suck up to me while we talked."

"I don't know, Val. We need an informant, I just don't like the way you're going about it."

"Nothing will come of it, I'm sure." In truth, Vermeulen wasn't, but the stakes were high and they wanted some results.

"Okay, then," Timmerman said. Vermeulen could hear a sigh before he ended the call and went back to the room where Vinke was waiting. He asked Smits to leave once more.

"I told you before that you've won the extended detention lottery and that your prize will be up to ten years in prison. Well, you've also won a far better prize. It's the get-out-of-jail prize. It's a one-time offer and it comes with one condition."

"What is that?" Vinke said, squinting.

"You spy on Beukes and Vanderfeld for us."

"What? No way. You leave my family out of it."

"The alternative is prison. Your choice. Maybe your wife won't take kindly to your being a dumb enough criminal to get caught. Maybe she doesn't even know. And imagine what her brother will think. Here he set you up with an easy deal selling stolen cars to Venezuela and you blow that and expose him. Believe me, you're better off helping us."

Vinke got up, all huffing and puffing. "Never."

Vermeulen waited.

Vinke started pacing. He mumbled to himself, gave Vermeulen deadly looks.

"You can't make me do this," he said.

"You're right. But I can make sure that you go to prison. I can also find a way to let Beukes know you ratted on him."

Vinke stopped, pale now. "You can't do that. I'd never rat on him."

"Well, here's a unique paradox, if you don't rat on him, he'll think you did. But if you do, he'll never find out."

"This is blackmail."

Vermeulen shook his head. "I wouldn't call it that. I'm giving you choices. You are perfectly free to choose what suits you best. Maybe some time in prison would do you good. You know, set you on the straight and narrow. Earn the respect of your wife, be an example to your son."

Vermeulen turned toward the door, reached for the handle. "Yeah," he said. "I think you're right, prison would be better for you." He opened the door.

"Wait," Vinke said. Vermeulen turned around. Vinke's face was ashen now, his body deflated. "I'll do it."

Vermeulen took a deep breath. They left the office together. Smits stood in the corridor, eyes wide.

"Where are you taking him?" he said.

"The task force will take over this case," Vermeulen said. "I got the okay from above. Feel free to check. And he needs his things back."

Smits shrugged with a whatever look on his face. "Meet me at the exit." He left. At the end of the corridor, he turned and hollered, "What do I do with the stolen cars?"

"How about returning 'em to their rightful owners," Vermeulen said.

The look on Vinke's face told him that his decision wasn't popular, but he wasn't going to let Vinke export those stolen cars. It's one thing to strong-arm a crook into becoming a rat. It's quite another to abet a crime. That really would come back to bite him.

CHAPTER FIVE

CELLULAR LEVEL

———— ◆ ————

THE MEMORY OF MEETING VINKE BACK in 2002 made Vermeulen antsy. As soon as he was done, he decided to walk back to his hotel. The exercise would do him good and he needed to walk off his nervous energy. The sun was well past its zenith and the wind had picked up. He shivered and put on the jacket he'd slung over his shoulder.

Gijzelaarstraat wasn't one of the boulevards of Antwerp. It was narrow, the sidewalk was in need of repair and there were no trees. Despite that, it was just the right street to make him feel like he'd come home.

Home.

It wasn't a word he'd thought about much since moving to New York City. So much of his job at the UN involved travel with all its drawbacks—hotels that felt alike, no matter where in the world, hasty meals that were forgotten as soon as the plate was empty, an army of hospitality workers who smiled in hope of a generous tip. For a while, his apartment at Gansevoort Street in New York City was as close to a home he had. Then he and Tessa moved in together, and he hadn't lived at the new place long enough to consider it home.

Against all expectation, feeling the uneven sidewalk pavers through the soles of his shoes brought back that feeling of home he'd longed for without knowing it. It was tenuous at first, not a rush of emotion. Lots of things were different from what he remembered. More cars, a lot more bikes that seemed to ignore all rules of the road, more people with browner skin tones. But there was that inkling that he knew how this city worked. A familiarity that made him lift his feet just a bit higher without having to trip first because his body knew the pavers weren't flush.

At the end of that first block, a smile had returned to his face. Of all the places in the world, he knew Antwerp best. No matter the accusations against him, this was the place to face them. He knew this city at a cellular level. Whatever they thought they had on him, he'd prove them wrong.

He reached Gillisplaats, dodged a mom on a cargo bike carrying two kids, and passed the old *Waterpoort*. At one point this gate had been part of the wall that surrounded old Antwerp. Since then, it had been moved so much that it had acquired the name "walking gate." It stood alone on its square, amid flower beds, looking a little lost. He continued along the green zone, past the Museum for Contemporary Art.

A bar with the clever name "Heming Way" caught his attention and he went inside. Despite the name, it wasn't a busy place, just a couple of tables were occupied. He climbed on a barstool and ordered a De Kooning without having to wonder if they carried his favorite beer. The bartender, who could have been Spanish or Latin American, drew the beer and set the glass on a cardboard coaster in front of him.

"Visiting the city?" he said.

Vermeulen raised his eyebrows. "Why do you ask?"

"You don't sound like you're from here, is all."

That deflated his good mood. "I lived here for twenty-odd years."

"Oh. Is that so? Must've been a while ago. Where'd you go?"

"New York."

"Ah, makes sense. Your Flemish has bit of that American twang. Welcome home."

The man turned and busied himself stacking glasses at the other end of the bar.

Some kind of welcome.

He refused to let the bartender's comment burst his bubble. Let them think what they want. This felt closer to home than any place he'd been. He finished his beer, left a few euros by the glass and walked out.

Along the way, he saw new construction in red brick that mimicked the old port storage buildings, narrow but tall, with peaked roofs. Despite their recent construction they fit into the streetscape as if they had always been there. They were a bit like him. He continued to the *Grote Markt* with the city hall to the West, the *Brabo Fountain* at the center and the *Onze-Lieve-Vrouwe-Kathedraal* to the East. Against the early evening sky, the cathedral was awe-inspiring. The tallest building in the city, its spire looked over the Schelde River on one side and the rest of the city on the other. The last time he thought about the cathedral was during his mission in the Côte d'Ivoire where he was astonished by the size of the local basilica.

He stopped at *Frituur* N. 1 and ordered a tray of fries with mayo, a *frikandel* and, a bottle of Jupiter. *Frituur* N. 1 was a busy place. The pile of fries that had gotten their first fry in beef tallow told him they expected a lot more customers as the evening progressed. He picked up his order, sat on a bench outside and was in heaven. There was nothing like Belgian fries. A couple joined him at the other end of the bench, spearing their fries with the tiny forks that had accompanied fries for as long as he could remember. He nodded to them, they nodded back and he returned to his reverie. After finishing his meal, he tossed the cardboard trays into the trash. It was getting cold. He rubbed his hands. Time to go to his hotel. He had to get unpacked and ready for the morning.

The walk from the *Grote Markt* to his hotel was only a few blocks, but it was along one of the less picturesque lanes. There were a few restaurants with outdoor seating, but the colorful umbrellas didn't quite make up for the sullen feel of the passage. It didn't matter much to him. The fast food was all he was going to eat that night. He looked into the window of a chocolate shop. One of those colorful packages would be perfect for Tessa.

As he turned back into the lane he saw that the couple who'd eaten their fries at the same bench were lingering farther down the lane. By itself, that meant nothing since there were other people walking one way or the other. Except, he'd just passed the same spot and there was nothing to see, no reason to linger. He looked right at them. The man met his stare, then turned his head to kiss the woman.

A couple of lovers?

Vermeulen's gut rejected that assessment. The gaze of the man had been too deliberate. The kiss that followed looked staged rather than real. It was time for evasive tactics, lead them away from his hotel. He took a right at the next intersection and walked east at a good clip. A block farther, he turned left and stepped into a restaurant entrance. Through the window, he saw that the couple had followed him. They stopped at the intersection and looked for him. The woman remained at the spot while the man proceeded in the direction Vermeulen could have gone.

Vermeulen walked past the bar toward the kitchen. He stepped into the wardrobe alcove and hid behind the coats hanging there. The woman came into the restaurant, lingered at the door and scanned the eating area. He waited. A server walked by, hesitated a moment and was about to ask something. Vermeulen put his index finger against his lips and gave him an impish smile. *Just a surprise, please don't spoil it.* The man smiled back and continued toward the kitchen.

When he peered past the coats again, the woman had left. He walked to the entrance and opened it. A party of three were about to enter the restaurant and the awkward dance past each other was enough of a diversion. He retraced his steps back to the street on which his hotel stood. Nobody followed him. Or, if someone did, they practiced far better surveillance than the couple had.

Back at his hotel, he asked the concierge, a Sikh man whose name tag read

"Devahu," if there had been any messages or if anyone had asked for him. The man shook his head. He walked the stairs up to his room, opened the door and decided he was too tired to unpack. With the jet lag, he was liable to wake up early anyway. He'd have enough time to unpack then.

He closed the door and saw an envelope on the carpet. His chest tightened. He opened it. There was another printout of a photo. This time they had cleaned the printhead. The photo showed him standing on the stoop of a building. Same coat as before, that envelope under his arm. It might have been taken on the same day. Again, the street or the house were impossible to identify. All he could see was the stoop and the door. That, and the house number, eighty-four. How many houses with that number could be found in Antwerp? A hundred? At least. Probably more, but he knew it wasn't any of those other houses. The pressure in his chest increased, because it could only be one building.

His phone buzzed. He picked it up. Another message. He tapped on the icon. The text was no surprise, *nummer twee.*

He sank into the chair, his heartbeat now rattling his ribcage. Whoever they were, they knew where he stayed and they knew that he'd returned. They even knew when he opened the envelope. All his evasive maneuvers had been for nothing. Either that, or the couple following him on the street was sent by someone else.

The sense of homecoming he'd felt while walking to his hotel was gone. Being followed by unknown characters and finding old photographs slipped under the door reminded him more of his regular United Nations work. Except, this time he wasn't the one investigating. He was the target.

He called Tessa, who answered right away.

"How are things, my love?" she said.

"Iffy, tending towards troublesome."

"Are you in trouble?"

"Not yet, but I could be. The judge is going to be a pain in the neck. And I'm being followed."

"By whom?"

"Not even a clue. A man and a woman. And someone is putting old photos under my door."

"You want me to come?"

"I miss you a lot, but, no, that's not necessary. I'll just tell my story and that should do it."

"Is that the best strategy?"

"For now, yes. Listen, I'm bushed, I gotta get some sleep. Talk tomorrow?"

"Sure, love you."

"Love you, too."

CHAPTER SIX

A TIME OR TWO

———◆———

AS HE EXPECTED, VERMEULEN WOKE AT the ungodly hour of four. His body was busy reassembling the scattered bits that hadn't yet traversed all the time zones. A cold front must have arrived that night because wind buffeted the window. He turned over and dozed off. He woke again at five to the sound of rain hammering against the glass. Autumn in Antwerp, altogether best spent in a warm bed. He closed his eyes once more. Which was a mistake, because the next time he opened them it was eight-thirty.

Damn.

He fired up the Nespresso machine the hotel had provided and hurried into the tiny bathroom. A hot shower and shot of caffeine later, he got dressed. Unpacking the suitcase had to wait. The rain still came down and a quick look out of the window told him it wasn't going to end anytime soon. Walking was out of the question. He called the desk and asked them to order a taxi.

Unlike in Manhattan, rain in Antwerp didn't bring out umbrella vendors at every corner. It was just a fact of life here. The concierge took one look at his thin coat and reached into a closet, producing a well-used loaner. Better than nothing.

He arrived at Smits's office right on time.

"You're cutting it mighty close," Smits said. "The interview room is a couple of floors up."

They hurried up the stairs and walked into the room five minutes late. Magistrate Mesman stood by the door, looking put out. The other people in the room were a man and a woman, both in their early thirties. The room itself was simple, the decor similar to Smits's office. A large table stood at the center with two chairs on one side and one on the other. A microphone was placed in front of each chair. Two laptops, already open, sat on the side with the two chairs. Three bottles of mineral water and three glasses were all the provisions they thought necessary.

The only good part of the seating arrangement was that Vermeulen's chair was facing the windows. Not that there was much to see besides gray clouds refracted by rain running down the glass, but he preferred that to looking at a wall.

"Now that you are finally here, Mr. Vermeulen, let's get started. Meet Assistant Inspector Hendrik de Haas, and Inspector Maya Dekker from the Federal Police. They will conduct the interview."

Both were in civilian clothes. De Haas looked like an even younger version of Mesman. The only differences were his blond hair, which was shorter, his tie, which was yellow, and the pink cheeks, which made him look like a farm boy in the big city.

Dekker's skin was the color of dark chocolate, she had short cropped hair and stood taller than De Haas. Her heart shaped face was unadorned except for a tiny diamond in her left nostril. Her ochre eyes felt piercing. The once-over she gave Vermeulen exuded suspicion.

Vermeulen stuck out his hand to greet them and said, "*Goedemorgen.*"

The two just nodded at him. The dark clouds outside were more expressive than their faces.

"I assume this chair is for me?" he said.

Dekker nodded.

Vermeulen took his seat.

"Well, it looks like everything is set. I'll be downstairs if you need me," Mesman said. He and Smits left the room.

Dekker and de Haas walked around the table and settled into their chairs, Dekker to Vermeulen's left. De Haas moved his microphone closer to his mouth. Its cord got caught in the grommet at the center of the table and he yanked it impatiently.

"It is Thursday, the twenty-second of October, two-thousand-fifteen. This interview is conducted by inspectors Maya Dekker and Hendrik de Haas. Also present is Valentin Vermeulen, formerly employed by the crown prosecutor. The time is nine-thirteen."

De Haas paused. Vermeulen didn't see a recorder, but that didn't mean much. A new building would have all that equipment built in. There was a mirror at one of the walls and it wouldn't be a stretch to assume that it was of the one-way variety.

"Well, Mr. Vermeulen. We are here to sort out a bit of a mess left over from your last case. As magistrate Mesman has explained to you, a citizen, Theo Vinke, has filed a wrongful death complaint. According to the complaint, you coerced his father, Frans Vinke, to serve as a confidential informant for the case in question. Mr. Vinke claims he has evidence that shows not only your coercion but also that you later leaked his father's name, which led directly to his being murdered by the syndicate. He's demanded compensation for the wrongful death."

He paused. When Vermeulen didn't react, he continued, "Ms. Dekker and I have not seen this evidence yet, which means this isn't quite a burning issue, more a smoldering one. But he is likely to retain a lawyer. In other words, the case has the potential to become a full-blown dumpster fire. We decided to deal with it before it does. And that's why you're here."

He paused and looked at Vermeulen with raised eyebrows. Since he didn't have anything to add, Vermeulen just nodded.

"Okay, then. Next item. We are here to protect the prosecutor's office." Again, the raised eyebrows. Vermeulen nodded. "You are here as a private individual. Sure, you're a former member of the office and, looking at your record, a successful one at that, but that's all in the past. What I'm saying is this, we can't guarantee that our interests and yours will coincide. You understand?"

What was there to say? Vermeulen was on his own. Nothing new there.

"So, do you mind telling us who you are, your address and your current profession?" de Haas said.

His voice was as bland as his face. Vermeulen couldn't tell if it was due to some strange sense of professionalism, boredom, or concealed enmity. This interview was going to be a slog. And however long it took, it would feel twice that.

"My name is Valentin Vermeulen," he said, matching the bland tone. "I live at 285 West 119 Street in New York City, United States. I'm an investigator for the Office of Internal Oversight Services of the United Nations."

"You've moved in the last half year, haven't you?" Dekker said with just a hint of a French accent. She didn't check with de Haas, didn't even make eye contact with her colleague, which meant that she was in charge of the interview. Good to know.

"Yes, I have. But I don't know why that would be pertinent to this interview."

"Your partner is living with you, isn't she?"

Vermeulen looked at Dekker. How did she know this? Tessa living with him wasn't a secret, but it wasn't public knowledge either.

"Yes, she is."

"A bit of a muckraker, your Tessa Bishonga."

"I take exception to that description. She's a journalist."

"No need to be modest. Quite a stunt she pulled with those secret GMO papers. Received a lot of attention. Even put the GMO proponents in Belgium on the defensive."

Vermeulen wondered again how they knew this. Yes, the case in Mozambique had made some headlines, but Tessa's name didn't feature in the reporting.

"Tell us what you do in your job." De Haas said before Vermeulen could reply.

"Again, I don't see what my job has to do with this interview."

"It's simply part of the background information."

"Yes, but my point is that what I do in my current job has no bearing on what you call a potential dumpster fire. That was thirteen years ago."

"I'm afraid, you'll have to leave it to us to assess what has bearing," de Haas said.

Vermeulen saw a faint smile on Dekker's lips.

"I investigate fraud in United Nations operations," Vermeulen said.

"Those investigations take you around the world?"

"Yes, they do."

"They put you in direct contact with criminals?"

"Sometimes they do, yes."

"How would you say your record has been at the United Nations?"

"My record has been exemplary." That came out with all the conviction he could muster.

"Does that exemplary record include your shooting a Russian diplomat in Vienna?" Dekker said. She made that question sound as if she was asking about his working hours. He hadn't paid much attention to the news coverage about that case a few years back. But he was pretty sure that his name hadn't been public knowledge. Some Belgian cop knowing about it put him on edge. They'd done a lot more preliminary research than he expected. It was time to strike back. He chose the right tone. Far from defensive but also not angry.

"Are you implying that my service has not been exemplary? You have no basis to make such an assessment."

"I'm implying nothing. Did you shoot a Russian diplomat in Vienna during an investigation?"

"Yes, I did. But the shooting was ruled self-defense. The man was running a human trafficking ring."

Dekker wasn't done yet. "Are you authorized to carry a weapon in the performance of your duties?"

Vermeulen felt the first drop of sweat running down his back. Dekker's strategy was obvious, but he wasn't going to let her under his skin. He unscrewed the bottle of water and slowly poured half of it into his glass. He closed the bottle again and took a long sip. Finally, he said, "No, I'm not."

"All yours, Hendrik," Dekker said.

De Haas took over again. "You headed an investigation in Mozambique?"

"Yes, I did. And I state again for the record, that all the work I did for the United Nations took place after I left my position here. It has no connection to the case that you are investigating."

"So noted. In addition to the cases we've mentioned, you have conducted investigations for the UN in Congo, Syria, Ivory Coast, Sudan, and, most recently, Turkey. Are there any more?"

How did they get this information? No way Suarez, his boss at the UN, would reveal that. OIOS did publish regular reports about its activities, but no names were attached to the cases. On the other hand, the Belgian ambassador to the UN could have asked personally and the Undersecretary General of OIOS might have leaned on Suarez to reveal that information.

"Yes, there were more, but they didn't involve in-country research. That work was done from headquarters."

Dekker jumped in again. "During those investigations my colleague just mentioned, did you use a gun each time?"

She knows. She wouldn't ask a question to which she doesn't know the answer.

A denial would change everything. It would turn the line between them into a wall, separate their objectives from his for good. No "we're all on the same side" talk afterwards. Dekker and de Haas would regroup and treat him like an uncooperative witness. It was too early for that. They hadn't even reached the meat of the matter. "I don't recall. You are talking about a thirteen-year span. It may have happened a time or two."

"Irrespective of how often it happened, you were never authorized to carry or use a gun, right?"

"To the extent that I did use a gun, it was always in self-defense or to protect an important source."

"I understand that, but, still, were you ever authorized to use a gun?"

"No."

She leaned back in her chair, clearly relishing the exchange. Vermeulen stared at the dark sky outside. It reflected his mood perfectly. But he'd be damned if he'd let her get the better of him.

"How did you manage to get a hold of all those guns? Not every place is like the US where you can just go buy one," Dekker said.

"On the occasion that a gun was used, again, purely in self-defense, it probably came from the criminals themselves. Criminals, I should add, who were trying to or had already defrauded the United Nations. Fortunately, most crooks aren't very smart."

His gut knew immediately that the last sentence was a mistake. More sweat ran down his back. *What an idiotic thing to say.* It made him sound like Dirty Harry, like a guy who wouldn't hesitate leaking the name of Vinke to the mobsters he'd ratted on.

"Let's leave that be for the moment," de Haas said. "Although it's oddly apropos. You know the dilemma of superior orders versus individual responsibility, right? Nuremberg trials and all that."

Vermeulen couldn't fathom where this new tack was taking them. He cocked his head and listened for more.

"You know the situation. Your bosses okay your strategy, but reality kicks in, things go awry, you have to improvise. Maybe go a bit farther than ordered, strictly speaking, but all in good conscience, since your bosses said so."

Ah, there it was, the first attempt to holding their office harmless.

"I assume you are speaking in hypotheticals, because that didn't happen during the case," Vermeulen said.

"So, no cutting corners, no improvised action that didn't make it into the reports?"

"None whatsoever."

"Good enough. Let's take a break," de Haas said. He added for the benefit of the recording the time the interview was interrupted.

Vermeulen stood up. "Is there a cafeteria in the building? I haven't had any breakfast yet."

Dekker nodded. "Come with me. I could use a coffee."

"What game are you playing in there?" he said as they walked along the corridor. "None of that has any connection to the Vinke issue."

"Just establishing who you are, as a person. No big deal."

"It looks very different from where I sit."

"I wouldn't worry about it."

Which really meant, worry about it. A lot.

CHAPTER SEVEN

TARTARE OF SALMON

———— ◆ ————

BACK IN THE INTERVIEW ROOM after a bland egg sandwich, Vermeulen braced himself for further digging into his recent past. To his surprise, that part of the interview was over.

"You were one of the prosecutors for a task force codenamed 'Brass Herring?'" de Haas said.

"Yes, I was."

"Why were you involved?"

"I assume I was brought in for my expertise in financial crimes. The case focused on cocaine smuggling which had increased dramatically since the 1990s. Since the coca bush only grows in certain parts of South America, we knew that cocaine could only come to Europe via sea or air routes. Given the quantities involved, the sea route was the most logical mode."

"Who arrived at that conclusion?"

Vermeulen shrugged. All he knew was that he hadn't. The questions also didn't relate to the reason why he was being interviewed. Not that it came as a surprise. He looked at Dekker, who stared at the wall as if she was bored out of her mind.

"That fact had already been established by the time I joined the task force," Vermeulen said. "The quantities seized were simply too large to have been brought by individual couriers on planes. It was commonly understood that such quantities had to come in bulk, which meant the sea route."

De Haas typed again on his laptop. Dekker stared at the wall with an expression that said she'd rather be anywhere but here.

"What quantities are we talking about?" de Haas said.

"Not sure I can recall these numbers." Vermeulen scratched his chin and looked out of the window. "I do remember that the numbers of seizures had gone up since 1998."

"Are we talking kilos or tons?"

"As I said, I don't have those numbers. I'd be speculating."

"Would two thousand kilos sound about right?"

"For what, seizures or totals?"

De Haas studied his laptop. "Seizures."

"I think it was a little lower, but your guess is as good as mine."

"That wasn't a guess," Dekker chimed in.

Vermeulen suppressed a smile. *Good, I'm getting under your skin. Two can play this game.*

De Haas seemed unaware of what was happening between Dekker and Vermeulen. "Those seizures, what percentage of the total inflow did they represent?"

"Again, I don't remember. All we knew at the time was that they were just a small fraction, maybe twenty percent."

"And why were you brought in? Shipping isn't exactly your expertise."

"For the second part of the equation."

Both Dekker and de Haas frowned.

"How the money got back to Latin America," Vermeulen said. "The Columbian cartels weren't running a drug charity. There were mountains of cash, mostly small bills. How did they transport it back to Cali? Digging into that question *is* my expertise."

De Haas was back to typing on his laptop. Why he did that was beyond Vermeulen. Everything said in the room was being recorded. He could just order the transcript and be done. Did he do it to look important or to use his laptop to hide? For all his professional mien, he was just a kid, not yet sure if he could fill out the shoes he'd stepped into.

Dekker on the other hand, had no such problems.

"How did you feel when you were asked to join the task force?" she said. "Must have been a big boost for your ego. Young prosecutor, working on local pissant stuff, gets the call asking him to join the big boys."

Vermeulen no longer wondered about her intentions. Responding with anger wasn't worth it. *Make light of it, then zing her when she makes a mistake.*

"It wasn't a big deal. I had consulted for other task forces before. It was simply another inter-agency effort. Age and size had nothing to do with it."

"But it wasn't your usual bailiwick."

"Listen, Ms. Dekker. You have my entire employment history on that laptop of yours. You can look up what I was working on. Many of my cases went beyond Antwerp." He stopped for a moment. "You do remember that the first effects of the Schengen Agreement materialized in the late nineties.

The abolition of passport controls let not only law-abiding Europeans travel without stopping at the border. Criminals exploited the same opportunities. What you call 'pissant' stuff involved a lot of cross-border issues." A pause. "But you wouldn't remember that, you were just finishing high school then."

He leaned back in his chair and watched her face. She maintained her bored facade, but her eyes spoke murder. He didn't smile, he didn't want to gloat. He'd only issued an ultimatum. *We can do this civilly, or we can do this the hard way.*

De Haas looked at Vermeulen, then at Dekker. It must've been dawning on him that something was brewing between the two, something that could affect the remainder of the interview, something he better got sorted out to prevent all-out war.

"Let's break for lunch," he said. He looked at his watch. "Be back here at two."

* * *

VERMEULEN HURRIED OUT OF THE PALACE OF JUSTICE. He wanted real air, even if it was wet and cold outside. The umbrella he'd gotten from the concierge turned out sturdier than it looked. Under its cover, he headed to the Schelde.

The walk wasn't very picturesque. He followed the street until he reached the quay road. Beyond it was only parking, some covered, some not. An uninspiring river front. All those cars had to be put somewhere. His search for a bench was unsuccessful, so he stood at the edge of the road and looked across the river to Linkeroever, a neighborhood with much taller buildings than the city proper, but also more green space and a nice waterfront for strolling and resting.

The rain picked up and he turned back to find a dry spot. A little restaurant, almost hidden at the corner of an office building, turned out to be a real find. Just a few tables. A man in white shirt and black trousers greeted him and handed him a menu printed on fine paper. The menu was short and the choices looked delicious. The waiter explained the options. He turned out to be one of the owners. He introduced his partner, the chef. Vermeulen chose a tartare of Scottish salmon over pasta with dill mascarpone. While he waited for the meal, he dialed Tessa's number. She didn't answer. It was too early in New York. He texted her a kiss instead. He would have to catch her up later with what was going on.

The meal came and he was not disappointed. Good food always lifted his spirits. He took his time eating. The owners asked how he liked the meal, he told them it was excellent. After finishing, he ordered an espresso and sipped it, looking at the rain outside. The sun, yesterday, was unexpected and he'd thought of it as a good omen for his time here. The rain today, pretty much the norm for this time of year, felt like reality kicking in.

* * *

AT TWO O'CLOCK SHARP HE WAS back in the Justice Palace, a bit damp, but refreshed. He couldn't say the same for de Haas and Dekker, who looked unhappy. At least he wasn't that.

"We've established that you had developed expertise in cross-border financial movements at the Prosecutor's office, which was the reason why you were seconded to the task force on cocaine smuggling. That about capture it?" de Haas said.

Vermeulen nodded.

"Who initiated that transfer?"

"I have no idea," Vermeulen said. "One day my boss told me to report at the task force. It operated out of a large office not far from the old Palace of Justice. I went there, introduced myself and was put to work."

"How many people worked for the task force?"

"Beats me. I'd say ten to fifteen people altogether. Mostly federal police officers and a couple of prosecutors. I didn't work with everyone there."

"Not a large group, then?"

"If you say so."

"Do you remember names?"

"I think Jan Smits was involved."

"Anyone else?"

"Why are you asking me? Don't you have that on your computer there?" Vermeulen said. "I'm sure your record is far more accurate than my memory."

De Haas looked at Dekker, who pursed her lips. De Haas went back to typing on his laptop. Probably something about Vermeulen's reticence in answering simple questions. Dekker snapped out of her bored state and pounced.

"As it turns out, Mr. Vermeulen," she said. "Our records aren't as complete as you assume. There are some key files missing. You wouldn't know anything about that, would you?"

Vermeulen said his "No" a little too fast.

"You don't remember the names of the task force members?" she said. "Not even the ones you worked with closely?"

"Jan Smits, as I said."

Dekker almost rolled her eyes. "Come on, he wasn't part of the task force. He just hung around the edges. Who else?"

Vermeulen made a show of thinking hard, staring at the wall, then at the rain outside.

"Well, there was Kees. Kees van Dijk. He was part of it. Really good cop, had a nose for crime."

"Who's had a stroke three years ago," Dekker said.

"Oh. He did? That's too bad. He was a good colleague." Vermeulen said, thoughtful, but careful not to go overboard.

"Any other name you might unearth in that archeological dig you call memory?"

Vermeulen took his time. Better to piss them off than lying outright.

"Cornelia Boogman. She was the admin, who held the whole thing together. Knew where everyone was, what they were doing. You should talk to her. She knew it all, down to everybody's first-born child."

Dekker was growing exasperated.

"She retired four years ago and moved to the Caribbean without leaving a forwarding address. But you knew that already, didn't you?"

Now it was Vermeulen's turn to be indignant. "I reject your insinuation. Yes, I figured that Cornelia might be retired by now, but not that she didn't leave a forwarding address." Although she'd always said that she'd be living on a sailboat, which would make that rather likely. But he didn't say that. Instead, he threw out another name. "How about Gerrit Graaf. He was from the drug crimes section."

"We've already talked to him. You know he didn't participate in the daily meetings. I'm getting tired of this game. Are you going to give us the names or not?"

"Why don't you tell me who you've got and I can tell you if I remember anyone else."

Dekker sat back in her chair and drank from her bottle, not bothering to pour the water into her glass. De Haas took that as his cue to change the focus.

"What about Alex Timmerman? That name ring a bell?" he said.

Vermeulen stroked his chin. "He was a federal cop, wasn't he? Yeah. I do remember him."

"Have you been in touch?"

Vermeulen frowned. "Why would I? I barely knew the man."

And that wasn't exactly true.

Chapter Eight

Two-Forty-Seven

———————— ♦ ————————

IT WAS ON A MONDAY MORNING BACK IN 2002 when Vermeulen first met Alex Timmermann. He was busy at the task force office on Justitiestraat when Timmerman stormed through the door, which slammed against its stop and bounced shut again. His hand shot out, almost striking Vermeulen in the chest. "Hey man, Alex's the name. Who're you."

Vermeulen shook the man's hand and thought he'd touched a live wire. "I'm Valentin Vermeulen, prosecutor's office."

Timmerman was a man of boundless energy. Vermeulen could see that right away. Always in motion, his foot tapping, his fingers drumming on the file cabinet, his entire body swaying, as if dancing to an invisible beat. And it was a lot of body that was swaying. He was over six feet, a sturdy chest, long arms, a solid man. His visage matched his body. He had blond hair, blue eyes and a grin as wide as the North Sea.

"Great to meet you, Val. You the money guy?"

"I'd prefer Valentin, if you don't mind. And, yes, I'm the money guy."

"No prob, man. You ever get away from behind your desk?"

Vermeulen wasn't sure what that was supposed to mean. He said, "Usually that's where my work is. So, I guess, no."

"Okay. I'm gonna change that. Be prepared for a few outings. I wouldn't know financial shit if it bit me in the ass. I end up collecting all the paperwork, folks like you get the pile and I never know what I found. Not a good way to run this task force."

Vermeulen agreed with that but thought that he could make that info available without running after crooks in the port of Antwerp. The last thing he needed was late night phone calls to go on a raid. Marieke, his wife, was already pissed about the overtime he was putting in. He nodded uneasily.

"Let's go," Timmerman said.

"What? Now?"

"Fuck yeah, just got a tip about a delivery from one of my informants. It's hot. We got to get to the Delwaidedok, like right now. I alerted the uniforms we want to nab the guys who are getting the dope from the container."

Vermeulen put on his windbreaker and headed for the door. Timmerman hustled him along.

"Why do you need me?" Vermeulen said.

"Because you need to check the waybill, manifest or whatever you call that shit. Note the consignee and all that. I can't do that and grab the runners."

"The what?"

"The runners. They are the crazy dudes who jump the fence, break open a specified container, grab the bags of cocaine and make a run for it. Good runners are so fast, you'll barely see them. Bad runners get caught."

"They're the least important link in the chain. Why grab them?"

"Because they are like contractors. They're not part of the syndicate and bound by some asinine oath. Good runners are scarce, which is why they have their pick of jobs with the syndicates. Catching one of them could crack a case wide open."

Timmerman motored down the Britselei at high speed. The unmarked VW transporter had flashing lights behind the grille and a siren. After Britain, the street names changed to Frankrijklei, and then to Italiëlei. Not for the first time Vermeulen wondered why the north-south connector through Antwerp read like a list of EU members. They reached Noorderlaan and Timmerman really stepped on it. They merged onto the A12. Timmerman turned off the siren. A few miles later, they exited near the Delwaidedok and approached, much slower, the entrance to the Overseas Shipping Company quay.

"They handle most of the trade with Latin America," Timmerman said.

He showed his shield to the man at the entrance booth. They were allowed to proceed. Past the booth, a police car was waiting for them. Timmerman waved at them to follow him.

Solid walls of containers occupied the rear of the quay. They were stacked six, seven boxes high. You'd have to be a mountain climber to get to those at the top.

"How the hell do the runners know where to find their container?" Vermeulen said.

"They know the ID number. It's painted on each side."

"Yeah, but look at this, there are thousands of containers. I wouldn't know where to start, and if it's the one at the top, that doesn't do them much good even if they find it."

"The syndicate has port workers on their payroll. For the right amount of cash, they'll tell you which row it's on. As to the height, I've seen containers opened at the top of a stack. Some of these runners are like mountain goats."

"Do you know where we're headed?"

Timmerman didn't answer. He sped along the center lane. The containers were arranged in rectangular blocks, divided by wide access roads.

"We're looking for row two-forty-seven, so keep an eye out on your side."

Only then did Vermeulen see the white numbers on the concrete, designating each row of boxes. They were at three-forty-five. They flew through another intersection. In the next block, Timmerman slowed down. They saw their number. Timmerman stopped. Each row accommodated six forty-foot containers, end to end.

"Looks like the port people on the take also have to make sure the container is at the end of a row," Vermeulen said.

"You got that right."

"There's a problem. Row two-forty-seven is on both sides of the roadway."

Timmerman swore. His informant didn't tell him which block to look for. He checked the container number on his sheet. "It's not one of these."

He raced around the block and checked the numbers there. They struck out again. Timmerman did one more turn around this block, same result. The container he was looking for isn't on its designated row. He swears again. "Goddamn informant, not worth a shit."

"Let's park the van and walk," Vermeulen said. "If I wanted to steal things from a container, I wouldn't want to do that in plain view of anyone who might be driving by." He pointed to the tall mast holding up a security light. "See that? It's right at the center of our row. There can't be a container there."

Timmerman looked at him and said, "That's why you're paid the big bucks. Let's go."

They parked the VW out of the way. The cops stopped behind them. Timmerman told them to wait. Their uniforms would scare the runners off. The two walked back to the row. Sure enough, their container was in the stack. An orange box, forty feet long, its door facing the light mast. It was the second box from the bottom.

As far as they could tell, the door hadn't been tampered with. The locking handle was in its retainer and they could see the customs seal in its place. The runners haven't been here yet. Timmerman radioed the cops and told them to hang back. The two of them withdrew and found a spot near the next security light that offered enough cover.

Timmerman had made it sound like the runners were about to empty the container. They stood, sat, lounged and paced for over an hour. Every five minutes, they checked the container. No runners. Elsewhere the dock was busy, gantry cranes unloading, stackers scurrying back and forth, engines roaring, horns blowing.

"Are you sure this is the container?" Vermeulen said.

"It's what the informant told me. The number is correct."

"Could the informant play on both sides?"

"Of course, he could. He hasn't so far, though."

"Maybe they've been here already."

"But the seal isn't broken."

"Do you know that's the original seal?"

Timmerman frowned and said, "You got one hell of a devious mind."

The seal was too far above to inspect.

"Looks fine," Timmerman said.

"It would if they put a new one on. I'd say we open the thing up."

"Oh man, in that case we might as well kiss this day goodbye. I'll have to get a warrant, then we'll have to get the company to cut the seal, witnesses, the whole fuckin' deal. Forget it."

"What about skipping the warrant? Cutting the seal doesn't take much."

Timmerman shook his head. "We can't cut the seal without a warrant. You know that, Val. I'm as flexible as the next cop, but I'm not breaking the law."

"You're right," Vermeulen said. "And please call me Valentin."

Timmerman radioed the cops, told them to go home. The two went back to the VW and climbed in. Timmerman slumped behind the steering wheel, dejected.

They drove off. As they passed row two-forty-seven, Vermeulen saw a movement on the topmost container. Just a gull. Or was it? It was too big, more the size of a mountain goat.

"Stop," he yelled.

Timmerman stomped on the brake. The VW screeched to a halt. Vermeulen was already outside and ran between the containers. He reached the light mast and looked up. The container doors were open and a rope was dangling from the top. Timmerman caught up, saw the rope too, pushed the radio button and told the cops to come back. Vermeulen ran to the other end, watched the top. Nothing. That didn't mean anything. Whoever was up there just had to lie flat and wait them out. Timmerman yelled to whoever is on top to come down. He might as well have told the gulls to stop flying.

They waited, but didn't see anyone. *Good runners are so fast, you'll barely see them.*

Vermeulen told Timmerman that the runners could be anywhere on top of the containers. Timmerman swore. They walked back to their van. Timmerman ranted. They climbed back into the VW and drove off.

Halfway back to town Timmerman said, "There's a leak, Val. I fuckin' know it."

"Please call me Valentin."

"Sure thing. There's a leak."

"I agree, someone must have warned them. They knew we were coming, hid atop the container, waited until we left, and took the coke."

Chapter Nine

The Kennel

─────────◆─────────

Back in the present, De Haas, tired of prying the names of the task force members from Vermeulen, continued to the next item on his laptop. "Where did you keep the files?"

"At the office on Justitiestraat. There was a whole wall of file cabinets, four drawer ones, if I remember correctly, steel, painted gray."

"Lovely that your memory serves you so well when it comes to the cabinetry," Dekker said.

De Haas shot her a warning look.

"Did any of those files ever leave the office?" he said to Vermeulen.

"Of course, whenever the presiding judge needed them."

"So you didn't make copies for the judge?"

"We may have. It wasn't my job. Cornelia would've handled that."

"Did you have any other locations where files might have been kept?"

For once, it was de Haas who posed the dangerous question. Vermeulen knew this was the moment of denial. "Not to my knowledge."

"And you held all your interviews at that office?"

"Yes, as far as I remember."

"Even when debriefing undercover officers? That seems rather careless."

"Oh, that." His face belied the tightness he felt in his stomach. "No, I don't think we did that there."

"Where did you debrief them?"

Vermeulen pursed his lips. "I don't remember debriefing anyone. As I said, I was in charge of financial records."

He could tell that his answer had turned the slow burn in Dekker to a raging fire. Her eyes spoke murder.

He shrugged as if to say, "What?"

Dekker burst out, "What about that secret apartment?"

Vermeulen flinched, struggling to keep his composure. *They know about the Kennel. Nobody was supposed to know about it.*

"Yes, we know," de Haas said, shaking his head.

Vermeulen looked out at the gray sky, willing himself to stay calm.

"You all would have gotten away with it, too," Dekker said. "The only reason we found out is because one of our assistants did a simple search for 'Brass Herring' and there it was, a line item in the current budget, well hidden under 'Miscellaneous, *Lease-apartment-op Brass Herring.*' I can't even fathom what bureaucratic cock-up makes us still pay rent on it."

"Why don't you tell us where it is?" de Haas said.

Vermeulen raised his eyebrows. "You know about the Kennel, but you don't know where it is?"

"Is that what you called it, the Kennel?" Dekker said. "Sounds like a sleazy bar. To answer your question, no, we don't know where it is because our files on task force 'Brass Herring' are incomplete. Whoever handled that lease did an admirable job hiding it. Well, not really hiding it, it was in plain sight. It just wasn't cross-referenced. Nothing connected to it. Tell us where it is."

The end of the road. No more fancy footwork, half-truths or evasion. Vermeulen took a deep breath. "The Kennel is on Verversrui."

Dekker hissed, "Who's brilliant idea was it to rent a place in the red-light district?"

Vermeulen raised his hands to protest his innocence of at least that charge. "I had nothing to do with that."

"Did you meet informants there?" Dekker's face had gotten darker.

"We did."

"What's the house number?"

"Eighty-four."

The very house number of the second photograph. It brought back mixed memories.

* * *

THAT WAS IN MID-JUNE, 2002. ALEX TIMMERMAN had asked him to come. There was a protocol for using the place. First, you're sworn to secrecy. No blabbing about it. Not at the office, not to your wife, lover, or kids. Vermeulen had no intention of talking about the Kennel, so the warning seemed a little over the top.

Second, you didn't just walk in. You pretended to look at the sex workers while checking one of the third-floor windows. If there were two anti-nuclear power decals on the pane, you could come up. If there was only one, you waited. This made good sense. Better to not walk in on a meeting with a skittish informant who was liable to jump ship if something felt fishy.

Third, you buzzed one of the sex workers. She'd leave her window and let you inside. That way your cover was maintained.

Vermeulen followed all these rules and walked up to the third floor. Timmerman was waiting for him and led him to the door on the left. Its only distinguishing difference was the extra metal flashing around the lock, meant to prevent brute force means of entry. Vermeulen stepped inside.

Bare would've been a generous term to describe the apartment. Besides a desk and four chairs, there was a file cabinet. On one wall hung a cheap print of Brueghel's *Bath of the Nymphs* in an even cheaper frame. Cornelia Boogman and Kees van Dijk were already there. She had soft brown eyes and a round face that was framed by auburn hair. She was in her late forties, a bit on the heavy side, had an encyclopedic memory and was hard as stone. Her motherly appearance had misled more than one newcomer. In short, she was perfect as the administrator.

Van Dijk was a portly man with a red face that spoke of high blood pressure or too much beer. His belly spilling over his belt hinted at the latter. He had a brush of a mustache and short, brown hair.

"Nice digs," Vermeulen said. "Is the back as pleasing as the front?"

Timmerman said, "Yeah, check it out, gourmet kitchen and a palatial bathroom with all modern conveniences."

Vermeulen did check out the back. The kitchen was a throwback to the nineteenth century. He half expected a hand pump to haul up water. He opened the refrigerator. It was empty, except for a carton of milk that looked fresh. On the counter stood a coffeemaker. Its glass carafe was coated with a brown film. He didn't bother with the bathroom.

Boogman, acting on her motherly instinct, had found a rag in the kitchen and was wiping the desk and four chairs. Her efforts did little to improve the ambiance. The place smelled like a mixture of mildew and rot. Some of that probably came from the nasty curtains that covered the street side windows, the rest from the carpet that felt squishy under his soles.

Van Dijk saw Vermeulen's expression and said, "I call it the Kennel. My grandfather used to raise Malinois dogs and his kennel smelled just like this."

Vermeulen nodded. A kennel full of sheep dogs would smell like this.

Timmerman asked them to sit down. "We're meeting here because there is a leak in the task force," he said. "Thanks to Cornelia for finding this nasty place on short notice. She buried the cost somewhere in the budget."

"Are you sure about the leak?" van Dijk said.

"Absolutely. Our string of failures can't be coincidences. Besides, Val found a new source. We can't have that exposed. Why don't you tell them?"

With the others waiting for the news, Vermeulen didn't remind Timmerman about using his full name. "Well, it wasn't really my doing," he says. "I got a call from a colleague at my regular office. He said that they had booked a two-bit crook on charges of larceny and possession of stolen goods, when the guy claimed to know a lot about how the drug syndicate moves money. My colleague wondered if the task force would like to talk to him. I went there, took one look at Frans Vinke and knew he was just another wannabe."

"Ain't that the truth," van Dijk said. "It never ceases to amuse me how the minnows in the sewer think they're helping themselves by pretending to be bigger shots than they are."

Vermeulen nodded. "I was about to leave the office again, when he said he knew how the syndicate launders money. That made me stop. I asked to speak to him alone and grilled him further. Much of what he said was vague. Just the kind of bluster you'd expect; big talk, little substance. But he mentioned two names that made me sit up. Beukes and Vanderfeld. One is the head of the syndicate and the other is his lawyer."

Timmerman picked it up from there. "Valentin calls me up. I do a little digging and, it's true, Vinke is small fry. Except, his wife is the sister of Beukes and he's got a son, Theo, who's engaged to Vanderfeld's daughter."

Boogman clapped her hands. "What a stroke of luck. Why was he brought in anyway?"

"Smallish stuff," Vermeulen said. "Possession of stolen cars with intent to fence them abroad. He claimed he didn't know the titles were forged but refused to name the sellers. He might've gotten some time in prison, but not a lot. I asked to speak to him alone and laid it on thick. Repeat offender and all that. Made it sound like he was going away for five to ten years. When he was ready to crumble, I gave him his way out. Spy on Beukes and Vanderfeld for us and you'll go free. He wasn't really happy about it, but he agreed. We walked out of the Justice Palace together."

"That's not really legal," van Dijk said.

Timmerman pressed his lips together, but didn't say anything.

Vermeulen said, "And not really illegal either."

Van Dijk didn't let it go, though. "We'll be in deep trouble if this comes out."

"I agree, it's gray," Boogman said. "But why should it come out? Vinke has every incentive to keep his mouth shut."

"Right, and we'll keep it secret," Timmerman said. "That's why we are the only ones who know Vinke. And it needs to stay that way. No mention of Vinke at the task force office. No paperwork. All discussions involving Vinke must happen here. No exceptions."

"Who's the leak?" van Dijk said. "You got to have a suspicion. Tell us."

Timmerman shook his head. "No, I don't. The only thing I know for sure is that you three are solid. And together, we're going to roll this operation up and stuff it in the nearest dumpster. In the meantime, not a peep to anyone about Vinke."

* * *

THAT SECRET HAD LASTED FOR THIRTEEN YEARS. The four of them had indeed been solid. Vermeulen was sure Dekker and De Haas wouldn't see it that way, but neither said anything. After the revelation of the Kennel, De Haas called it a day. Vermeulen walked back to his hotel, not looking forward to a long evening alone. The low clouds made the afternoon feel much later than the time on Vermeulen's watch. At least the rain had taken a break. He didn't feel like eating yet, but he stopped at a night store and bought a bottle of *Oude Jenever*.

Back at his hotel room, he asked Devahu, who seemed to be on concierge duty all the time, if anyone had stopped by or asked for him. Of course, nobody had. He didn't believe that anymore. He opened his door, and, sure enough, there was another envelope on the floor. It contained another photo. This printout was crisp and he could see his features clearly. What had possessed him to grow a mustache then? It looked ridiculous. This photo showed him walking in the opposite direction of the first photo, against the same wall, but without the envelope in his hand.

He looked at his phone, expecting the inevitable ding. Another text message arrived and, just as he expected, it said, *nummer drie.*

He got a glass from the bathroom and poured a few fingers. He sipped it first, not having had any *Jenever* in a long time. The malty taste with the spicy juniper note was exactly as he remembered it. He downed the glass. The burn down his gullet felt good, but it didn't change his mood.

He poured another drink, but decided to hold off. Instead, he dialed Tessa's number. She answered

"How are things?" she said. "You miss me yet?"

"I started missing you as soon as I boarded the airplane. It's only gotten worse since."

"Right answer. I miss you too. What's going on? Are you in trouble yet?"

"Getting there. No doubt. The son of a former informant is suing the department for damages. He claims I leaked the name. The judge heading the investigation wants to make an example of me and hold the department harmless."

"Oh my," was all Tessa said. "Are they crazy? You didn't, right?"

"Leak the name? No. They're making it sound as if I sent a note to the head of the crime syndicate, telling them who the informant was. It's total bullshit."

"So it's the son's word against yours?"

"Yup. Except he claims to have evidence. I haven't seen it yet."

"What's your strategy?" Tessa never dwelled on misfortune. Getting through it was more important.

"Right now, I don't have one. They are quizzing me about every little detail of the task force back then. Problem is, we didn't tell anyone back then that we even had this informant. There was a leak somewhere and we didn't want him compromised. Some of the paperwork is missing."

"And you have been reluctant to tell them about it. So now they are even more suspicious."

All he could say was, "Exactly."

"When will you learn that your stubbornness will get you into trouble?"

"It didn't when I found you on that lifeboat in Maputo harbor."

"And I'm grateful for that. But you've got to learn when to be like bamboo rather than rock."

He heard her sigh and knew she was right. "I know," he said, much quieter now. "I started cooperating. In the meantime, I'll have to piece together what happened back then. There has got to be a clue as to why the son is trying to put me on the hot seat. Once I see his evidence, I know how to defend myself."

She was silent for a minute. "You want me to come yet?"

"No. This is my mess. I'll sort it out. I have a week."

"Let me know if I can help. I can research things from here."

"Will do. And now I want to get some rest. Love you."

"Love you too."

He ended the call and downed the glass of booze. A nice buzz made him mellower. A little too mellow. Some food would be good before drinking more. He took off his shoes, leaned back in the chair that wasn't meant for lounging, and put his feet up on the bed. He closed his eyes.

Chapter Ten

Bath of the Nymphs

---◆---

WHEN HE WOKE—AGAIN IN THE DARK OF THE PREDAWN—he found himself on the bed with no memory of having left the chair. He was wearing his clothes. His neck was sore and the *Jenever* had left him with a touch of headache. It was too dark to assess the weather outside, but the lack of stars or moon gave him little hope the sun would come out later.

The Nespresso machine came to his rescue and the hot coffee pushed his body into the vicinity of a living being. He needed a strategy. Not just for Dekker and de Haas, but also for these envelopes and texts. The way a text arrived just after he opened an envelope was uncanny. At first, he thought that whoever texted him was tracking his phone. But that'd only tell them that he was in the room, not that he opened the envelope. They had to be surveilling his room. True to the low countries' Calvinist habit, he hadn't closed the curtains since he had nothing to hide. He looked out of the window. Too dark to see anything. He pulled the curtains shut.

The alternative would be a spy camera. That thought did more than the espresso to kick his circulation into gear. Cameras had gotten so small, they could be anywhere. The video signal had to be broadcast as well, since they knew in real time when he'd opened the envelope. They probably piggybacked on the hotel's WiFi.

He searched his room. The smoke detector and sprinkler head were clean. Next came the two lamps. Neither had any suspicious additions. He used his penknife to remove the air-conditioning vent. Again, nothing. The light switch box was empty. The outlets were rather low for a camera, but he checked them anyway. Nothing. He lifted the two mass-produced paintings from the wall. Nothing there, either.

He sat back down and took a deep breath. He was overreacting. Sometimes, surveillance is low tech, like the couple that followed him. The window across the street was the most likely answer to his question. He was satisfied with his conclusion until he looked at the TV. It was attached to the wall by a mounting device that let him adjust the angles. The screen wasn't very large. He examined the bezel and found that it contained a camera at the top center. If someone hacked the hotel video system, they'd be spying on him without ever having to install a spy camera.

Another moment of decision. Disable the TV and let them know that he found out, or pretend he hadn't found it. Pulling the plug would safeguard his privacy, not a trivial thing. Keeping it operating would allow him to manipulate his watchers, but it also meant he had to be cautious. All telephone conversations would have to be elsewhere, except for those he wanted them to hear. He left the TV plugged in.

* * *

VERMEULEN STOPPED AT A SMALL RESTAURANT and ordered a breakfast of rolls, cheese and jam, accompanied by more coffee. Better to be fortified before visiting the Kennel. This day wasn't going to be pleasant.

Devahu, the concierge, who looked like he'd been on duty all night, consented to lend him the umbrella one more day, but intimated that he should find his own if he planned on staying longer. The weather forecast wasn't encouraging. Vermeulen took a taxi to Verversrui. There was a fine drizzle in the air, the kind that doesn't look like rain but would make you wetter than a fish in no time. The sun was only a distant memory.

Verversrui was the center of the official red-light district of Antwerp. In the tradition of Amsterdam, several buildings had street-level windows, through which customers could check out the sex workers. This early in the morning, most windows were empty, but some had their red lights on. Prostitution was a twenty-four-hour business.

There was a police sub-station at the end of the street. Across from it, a sign advertised a medical office. Two women, one black and one Asian-looking, hurried along the street under their umbrellas. He couldn't fathom how they stood the cold weather in such skimpy clothes. They were probably headed for their windows. When they smiled at him, he smiled back. No, he wasn't a customer. He passed what looked like a brand-new bordello, called Villa Tinto. It looked all shiny and the illuminated windows at street level weren't decorated as garishly as some.

The Kennel was right next door. The wall of the building had been painted, but the house number, eighty-four, was unmistakably the same as the one in the photo. The ground floor also sported three windows. Not as classy as the place next door, but not shabby either. A blonde prostitute was sitting in the middle window, her red light on. She wore a G-string and rainbow-colored pasties. Not much was left to the imagination. She smiled at him. Vermeulen smiled back, but shook his head. He opened the outside door. The vestibule on the other side was just as seedy as he remembered, chipped tile floor and stained wallpaper. There were buzzers for each of the windows, plus six mailboxes next to intercom buttons. The Kennel used to be on the third floor. He checked the names on the mail boxes. They weren't familiar. No surprise there. There was no name for the first apartment on the third floor. He was tempted to punch in his code—the landlord had changed the lock at their request because the sex workers got tired of opening the door for them. Funny that he should remember it after all these years. He decided it was better to wait for Dekker and de Haas.

* * *

THEY FINALLY SHOWED UP AND CROWDED INTO THE VESTIBULE.

"You're early," de Haas said, as if Vermeulen had tried to make them look bad. He didn't bother to answer. Dekker's expression could only be described as distaste. Vermeulen couldn't tell whether it was the vestibule, or the fact they were meeting in the red-light district. They looked at him expectantly.

"Well, open up," Dekker finally said.

"You don't have the code?" Vermeulen said.

"Of course not. We didn't know where this place was until you told us yesterday."

"What makes you think my code from thirteen years ago still works?"

He knew the answer. Bureaucracy. Nobody would've bothered to change the code since nobody was using it anymore.

He punched in six digits and hoped they wouldn't work. No luck. The lock made a clicking sound, he turned the lever and the bolt retracted. Dekker pulled the door open.

The stairs to the third floor hadn't changed one bit. Worn wooden treads, covered with a threadbare runner, a third of the rods missing or loose. The wallpaper was faded beyond recognition and gouged by generations of careless tenants.

The two doors on the third floor hadn't aged gracefully. Their varnish was splotchy, the metal flashing dull. Vermeulen repeated his code entry, wondering why they'd use the same code for both doors. Probably for the same reason that it hadn't been changed.

The door sprung open. The stink was as bad as he remembered. The curtains hadn't been changed. The carpet still felt squishy. The four uncomfortable chairs and the desks were still there, but not where Vermeulen remembered them. They were scattered as if someone had moved them to vacuum and forgotten to put them back. The file cabinet was the farthest from its usual spot. Since there had never been a vacuum in the office, the furniture must have been moved for a different reason. The Brueghel, more faded now, hung on the same nail, but crooked.

Someone had been here.

Dekker wrinkled her nose as she looked around. Vermeulen thought she was about to say something, but she refrained.

"You do understand that this place was perfect for its purpose," Vermeulen said. "The people who were debriefed here existed in this milieu. It'd have been suspicious if they'd gone to Zurenborg."

De Haas nodded and sat in one of the chairs.

"Why are we here?" Vermeulen said.

De Haas pointed to the file cabinet. "We're looking for the missing files. When we find them, you'll help us sort through them."

Vermeulen shook his head. "I'm not your file clerk. You want to know things from me, ask me."

"Your memory seems rather selective," Dekker said. "The documents will help your recall."

She walked over to the file cabinet. It was locked. She didn't have a key. Neither did de Haas. They turned to Vermeulen. For a moment they looked just hopeful enough that Vermeulen could only say, "You don't really expect me to have that key on me?"

Dekker's face went back to her stoic expression. "Of course not, we're not stupid."

Vermeulen bit his tongue and said, "Of course." But he couldn't quite keep from smiling. "What did you expect, then?'

"That you'd tell us where you kept the key," Dekker said. "I don't believe for a moment that you all handed off the key to each other when you needed it."

The smile on Vermeulen's face died in an instant. Just when he thought he'd gotten the better of her, she threw him another curveball.

"So where did you keep the key?" Dekker said.

"The spot changed, depending on who was working here," Vermeulen said. "It could be anywhere."

"No, it couldn't," Dekker said. "It could only be in one of the locations you chose, so, show us."

Vermeulen walked to the desk, opened the pencil drawer, slid his fingers under the top edge and shook his head. "It's not where we usually kept it."

He looked at the other drawers. The dust on the handles had been disturbed. Someone had definitely been at the Kennel.

"You really haven't been here before?" he said.

The two shook their heads.

"Like she said. We only learned from you where it is," de Haas said.

"Well, someone has. There should be thirteen year's-worth of dust on these drawer handles and there isn't."

He tried the drawers. No key there either. The drawers were empty. They had always been.

"A most ingenious hiding place. Who would look there?" Dekker seemed to enjoy herself for once. "What about the kitchen? Maybe inside the water reservoir of the coffeemaker."

Vermeulen would have looked there next, but she preempted that diversion rather effectively. He shrugged again. He went to the toilet, lifted the lid of the tank, and walked back into the office. "Not there either. I'm running out of ideas here."

Dekker stepped up to the *Bath of the Nymphs* and ran her finger along the top edge of the frame. She rubbed the tips of her fingers together, while looking at the painting. "What is it with old European painters and naked women?" she said.

Vermeulen decided that the question was rhetorical and didn't say anything. Timmerman had been wrong. The Breughel print wasn't much better than a pin-up.

She looked at her fingers. "You are right, there should be more dirt on the frame." She lifted the print off the nail. The key was taped to the back of the frame.

Vermeulen shook his head. He'd never put the key behind the painting. Anyone coming here without authorization would have put the key back where they found it. Maybe Timmerman switched the hiding place. He would've been the last one to use this place. Either that, or whoever had entered in the meantime.

"Are you sure nobody from the police or the judge's office has used this apartment since two thousand and two?" Vermeulen said.

Dekker and de Haas looked at each other. Dekker said, "We looked everywhere and found no reference to this place except that budget item."

"Could another division have used it? It seems weird that there's still a budget line for this place if nobody uses it."

"You'd be surprised," de Haas said. Dekker shot him a glance and he stopped.

Who could have been here? The more Vermeulen thought about it the less sense it made to him. Until he thought about the photos slipped under his hotel room door. Obviously, someone out there knew about the Kennel. And they wanted him to know that too.

Chapter Eleven

Impartial Facilitator

———◆———

O NLY TWO DRAWERS OF THE FILE CABINET contained any documents. De Haas lifted four binders out and spread them on the desk. Dekker picked up one of them, flipped the pages inside, put it back, and repeated the examination with the others.

"Why aren't these with the rest of the case files at the office?" she said.

Vermeulen stared at the binders on the desk. Made of thick black marbled cardboard, the first one had a two-inch spine, the other three were half that thickness. Each labeled with the case number and a sequence number. Now he understood how they knew that files were missing. The sequence numbers were a dead giveaway. He picked up one of the folders, fingered it as if looking for an appropriate response.

"Your guess is as good as mine," Vermeulen said. "Probably crossed signals, I thought someone else was going to do it and they thought I would. Something like that. Remember, the case was over, we won a conviction. Everybody moved on."

"How about this? You stored these files here to keep them out of the official record. Sounds like a hell of a better guess than yours."

"Yes, it would, if it were true."

"Of course, it's true. There was no reason to have files at this location. It's not secure and not according to protocol. It's not a question of leaving documents behind. You brought them here from the task force's headquarters."

Vermeulen looked at de Haas, who said nothing, but seemed to enjoy the back and forth. He turned back to Dekker. "No, I didn't."

"Let's not split hairs. I meant someone on the task force brought them here. That's obvious. What I'd like to hear from you is when and why they were brought here."

"I don't remember when they were brought here. It doesn't matter anyway. Not now. What matters is the why. There was a leak somewhere in the office. The syndicate was always a step ahead of us. We'd get a tip, we run to the port as fast as possible, but we get nothing. Someone had already warned them."

"It couldn't have been a bad tip, or incompetence on your side?"

Vermeulen straightened. "Listen, Dekker. You may drag me all the way from New York and pester me with your petty inquiry, but you may not insult my competence. I've done more for justice in Belgium than you ever will with your sad little crusade. Why aren't you out there prosecuting drug smugglers and money launderers?"

He shook his head and walked to the window and looked down at Verversrui. Foot traffic had picked up.

"What about . . ." De Haas' attempt to defuse the situation was cut short by Dekker.

"What you call a petty little crusade cuts to the soul of the prosecutor's service. It's cowboy methods like yours that sully the reputation of the justice system, that are responsible for the low esteem with which Belgians regard us. If all I ever do is make an example of you, I'll happily retire knowing that the judicial branch in Belgium is better for it. And believe me, I will."

"In your dreams," Vermeulen shouted and walked to the door. "I'm done with this."

"And I'll get an arrest warrant in less than an hour. Maybe sitting in a cell will bring you to your senses."

"Shut up, the both of you," de Haas said. It was loud enough to startle Vermeulen. He spun around and saw that Dekker had the same reaction. "Stop throwing threats around, Dekker. You won't get an arrest warrant, so don't pretend you could. And you, Vermeulen, quit stalling. I'm tired of having to drag every word from your mouth. We could have this sordid matter settled in less than a week. We've already wasted a whole day. I have no intention of wasting more time."

De Haas was the perfect 'good cop' of the pair. Vermeulen decided to throw him a bone. "You are right, not every tip worked out, but the pattern was unmistakable. The syndicate knew when and where we were going to be. We found a new informant and we needed to keep him secret even from the other members of the task force, because lives were at stake."

"So you rented this dank dump for the debriefings?" Dekker said. "How did you explain that to the people at the top."

"I didn't. I believe it was Cornelia Boogman who managed that. But I'm not sure. When I showed up here for the first time, it was all done."

"Let's look at these files, then," de Haas said. He opened the first binder, pressed the buttons to open the rings and lifted a stack of papers to the desk. He handed them to Vermeulen. "Have a seat, your real job starts now. You need to flag anything that has any bearing on Vinke's death." He handed him a package of pink page flags.

Vermeulen looked at the top sheet. It was a memo from Timmerman to the three people he trusted, Vermeulen, van Dijk and Boogman, summarizing their meeting about Vinke and the leak in the task force. He suppressed a groan, and stuck one of the page flags to the right margin. The thought of going through the record of what, at the time, had been the riskiest investigation he'd been part of made him feel him a bit queasy. And not just because the Kennel smelled so bad.

* * *

DE HAAS HAD GONE OUT FOR COFFEE. The one thing they'd all agreed on was that the coffeemaker in the kitchen was irredeemable. Dekker sat in a chair and glowered at no one in particular. Vermeulen started on the next document. No author was listed, but he remembered that it had been prepared by van Dijk. A background paper, detailing the familial connections between Vinke, Bastiaan Beukes, the syndicate leader, and Jordi Vanderfeld, his lawyer.

Vinke's wife, Ingrid, was born a Beukes, the oldest child. Her brother, Bastiaan, was three years younger. The family background didn't include anything remarkable. Beukes *père* was a crane operator at the port before it got all containerized. His only brushes with the law were a couple of drunk and disorderlies. But that didn't mean much. Everybody in Antwerp knew that a strategic drop of a pallet onto the quay yielded a bounty of goods that were perfectly sellable and would be written off as shipping damage.

Bastiaan Beukes didn't follow in his father's steps, at least not immediately. He went to school and studied accounting. Then he got a job at the port, a few pay grades above his dad, who was proud of his son's achievements. During this time, Beukes learned all about port operations. He moved on to the Overseas Shipping Company just about the time cocaine first made its appearance on the European black market. In 1990 he was fired from OSC. No reason was given. He opened his own import/export company, *Globaal Handelsbedrijf*, which became the front for whatever illegal activities he undertook. He did well and rose in the Antwerp underworld.

According to van Dijk, Ingrid and Bastiaan were very close and talked to each other on a regular basis. He also mentioned that Bastiaan wasn't terribly happy about Ingrid marrying Vinke. Vermeulen remembered van Dijk pointing out that Vinke might not be the best way to get to Beukes. Timmerman had waved him off. If Vinke himself couldn't get close to Beukes, his wife could. Sometimes love trumps family.

Jordi Vanderfeld was an altogether different case. According to the report, Vanderfeld grew up in an upper-middle-class family. His father was as far from the underworld as one could get in Antwerp. Jordi was smart, skipped a grade in high school and graduated youngest in his class from the same law school as Vermeulen did later. He married young and divorced only a couple of years later. He'd been single since and had one daughter. His reputation for a mind sharper than a razor made him the go to lawyer for the upper crust of the underworld.

Vanderfeld didn't belong to any particular faction. Instead, he played the role of the impartial facilitator. He was rumored to have drafted the agreement between two crime families that became the foundation of the syndicate. He was also Beukes's lawyer for all things personal and business.

Vermeulen remembered meeting him more than once. He was short and fat—there were no other words to describe him—but his tailor somehow managed to craft clothes that made him look imposing and powerful. He was certain that Vanderfeld had managed the money laundering. It took someone with his brain to set up a laundromat that could have escaped official scrutiny for so long.

That Vinke's son, Theo should end up engaged to Vanderfeld's daughter, Nora, was as much a surprise as his father marrying Beukes's sister. Theo and Nora met at a concert, she a law student, he figuring out how to make a living. Neither knew of the other's connection to the criminal underground. Theo wasn't happy that his father tried to keep him away from that world, and Nora knew little about her father's involvement with the top tier gangsters.

Vermeulen got up and walked to the window to look down at Verversrui. The past started sliding into place like a Rubik's cube. Had Theo become a criminal? Jan Smits didn't think he had. Had Nora found out about her father's bread-and-butter clients. He didn't even know if Theo and Nora were still together. He had better find out.

"Worn out already?" Decker said.

Vermeulen contained an urge to snap at her. He kept looking out of the window.

"There's a lot more to review," she said.

Vermeulen turned to her. "You are welcome to join me. It'd go much faster."

"You are the only one who can make sense of it."

"Listen, by now you should have realized that neither I nor my colleagues did anything illegal. We were worried about a leak and so we kept this part of the operation under wraps. But it was within the confines of what had been authorized by the judge."

"I don't know that. Vinke was killed shortly after the operation ended. His son claims that you leaked his name. If that's true, you might as well have signed his death warrant."

"I didn't leak his name. How often do I have to say that? I had no incentive to do so. No informant would ever work with me again. It would have been stupid."

"Maybe your well-known temper got the better of you."

Just hearing someone who didn't know him at all talk about his temper was enough to push his blood pressure up. He caught himself, turned back to the window, and breathed out slowly.

"You know nothing about my temper," he said as calmly as he could.

"I've heard enough."

"Maybe you should base your assumption on what you see before you rather than relying on rumors."

The next row was about to happen. The funny thing was, she was just like him, stubborn and convinced of being right. He decided to take a step back.

"I do need one piece of information. Do you know if Theo Vinke and Nora Vanderfeld are still together?"

Dekker gave him a surprised look, nodded, as if understanding that he'd deescalated, and took her phone from her bag. She dialed a number and relayed his request to whoever answered. Vermeulen sat back down and took the next document from the binder. It was a summary of his first meeting with an undercover cop. He hadn't thought about any of this for thirteen years, but just one glance at the paper and the past slid into focus, as if someone had twisted the lens on a camera.

CHAPTER TWELVE

FOUR AND A HALF POUNDS

———————◆———————

IT WAS THE THIRD WEEK OF JUNE 2002 and Alex Timmerman had asked Vermeulen to sit in on a meeting at the Kennel.

"So why did you ask me here?" he said.

Timmerman sat in one of the cruddy chairs. "I want you to meet one of the undercover cops. He's got information of a financial nature. You're the money man."

"I figured that. Could you be more specific?"

"Euro conversion. You know that since the introduction of the euro last January, crooks all over Europe have a problem, how to exchange their dirty money for clean euros. Bringing bags of cash to the bank and exchanging it will get you a lot of questions."

The buzzer sounded. Timmerman opened the apartment door and waited. A few moments later, a young man with stringy long hair and patchy beard stepped inside. He was dressed in workday clothes; jeans, washed-out cotton shirt and leather boots.

"Who's he?" the man said.

"He's from the prosecutor's office. He needs to hear what you have to say."

Vermeulen stepped forward and stuck out his hand. "Hello, I'm . . ."

The man interrupted him. "No names, the less I know, the better."

He sat down. "Here's what's going on. Since January, Antwerp criminals have used a variety of tricks to convert old money into euros. The standby has been paying loads of people to go to banks with relatively minor amounts of cash, usually no more than three thousand euros worth. By doing what everyone else is doing, they're blending in and are counting on banks being too busy with the conversion to pay attention."

Vermeulen nodded. "Yeah, I heard that, but that's pretty cumbersome. A lot of people who need to be paid. And there's a chance of getting caught and then ratting out the superiors."

"The other strategy is buying things, gold, diamonds, real estate," the undercover cop said. "They hold these assets for a little while, then dispose them and get euros back."

Vermeulen had heard that too.

The undercover cop continued. "Finally, they've been using loan sharks. Get this, they lend money to people interest free as long as they pay back the loan in euros. Still, that too takes time and there's of course some leakage."

"So how does that affect payments to drug cartels?" Vermeulen said. "They take dollars. What you're telling us has little to do with that."

"Hold on," the cop said. "What's the big new feature of the euro that has even the Cali Cartel interested?"

Vermeulen was not impressed. "It's the five-hundred-euro bill. Yes, we know. It means the volume of cash shrinks to a fifth. Bulk cash smuggling will be much easier. A million dollars in hundred-dollar bills weighs about twenty-two pounds. A million euros in five-hundred-euro bills weighs four and a half pounds. But has the Cali Cartel accepted Euros?"

The undercover cop said, "Yes, because it's much easier to stash in a false bottom of a suitcase."

Vermeulen wasn't sure. "You'd think so, but I think that's still risky. The increased airport security since 2001 makes smuggling cash via air couriers to Latin America much more difficult. We're back to the sea route."

"How are they getting all those high-denomination bills?" Timmerman said.

"Money service businesses," Vermeulen says. "They take your small bills, count 'em, sort 'em and exchange 'em for large bills. All for a fee, of course. Not illegal *per se*, unless it's done for the purposes of money laundering. What I do want to know is how the cash gets back to Colombia."

The undercover cop shrugged. "I don't have anything solid on that. I assume it goes with the return freight. We get bananas plus a load of coke and they get whatever they buy from us plus the cash."

He got up. "That's all I got." Timmerman brought him to the door. They whispered something. The cop left. Timmerman came back.

"I gotta say, I'm underwhelmed," Vermeulen said. "None of this information is news. Are you sure this guy's digging deep enough?"

"He's doing as much as is safe. Ask too many questions and you're dead."

"I get that, but he's also wrong about the cash smuggling. It's not simply the reverse of the coke smuggling. Maybe at the macro level, but not at the practical level. Think of how the cocaine gets into the country. Runners break open a container and pull out a million euros worth of cocaine. They turn it over to the syndicate for a nice fee, and they're done. No trust required."

"What do you mean, no trust required?" Timmerman said.

"Say a runner decides to keep a million euros worth of coke, thinking it's worth a lot more than the fee he gets. How's he going to turn the coke into cash? Selling it by the gram? The syndicate will kill him before he's made any money."

Timmerman frowns and says, "But that's the same with cash."

"No. Having a million euros means you can disappear fast. No transactions required. The syndicate would never trust a runner to put cash into a container. No, it happens before the container ever makes it to the port, before it's sealed for customs. We need to find out where that is."

* * *

Later that day, Vermeulen again sat at his desk in the office on Justitiestraat. He was tired of Timmerman calling him to this and that meeting. The man seemed way too impressed by the mediocre information brought by his assorted contacts in the underworld. They were offering chickenfeed and Timmerman sold it as pure gold. Had nobody told him that his intelligence sucks? Being new to the task force, Vermeulen didn't want to step on his toes.

He knew that the amount of money that flowed back to Colombia exceeded whatever scale Timmerman and his undercover cop imagined. The estimate of cocaine coming into Antwerp back then ranged from five to ten tons over the last twelve months. Vermeulen considered the upper limit a safe bet. The street price hovered around 48 euros per gram. That put the cash received at around four-hundred eight million euros. Not all of that went back to Colombia, of course, but applying the retail rule of thumb of a fifty percent markup, that still left well over two-hundred million euros that needed to be repatriated across the Atlantic.

The sheer amount made smuggling by couriers impossible. Too risky. People were unreliable, they got caught, they stole it. The next option was stuffing it in containers. Less risky, but that required access to the infrastructure of shipping.

Vermeulen yawned and stretched. He got up to refill his coffee cup. On the way back, he stopped at Boogman's office.

"Hi Connie, the task force must have checked on Beukes's trading company, can you tell me where I can find that information?"

"There should be a binder labeled *Globaal Handelsbedrijf* on the shelf. Good luck. We've subpoenaed their records so often, Jordi Vanderfeld joked that they should just keep a second set right here."

"That's not funny."

"I know, because we know they have a real second set hidden somewhere."

"So, you didn't find anything fishy in those books?"

Boogman shook her head. "Nope. Sure, there were the usual errors and omissions, but nothing that amounts to money laundering. On that front *Globaal* is as clean as a whistle."

"Well, I'll give it another look."

He put the cup down on his desk and went off to find the binder. Back at his desk, he paged through it: columns of text and numbers, a few notes scribbled here and there. Vermeulen drank coffee and pondered the information.

The most effective swindle is the kind that doesn't look like a swindle. So whatever *Globaal* had declared to be in those containers probably has been shipped. Sure, customs checked only a small fraction of the outgoing shipments, but a smart smuggler wouldn't rely on chance. They'd have a foolproof method. He started to look for a pattern.

First came more homework. Trade statistics. What was shipped from Belgium to Colombia? He called the Ministry of Trade, where they told him with unmistakable pride that all that information was on their website. At least one arm of the government was on the ball technologically speaking. He couldn't say the same about the prosecutor's office.

Weirdly enough, Belgium's top export to Columbia in 2002 was human and animal blood. If he were writing a crime novel, he'd have his plot right there— the mob kills people, then sells their blood. But he wasn't. It was probably something medical or other. Definitely with stringent safeguards, what with AIDS and mad cow disease.

He skipped down the list until he was stopped by something familiar. Belgium was shipping coated paper to Colombia. He thought he saw something about paper in *Globaal's* books. He checked. Yes. There it was. Two twenty-foot containers with rolls of coated paper. Paper is heavy. One could easily add a few million dollars or euros, nicely shrink-wrapped, and it wouldn't even register on the scale.

He kept on digging. *Globaal* wasn't a large firm by any stretch, but they were shipping an astonishing array of things. Antique cars, Dutch licorice, cheese, beer, electronic parts, vegetables, fresh and frozen. They even handled people's households when they moved to Latin America. Many consignments were small and got lumped together to fill a container. Either there's a market for that—ignored by the big firms—or *Globaal* was doing this because they just needed plausible transactions to explain their illegal earnings, probably a combination of both.

In all this olio of transactions there was only one constant, two containers of coated paper. They appeared far more regularly than any of the other shipments. And always to the same consignee.

Coated paper. Junk mail is printed on coated paper. Maybe Colombian marketers have just discovered that bane.

He called the customs office. Is there a way to find out when a container from a specific consignee is scheduled to be loaded? Oh, sorry, customs isn't a public information service? My mistake. Yes, I'll try the port offices.

The folks there weren't a lot more helpful.

"We could try," the man on the phone said. Vermeulen heard the emphasis on the word *could*. "But I'll be honest. You won't get what you need. Each line handles its own loading schedule. They transmit what's on board just before the ship leaves. By the time we find out and could tell you, the ship is already on its way to the North Sea."

Vermeulen explained that he's looking at a small shipper, not a big line.

"That's even worse," the man said. "The small ones just play it by ear. They are cheap because they don't guarantee arrival by a certain date. They load at the last minute when a slot opens up on a ship going their way. That's how they get the lowest rate from the shipping lines."

Vermeulen sat and contemplated yet another dead end. He wasn't given to swearing, but would've very much enjoyed an outburst just then. Instead he texted Timmerman.

Set up a meeting with Vinke. I need to know when the next paper shipment is going to Cartagena.

CHAPTER THIRTEEN

PAST PERFORMANCE

———◆———

R EMEMBERING THE PAST OF 2002 wasn't any more interesting than being in
the present. The afternoon at the Kennel dragged on. De Haas and Dekker
had taken turns watching Vermeulen. Except for reliving the past—which he
could've done without—looking through these binders was a complete waste
of time. There wasn't going to be a smoking gun in these folders. At least the
information would be handy if he needed to defend himself.

He'd looked through a series of status reports that contained nothing
important, when Dekker returned from wherever she'd gone. De Haas promptly
took off.

"I have that information about Theo Vinke you asked for," she said. "He's
still married to Nora Vanderfeld. They have two daughters. Why did you want
to know?"

"Just checking."

Theo Vinke was in the sphere of organized crime. Despite Smits's
protestations to the contrary, Vermeulen didn't believe for a moment that Theo
was not involved in criminal activities. A bunch of snack concessions were the
perfect front to hide his illegal doings.

That brought up the question why he wanted to draw attention to himself.
What did he have to gain? Possibly money, but only if the department was
held responsible. Vermeulen himself had no assets that could be tapped. His
retirement funds were off limits, he didn't own a house. It just didn't make
sense. Unless Theo was out for revenge. Did the evidence he received from his
dead father-in-law trigger an itch that he just wanted to scratch? Nah, that was
too farfetched. On the other hand, you never knew how long someone could
carry a grudge.

It all boiled down to the fact that Vermeulen was missing something. He took a piece of paper and started sketching what he knew. First, he'd been watched ever since he arrived, the watchers even knew his phone number, which wasn't public. Second, someone had been at the Kennel recently, moved the furniture and opened the file cabinets. Third, the judge and the cops were eager to push whatever blame there was onto Vermeulen.

"What are you writing?" Dekker said. She was sitting near the window and staring at the rain outside.

"Some notes. Listen, is this assignment some sort of punishment for you?"

She looked up, but didn't say anything.

"I mean, the only thing worse than having to read these old files has got to be watching me do it. De Haas, sure, he's new. I can see how he ends up here. The crappy jobs always go to the new guy. But you? You've got experience. You've been around the block, as we say in New York. I can see that. It doesn't make sense for you to be here, unless you crossed your boss or Mesman somehow."

She turned back to the window, staring at the dark clouds long enough to make him think she hadn't heard him. He knew better. When she turned again, her face was a mask.

"It's none of your business. Just keep reading."

"You're right about that. I'll go back to my work, but, hey, if you ever want to talk about it, let me know. I'm not in the department anymore, and I'll be gone by the end of the week. Nothing will come back to you."

He stretched and got up. "On a totally different note. Okay if I go and get some coffee? I'll bring you some."

Dekker nodded absentmindedly. He got up and headed for the door.

"Wait for me," she said. "I'll come along."

"Good. I wouldn't know where to go anyway."

They headed downstairs. The rain had turned into a faint drizzle and they left their umbrellas inside the front door. On the street, Dekker headed to the left toward Falconplein. Vermeulen walked next to her. Halfway down the street, she said, "You are right, this isn't my dream appointment. I was set to move to EUROPOL as the Belgian liaison officer for their task force on organized crime. I was looking forward to it."

"What happened? That assignment sounds tailor made for you."

"Long story and too boring. But I ended up babysitting you."

They reached a restaurant that was a poor imitation of an American Diner. Vermeulen hoped that the coffee would be better than the appearance. He ordered two large cups and added an *Appelflap*. "You want one too?" She hesitated, but he told the server to wrap up two of the triangular apple pastries.

She made ready to get her money out, but he stopped her.

"You'll have to fill papers in triplicate to get reimbursed. Consider it my peace offering."

On the way back he said, "I am curious as to what happened. It must've been significant to make such a dent in your career."

"I can't really say. It's being investigated. Let's just say a piece of evidence disappeared. I don't have it, never even handled it, but my name showed up last in the chain of custody."

"Looks to me like you were set up."

"Doesn't it, though. I can't make any sense of it."

"Maybe de Haas is unhappy about you moving on."

"Him?" She gave Vermeulen that *are you serious* look. "Please. He doesn't have the imagination to be devious. He's sucks up to his superiors, which is all he's good at." Dekker stopped. "I shouldn't have said that. I'm sorry. Please ignore that."

"I understand your being bitter. We all trust our colleagues; how else could we do our work. To be knifed in the back feels doubly wrong."

Dekker nodded.

They climbed up the dingy staircase and greeted the stink of the Kennel with a sigh.

"It is what it is," Dekker said. "Back to work for you."

"Not before I have my coffee and my *Appelflap*." He went into the kitchen, came back with a towel, pushed the binders to one side and wiped the surface of the desk. "There you go, please join me. Beats balancing things on your thigh. I don't want my *Appelflap* to fall on the toxic carpet."

She smiled and sat at the other side of the desk.

After finishing the coffee and pastry, Vermeulen went back to the files. The next document was the summary of his second meeting with Vinke. He compared the dates. The meeting took place just one day after he'd texted Timmerman with the request. Vermeulen remembered that even back in 2002 he'd thought that was too fast.

* * *

HOW DID TIMMERMAN ARRANGE A MEETING with Vinke so fast? Vermeulen went back to the Kennel on a day after meeting the undercover cop. Frans Vinke was already waiting there with Timmerman. Vinke looked much better than when Vermeulen last saw him. His face was polished and fresh, if a bit ruddy. The buzz cut that made him look quite unlike a member of the special forces. That detention pallor was definitely gone. His clothes looked newer, too. Creased jeans—somehow mobsters thought them to be the height of fashion—a white T-shirt and a light black motorcycle jacket casually slung over the back of the chair he sat on.

"It's you, huh?" he said when Vermeulen enters. "Let me tell you, I don't like it. No, I don't. Rat out my own family? That's what you want me to do? No way."

"Spare me the crocodile tears," Vermeulen said. "Your track record tells me that you never had any compunction throwing people under the bus if it helped you."

Vinke pouted. "You know what they say on those investment statements, 'Past performance is no guarantee of future outcomes.'"

"Yes, but your past is the exact opposite of what they are referring to. It would pretty much guarantee the same outcome. But what would you know about investment contracts anyway?"

Vinke hesitated, then mumbled something about having to worry about retirement. He didn't fool Vermeulen.

"Looks like Beukes has finally given you a job," Timmerman said. "Took a while, didn't it? I figured marrying his sister would get you a job sooner."

Vinke shrugged. "He's wary, is all. Likes how his company runs. You'd do the same."

"He made peace with you marrying his sister?"

Vinke got red in the face. "What you talking about. He never had no problem with us marrying."

"Not what I heard," Timmerman said.

"Who'd you hear it from."

Timmerman ignored the question. "How does Ingrid like having a stepson? She and Theo getting along?"

"Theo doesn't live with us."

"Ah, that should help. Frankly, I don't get what she sees in you. But love works in mysterious ways, or so they say."

"Just leave Ingrid out of this." Vinke was getting all squirmy on his chair.

Strange, his marriage seems a touchy subject, Vermeulen thought.

"Don't worry," Vermeulen said. "Tell us what's happening at *Globaal Handelsbedrijf*?"

Vinke turned a bit sulky. "Beukes doesn't let me near any of the incoming trade. That part of the operation is off-limits for me."

"He doesn't trust you?" Vermeulen said.

"Maybe." Vinke seemed genuinely upset by that. "And I'm family. He trusts strangers before trusting his own blood."

"Come on, let's not get carried away, you married into the family. Whatever you do, don't make a fuss about it. Be the nice brother-in-law, don't rock the boat. Work on earning his trust," Timmerman said, sounding worried.

Vermeulen didn't share that concern. He'd milk Vinke as long as he can, and wouldn't lose sleep over his eventual discovery.

He said, "If you don't get near the incoming goods, what do you get near to?"

"Everything else. Whatever's shipped out." Vinke found his bluster again.

"What do you do exactly?"

"Well, this and that, you know, keep an eye on things, making sure that everything is on the up 'n up."

"In other words, nothing. You have a no-show-job." Vermeulen shook his head, wondering if he'd made a mistake recruiting Vinke.

"The hell I do. I show up for work every weekday, and on time. Beukes is a tough boss."

"Where do you show up?"

"The *Globaal* main port office. Across from *Churchilldok*."

"Are there other offices?"

Vinke shakes his head.

"Good, then tell me about those paper shipments," Vermeulen said.

There was spark of recognition in Vinke's eyes. He quickly put on a puzzled look. "What do you care about paper shipments? I thought you were after drugs?"

"Just answer the question."

"Paper shipments usually are loaded at the *Delwaidedok*. Just a couple of twenty-foot containers, like every three weeks or so. It's not a big-ticket item, I wonder why he bothers."

"What are the big ticket items?"

"Medications, plastics, old cars. Beukes is always looking for new opportunities."

"When's the next paper shipment?"

Vinke scratched his chin, pretending to wrack his brains.

"Come on," Vermeulen said. "I don't have all day."

"It varies."

"Listen," Vermeulen said, louder now. "If you don't know anything, I have no use for you. Remember those ten years in prison. I can easily toss you back to Smits and the stolen cars."

Vinke crumbled. "In two days."

"Who supervises the loading?" Vermeulen said.

Vinke shrugs. "The paper factory? All I know is the containers are brought to the dock and then they are loaded on the ship."

"Where's the factory?"

"Zaventem."

"Does Beukes pick up the containers, or does the factory bring them?"

"Beukes doesn't pick up containers. He's the boss."

"You know what I mean. *Globaal* picks them up?"

Vinke nodded.

"Where are they now?"

"I don't know. They're supposed to arrive tomorrow. Get loaded the day after."

Vermeulen threw out the most important question. "You wouldn't know the container numbers, would you?"

Vinke shook his head, but, eager to please, said, "I can find out."

"Do that and text them to Timmerman. You do have a burner, right?"

"He does," Timmerman said.

"Okay. We need those numbers right away."

Chapter Fourteen

Percentages of Guilt

———◆———

Back in 2002, it was the waiting that bugged Vermeulen. Now it was the sheer tedium of watching the clock march forward while reading old files. He knew they wanted to pin Frans Vinke's death on him. That meant he had to continue to prove his innocence. Vermeulen took that to heart as he walked back to his hotel. What a way to end what had been a miserable week all around. Even worse, he now faced a weekend with nothing to do but wait for the trudge to continue on Monday. At least there'd been a tentative thaw in his dealings with Dekker.

The forecast for Saturday and Sunday was more rain. Not that he was going to do any sightseeing. At least he'd have time to buy an umbrella. Being stuck in a strange hotel room for two days was not his only option, of course. But as miserable as it sounded, it was less daunting than the alternative, contacting his ex-wife Marieke. He'd wanted to call his daughter Gaby ever since he arrived, but hadn't because he was certain she would tell him to meet with Marieke. It was the last thing he wanted to do.

Halfway to his hotel—he'd chosen a different route to foil whoever might be following him—he decided he needed to eat something. He didn't really care about what he'd eat. The next restaurant would be as good as any. That turned out to be a literal hole in the wall. The place was barely wider than the entrance. The inside was dark and stank of cigarette smoke. Three bare forty-watt bulbs hung from the ceiling. Three small tables stood on two legs each and were bolted to the left wall. Instead of chairs, stools stood at the short ends of each. The tables were bare, gouged and full of stains. The walls were a dirty beige, the ceiling even darker from centuries of cigarette smoke. A narrow path to the right led to a dark curtain.

Two men sat across from each other at the farthest table, smoking and drinking beer. The one facing Vermeulen gave him the once over and said something to his companion. That one turned around and repeated the assessment. Apparently, Vermeulen didn't warrant further concern because the second man shrugged and turned back to his table mate.

Vermeulen stood for a moment, thinking he should move on. This wasn't a place where strangers came to eat. But he was a stubborn man so he sat the hell down. As nasty as the place looked, it had more character than the bright trendy places that could've been anywhere in the world. He only hoped the food passed health department standards.

A figure emerged from behind a black curtain. The woman was short, but so wide she had to sidle past the tables. She wore a short-sleeved blouse that might have been white at one point, straining against the buttons, an apron the color of dirt over a brown skirt.

"You want to eat or drink?" she said.

"Both, if that's possible."

She nodded, turned back and disappeared behind the black curtain.

He settled on the stool and expected her to come back with a menu. She didn't. He waited, checked his watch, and waited some more. After seven minutes she came back carrying a chipped plate with *Stoemp*, slices of fried *Bloedworst*, and apple sauce in one hand and a bottle of beer in the other. She put both down hard enough to make the beer foam up. She pulled a fork and knife from her apron and dropped them next to the plate.

"Fifteen euros," she said and handed him a shred of paper with the numbers one and five scrawled on it.

Vermeulen pulled out his wallet and handed her a twenty-euro bill. She took it and disappeared behind the curtain. He waited for his change, but the woman didn't come back. He probed the mount of mashed potatoes and carrots with his fork. The first mouthful transported him back to his mother's kitchen on the farm. The mash was smooth, but not food-processor fine. Just enough salt and pepper, a little cream and nothing else. So far so good.

Bloedworst could be hit or miss. Getting blood sausage right depended on the artistry of the butcher. He didn't hold out much hope that anyone in the mechanized food industry still knew that art. The first bite proved him wrong. Just the right mix of blood, flour, and specks of suet. The dusky flavor brought back images of the annual pig slaughter on the farm. The most vivid was of an eviscerated pig spread wide and hanging by its front hooves from hooks next to the barn door.

He ate with increasing gusto while the flood of memories took him back. He'd only learned later that his father had struggled all along. His parents managed to keep that reality to themselves. He spent his childhood outdoors, around animals, on the tractor, in the meadow, playing the grass trumpet with blades of grass between his thumbs, or searching for eggs in the chicken coop. He had his chores, which he did more or less to his parents' satisfaction. He thought of it as a solid childhood. Words like happy or sad didn't really fit. There were ups and downs—life was like that—but it had grounded him in the world.

He finished the meal and wiped his mouth with his hands since he hadn't received a napkin. The two men had left after finishing their beers. No other patrons had come inside. The woman hadn't appeared again. For a moment he wondered if he was dreaming the entire episode, as if the restaurant existed apart from time and space. He stood up and shouted, "Thank you, it was delicious." A grunted "Bye" was the only response he got.

He stepped out of the door and back into a reality in which he knew he had to call Gaby. He took out his phone and dialed her number.

"I was wondering when you were going to call," Gaby said.

His daughter worked in the Düsseldorf office of a Belgian logistics company. She headed their Africa bureau and Vermeulen couldn't be prouder of her achievements. The only sore point between them was his unwillingness to speak to his ex-wife. Ever since they reconciled some five years ago, Gaby had made it her mission to get her parents to make up. Which was the reason why he hadn't called her first thing after arriving in Antwerp. She'd have dropped everything and arranged a parental conclave to *talk things through*. Since Vermeulen didn't think there was anything to talk through, it was going to be a train wreck. A good enough reason not to call.

"You talked to Tessa?" he said.

Tessa had met Gaby a few years back in Vienna, after Gaby had been in a skiing accident. They'd become good friends, which meant Vermeulen couldn't really keep anything from one or the other.

"Have you talked to Mom yet?"

"Haven't had the time. This thing here is far worse than I expected, they're trying to pin responsibility for a murder on me."

If he thought his dire situation would get Gaby off the Mom thing, he was wrong.

"All it takes is a short call. Is that too much?"

"And then what? Set up a meeting, have dinner? Agree that the divorce was a big mistake? As much as you would like that, it's not going to happen. A lot went wrong back then. We were both at fault and rehashing who was responsible for what, assigning percentages of guilt, won't help anyone. Pulling off scabs just starts the bleeding again. It's better to leave them alone."

It was the most he'd said to Gaby on that topic in a long time. She was silent. Damn. He'd gone too far. But he was tired of deflecting her attempts to get him to engage with Marieke.

"I see," she said. "Sorry to trouble you. Hope you have a nice stay in Antwerp."

"Wait. Don't hang up. I'm sorry, Sweetheart. That was harsh and selfish. I know you'd love nothing more than have your parents get along again. I'm not saying that's never going to happen. Scabs fall off when they've done their jobs. But we've got to give them time."

He held his breath, waiting for the hiss of a disconnected call. It didn't come. He breathed out.

"As much as I appreciate your medical analogy, it fails," she said. "While the scabs are there, the body is busy working on healing. When the healing is done, the scab comes off. I don't see you do anything that would promote healing. In your case, the scab will just become infected and fester forever."

"*Touché*," was all he could say. He knew better than to argue with his daughter.

There was more silence. He took it as a good sign that she wasn't ending the call.

"Will you come this weekend?" he said.

"Only if you agree to meet with Mom."

"As long as you are there, sure."

"Are you afraid of her?"

"I'm afraid of reliving the pain I've tried to forget for thirteen years," he said.

"Don't you think Mom is in the same boat?"

"I don't know. Maybe. The last time we met, I had no sense of that."

"I'll call her and see if she's up to it."

"Please come either way. It's only a couple of hours by train."

* * *

HE OPENED THE DOOR TO HIS ROOM with trepidation, anticipating another envelope with an old photo. There wasn't one. He exhaled. This whole surveillance thing made little sense. If someone was trying to unsettle him, they'd succeeded. For a day and a half. After he told Dekker and de Haas about the Kennel, there was nothing more to hide. Well, almost nothing.

Three photos, three text messages. And then, nothing. Someone had photographed him going to and leaving the Kennel. The secret place wasn't as secret as they thought it was back then. Someone kept an eye on it and photographed him. It felt almost like a private detective had been collecting evidence on a philandering husband.

Was that it? Some PI shooting photos of everyone who entered a house of prostitution on the off chance it could land him a job. Nah, couldn't be that. How would the PI even know whether or not the man in question was married and how to find the aggrieved spouse? The surveillance had to be more targeted. But the PI scenario gave him another idea. If they'd taken photos of his comings and goings, they'd have taken photos of everyone entering and leaving, including Frans Vinke. For what purpose? And why send them now and not back then?

His first assumption had been that Theo Vinke sent them, but that didn't make sense. Theo was looking for revenge, a payout, or both. These photos didn't bolster his case. All they did was show that the task force had used a secret meeting place. There was no logical connection to the claim that Vermeulen had leaked the name.

What if Theo Vinke wasn't the sender? The photos showed that the Kennel wasn't a secret, that someone knew Frans Vinke went there to meet with police. Who would want him to know that?

He stood up, fetched the bottle of *jenever* and poured himself a finger. He stepped to the window and looked out at the night streets. There was a lot of foot traffic. Friday night meant a larger than normal crowd, even with the drizzle that persisted into the evening.

As the pale amber liquor burned its way down his throat, it struck him that the photographs proved his innocence. Somebody knew that Frans Vinke was a rat before the investigation was finished, before Vermeulen was supposed to have leaked the name. The warmth of the booze and relief spread through his body. Who could that be? Beukes and Vanderfeld were the logical candidates. Vanderfeld was dead. Beukes, then. He couldn't think of a single reason why Bastiaan Beukes would want to help him.

If only Tessa were here. She'd have the clear grasp of an outsider about the whole matter. And she'd enjoy standing there with him, sipping the *jenever* and looking at the old city at night. He did the next best thing and called her. She was on her way to a meeting and couldn't talk long. He told her that he'd spoken with Gaby.

"I'm glad you did," she said. "It sure took you a long time."

"That's because I dread what's coming next."

"Don't be so dramatic. You don't have to meet her. You could just talk on the phone."

"That wouldn't be enough for Gaby. She wants her parents to make up."

The moment he'd ended the call, his phone rang again. This time the caller was Jan Smits.

"Hey Valentin, how are things going. I hope Dekker and de Haas aren't pestering you too hard."

"Hey Jan. It's a pain, but you know that already. Anything new you can tell me?"

"No. Now that those two are at it, I don't hear much. How's it being back at the Kennel?"

Vermeulen hesitated. That was odd.

"How do you know about the Kennel?" Vermeulen said.

"That's where you three are meeting. Mesman told us that the investigation had moved there. You find anything interesting?"

"There isn't anything interesting. Listen, thanks for checking in. It's been a long day. I need some rest. See you around."

He ended the call, but that didn't end the strange feeling he had. They way Smits had asked about being back at the Kennel sure sounded like he'd known about the dank apartment all along.

CHAPTER FIFTEEN

ERRARE HUMANUM EST

———◆———

THE SAME WOMAN WHO'D FOLLOWED HIM two nights earlier stood, half hidden by a tree, across the Vrijdagmarkt, a little square where people sold second-hand goods every Friday morning. Since it was Saturday, the square was empty. Vermeulen caught sight of her when he turned the page on the *Gazet van Antwerpen*. The cafe had free copies. With the paper as cover, he tried to locate her companion. Either the man wasn't around, or he was better at remaining invisible. She wore a teal raincoat, made from some modern waterproof material. The hood covered her hair, but he recognized the sharp nose and the narrow chin.

He took a deep breath and exhaled again. As if the whole document search wasn't annoying enough. No, he had to deal with amateur spies, too. He'd had it. Enough of this nonsense. It was time to find out who was after him. Although a confrontation was tricky—the last thing he needed was being arrested for harassment—it was better than trying to follow her. Who knew where he'd end up?

The next question was where to confront her. The Vrijdagmarkt wasn't a good place. She could just walk away if he approached her. And running after her was exactly the scenario he hoped to avoid. No, a confined place preferably with controlled access would offer more options. He pulled out his phone, tapped the map app, and, for once, was lucky. The Plantin-Moretus Museum was just a couple of hundred yards away at the western end of the square. He checked the museum's website. It was the home and print shop of one of the earliest publishing dynasties, dating back to the fifteen hundreds. The fact that it was a UNESCO World Heritage Site only made his visit there more believable. And it opened at ten on Saturdays. He signaled the waiter for another cup of coffee and continued reading the newspaper, while keeping an eye on the woman.

At ten o'clock, he folded the paper and put it back on its rack. The woman was there. She'd switched to a different tree. Standing outside in the wet weather without moving was suspicious. She made it look like she'd been stood up, tapping her phone, staring at its screen, looking at the sky, then at the ground, shaking her head, and repeating it again. She called someone, or pretended to do so. It was pretty convincing.

He paid the waiter, left the change for a tip and ventured outside. The rain had started again. He hadn't acquired an umbrella yet, so he hurried across the square. If the woman was good at her job, she'd be after him in no time, just like he planned.

A small line had formed at the entrance of the museum, but he got in quickly, paid the entrance fee, glad to be in a dry place. The cashier gave him a floor plan of the museum and asked if he wanted to rent an audio guide. Vermeulen declined, but he stopped in the gift shop, buying an umbrella. It was black with the phrase *Errare humanum est* printed all over it in white letters and different typefaces.

He followed the suggested path through the first floor. The plan helpfully labeled important exhibits as *must see*. The Museum was kept as close to the sixteenth century style as possible. Dark wood dominated every room, be it the wainscoting or heavy pieces of furniture. In the Big Drawing Room, he lingered in front of a Rubens portrait of Christophe Plantin, the founder of the press. Since it was one of the *must-see* items, he examined the painting from many angles, glancing into the adjoining room until he caught a glimpse of the woman.

The next room, another drawing room, led to a colonnade that bordered a formal garden on the left, and more exhibits to the right. Vermeulen took quick steps forward and hid behind one of the columns. He heard steps on the stone pavers. No one followed him to the garden. It was too wet to admire the expertly trimmed boxwoods. He waited a few minutes to allow the woman to make her way to the next room, then followed her.

She stood inside, her hood flipped down, revealing black, straight hair, cut to medium length. She wasn't focused on the books, prints and maps on shelves, a simulacrum of the sixteenth century shop. Instead, she peered around a corner into the next room, trying to catch sight of Vermeulen. She turned to look backward. Vermeulen stepped back behind the door frame. Had she seen him? Her next move would depend on that. If she had, she wouldn't confront him. No watcher would. She'd disappear and hope to pick up the trail elsewhere. Or someone else would step in. If she hadn't seen him, she'd hurry forward to catch up.

He looked again at the plan. The garden and the rain were the best cover, and she should come out into the colonnade again after walking through the next exhibits. He cut across the gravel path surrounding the boxwoods and stopped next to the last column, his new umbrella now opened to hide his face. He saw the teal raincoat, stepped toward it, raising the umbrella at the same time. The woman recognized him, stopped, her eyes darting left and right. He took advantage of the moment, grabbed her by the elbow before she could step back, pulled her closer as if to offer her shelter under the umbrella. He turned with her toward the boxwoods. Just a couple braving the weather to admire the gardens. By the time she offered any resistance, they were already partway toward the center of the garden and out of earshot.

"Who are you?" he said. "Who told you to follow me?"

"Let me go." She tried to pull her arm from his grip but didn't succeed.

"You've been following me since I arrived. Where's your partner? He got the day off?"

"I don't know what you are talking about."

"Stop pretending. I know you're following me, so tell me who sent you and I'll let you go."

"I'll scream," she said. Her eyes were glaring and she flashed her teeth through her twisted lips. He had no doubt that she was a formidable screamer.

"I'll scream back. I'm good at it, too. It'd just be a couple having a fight at the museum. Happens all the time. Worst case, they throw us out, but you won't get rid of me."

She seemed to relax, but Vermeulen didn't fall for the trick. He held onto her elbow.

"Just tell me," he said.

"What if I don't? You going to slap me? I doubt that very much. There's nothing you can make me do. Let go."

"You are right. I can't make you say anything. But I'll follow you and you'll lead me to your employer. And believe me, that's a lot easier when I don't have to hide. Your boss will know that your cover is blown. I'm assuming he won't take kindly to it."

"Nonsense, I'll just call him and tell him you went home."

"I'll follow you. Just think of me as your shadow from now on."

She jerked free of his grip and pulled her phone from her purse. "I'm calling him now."

She tapped a few times and put the phone to her ear.

"Hi," she said. "It's me. Vermeulen's found me out and wants to know who you are."

She listened a moment, wrinkling her brows, and handed the phone to Vermeulen.

Vermeulen identified himself.

"You're quicker than I expected," a male voice said. "I guess Nora didn't quite blend in as much as I hoped."

Despite the familiar demeanor, Vermeulen hadn't heard that voice before. "Who are you?"

"Come on. Put two and two together. It's Theo, Theo Vinke."

That would make the woman Nora Vanderfeld. "Why are you following me. You are already suing the department. What do you want from me?"

"The department will cover its ass and blame you. That's all they're interested in. If you haven't figured that out yet, you will when the evidence comes out. You'll do what every smart person would do, you'll try to skip town and go back to New York. I want to make sure you don't. That's why I need to know where you are at all times."

"What evidence?" Vermeulen said.

Vinke didn't elaborate. All he said was, "You killed my father. I'll make you pay."

"How? You're going to arrest me yourself?"

Nora stood and frowned.

"I'll figure something out," Theo said and ended the call.

Vermeulen looked at Nora. "What is he talking about? What evidence?"

She shrugged as if to say, "Don't look at me. Not my idea. I'm just the helper."

Chapter Sixteen

Cold Turkey

————— ◆ —————

AT NOON, GABY CALLED. "I'M ON THE TRAIN FROM DÜSSELDORF, will arrive in Antwerp close to two. We're meeting with Mom tomorrow for brunch at a restaurant. You know, neutral ground. If that goes well, we might have dinner together, too. Sound okay?"

Vermeulen swallowed. There were other things he'd rather do. Anything, really. Even being bored in his hotel room. But he wanted to honor Gaby's wishes. Being civil for a couple of hours was the least he could do. As long as he ignored Marieke's barbs, he'd be fine. After brunch, he'd politely decline to join them for dinner. Gaby was hoping for more, much more, but a daughter is entitled to be unreasonable when it comes to her parents, no matter what her age. "Sure," he said. "Sounds like a good plan."

Despite the weather, he decided to walk to the Centraal Station. His new umbrella held up well and he had plenty of time. He stopped at a *Frituur* that had a glassed-in seating area and got his fix of fries with mayo and added a *Curryworst*. They didn't taste nearly as good as the previous fries he'd had. It had nothing to do with the quality of the food, more the state of his mind. He couldn't shake the feeling that he was besieged on all sides. Meeting his ex-wife was another burden added to an already considerable load.

When Gaby got off the InterCity train, all that *Angst* that had tormented Vermeulen blew away like wisps of steam on a cold day. She'd let her hair grow longer, which brought out the curl he'd always loved when she was little. She put down her bag, they kissed each other on both cheeks, hesitated a moment, then hugged.

"It's good to see you," he said. "Thanks for coming."

"I hope you'll say the same tomorrow evening."

He smiled. "I know I will. Tomorrow will be whatever it will be, but you are here now and I'm glad to see you."

"And I you."

They walked into the main station building and stopped at the exit doors.

"Where do you want to go?" she said. "The weather isn't much for walking around."

"Hmm. I don't know. My hotel room is far too small. Any museum you want to see?"

She shook her head. "Too exhausting. I either need to walk at a good pace or sit."

Outside the rain had stopped, but the wind felt raw on his skin. Gaby pointed to the entrance to the zoo. "Hey, let's walk in the zoo. Haven't been here in ages."

"Sounds great."

She left her bag in a locker at the station. He bought two tickets and they wandered past the small monkeys and okapis, toward the valley of the great apes. The drizzle stopped and Vermeulen folded his umbrella.

"Tell me what you are doing here," Gaby said. "Tessa mentioned an old case and you being accused of something, but I couldn't quite understand what that was all about."

Vermeulen took a deep breath and recounted everything that had happened so far. Occasionally, she interrupted and asked for clarification. When he was done, they walked in silence for a while.

"The only thing that sounds fishy to me is you tricking Frans Vinke into ratting out his gangster family," she said. "I don't know the law, so I don't know if that was illegal, but it was just a shitty thing to do."

"Not if you knew Vinke and what was going on at the time. Cocaine . . ."

". . . was coming in like a flood. I know, Dad. I was there. Cocaine wasn't my thing, but you know that. If the likes of me hadn't been buying the stuff, there wouldn't have been the criminal network to bring them in. The real problem wasn't that drugs were coming in, the real problem was so many of us feeling compelled to shoot up, snort or smoke that stuff."

The matter-of-fact manner in which she described her own heroin addiction took Vermeulen by surprise. He didn't know what to say next. The memory of searching for her after she'd run away from home flooded his mind, the anguish he'd felt back then still turning his stomach hollow. She'd been one of the army of teenagers who'd gotten hooked for one reason or another. Finding her had only replaced the anguish with pain.

"You look surprised," she said. "Yes, I liked heroin. The high was unlike anything else. All that shit around you, that miserable world, that lack of future, that dad working eighty hours, just melted away. Instead, the world smiled at you. The birds sang. It was bliss. Not a day goes by when I don't remember that feeling."

"Until you needed the next dose."

"Yeah, there was that. Heroin lasted longer than cocaine. At my stage, I was okay with one hit once a day. Coke lasted maybe an hour and then you needed another bump. That was the main difference for me. Coke just gave you a short buzz. A little pleasantness. Maybe better sex. Heroin took you away from it all."

She looked at Vermeulen whose face must have given away his incredulity. She'd never talked about her drug addiction so openly. They'd walked past the apes, the restaurant and reached the buffalo savanna, where they lingered.

"It's okay, Dad. I'm not proud of those days. I was lost. Between yours and mom's incessant fighting, you always being gone and just the normal sixteen-year-old cynicism about life, the universe, and everything, I'm amazed I got out of it."

He was about to say that he'd been the one who'd yanked her away from that world and got her clean, but held his tongue.

"The point is, I wasn't the only one," she said. "There were tons of teenagers and older people who needed to get high. Nobody ever asked why that was the case. Everybody, you included, blamed the drugs. What we needed was a conversation, an ear, anyone who'd listen. What we got was prison, clinics and the war on drugs. And you were part of that."

He swallowed but remained silent.

"I hated you for taking me away from that," she said. "Rehab was hell. Every day, I scratched a notch into the wall of my cell . . ." She shook her head in response to Vermeulen opening his mouth. "No, don't tell me it was a medical facility. It was a cell. Many before me had scratched notches into the wall. Each notch represented a deeper circle of hell to which I condemned you. You dumped me into that cell, cold turkey, without maintenance dose. Like it was the Middle Ages."

She looked out at the animal enclosure. "Like those buffalos. Locked up. At least they don't know any better. Who knows, maybe they do."

Vermeulen wanted to explain all the reasons why he had to do it back then. She held up her hand.

"Don't, Dad. Please don't argue. That's how it was for me. No matter what you thought. No matter what your intentions were. It was hell. And it didn't have to be that way. That's what I want you to know. You could've gotten me back a different way. Maybe you didn't know better but you also didn't ask."

What was there to say? He'd done what he thought was best. He'd always thought that her anger came from his valuing work over family. Now he saw that it was only partly true. Abandoning her at that facility had kept them from talking for almost eight years. Even now, it lurked in the depths of their relationship.

"I'm sorry. I should have asked," he said after a long while.

Gaby nodded, took a deep breath, closed her eyes, and exhaled.

"You didn't leak Vinke's name, right?" she said, a different Gaby now, as if she'd shaken the past off.

"No. But it feels like that doesn't matter. His son Theo has me followed because he wants me to pay for his dad's death. He says he has evidence. I can't even imagine what that could be."

"Do those cops know that you coerced Vinke into being an informant?"

"Not quite in those terms."

"You should come clean on that. It's better if you tell them. If they find out on their own, you look even worse."

Vermeulen knew that, of course. As a general rule it's always better to admit wrongdoing before it's found out. But he was also thinking like a lawyer, and as a lawyer it's not smart to admit to something without having a solid reason to do so. He hadn't found that reason yet. He didn't say anything.

"Cheer up, Dad. The worst that can happen is that they reprimand you for your unorthodox methods. And they can't even do that since you don't work there anymore."

"From your lips to God's ears."

She smiled. "Hey, looks like it cleared up some. Let's get going. I want to see the giraffes. They are my favorite animals."

They wandered through the zoo until Gaby told him she was going to meet some old friends before going to her mother. They hugged good-bye.

CHAPTER SEVENTEEN

RUBBER FIG

---◆---

VERMEULEN ARRIVED AT THE *FELIX PAKHUIS* shortly before eleven on Sunday morning. It was an old warehouse along the *Willemdok*. It had been renovated to house a restaurant, an events center and space for business function. Gaby had told him that the restaurant had the best brunch buffet in Antwerp. He stepped under the awning over the entrance and shook out his umbrella. *Errare humanum est.* What had possessed him to buy an umbrella with that phrase? If erring was human, he had to be super-human. Damn! This brunch was a mistake, the whole Antwerp episode was due to his mistake. His job at the UN was due to his mistake. Never mind the rest of his life. That's a hell of a lot of erring for one human. Better not to commit another one and get out of here. His umbrella only half open, he saw Gaby and Marieke approach on the sidewalk. Too late.

"Are you already apologizing?" Marieke said. She had cut her hair shorter since he last saw her. Other than a few wrinkles, she was aging well. Her brown eyes still had that sparkle that he'd fallen in love with so many years ago.

Since Vermeulen hadn't said anything yet, he was confused.

"The umbrella, Dad. 'To err is human.'"

"Oh." He breathed out. "No, I needed an umbrella at the Plantin Museum and this was the only kind they sold."

Despite Gaby's explanation, the tone of Marieke's voice pulled him straight back to 2002 and that fateful Friday afternoon.

* * *

Vermeulen rushed up the stairs to their apartment. He was late, again. He opened the door, Gaby lay spread over the sofa reading a magazine. She looked up and said, "You're late. Mom is furious."

He shrugged apologetically.

"I don't really care," she said. "But I'd really like it if, this time, you two wouldn't have another screaming match. I could use some peace and quiet."

"I'll try."

Gaby rolled her eyes and gave him a look that said, *You're pathetic.*

Vermeulen walked past the dining table into the kitchen. It was cramped, like most kitchens in old apartment buildings. Marieke was standing by the stove. Steam roiled up from a pot of boiling water. It was hot. A bowl of green salad was standing on the counter, ready to be eaten. Next to it an open package of spaghetti. The empty frying pan was waiting for something to be fried. He froze, his stomach clenched. He'd forgotten to bring the ground meat and the tomato sauce.

Marieke knew already. He'd been late and forgotten to bring home groceries before. And not just once or twice. She looked at him, her face taut with a lethal mix of resignation and anger. Without saying a word, she dumped the green salad into the trash can. Next, she grabbed the pot and dumped the boiling water into the sink. Steam and hot water made a mess of the sink and the backsplash.

"Wait," Vermeulen said. "I'll . . ."

She turned to leave the kitchen. He stood still, blocking the door.

"Get out of my way," she said.

"The hell I will. You've never forgotten anything?"

"Get the fuck out of my way."

The curse did it for Vermeulen. "Right, throw a tantrum. How very adult of you."

Marieke pressed her lips together. Vermeulen could see how hard she tried not to say anything. He wasn't not impressed. "I've forgotten to buy groceries. Big deal. We'll go and have a pizza or something."

She still didn't say anything.

"Come on. I have way too much on my mind. Work is hell. You could cut me some slack."

The pinched look on her face gave way. Whatever she'd tried to hold back, it was too much and it burst out in a violent rage.

"Cut you some slack? What the fuck you think I've been doing for the past ten years. There's no goddamn slack left. You've used up all the rope."

"Oh yeah? Well, I have news for you, Misses Long-Suffering Perfect. I bust my balls earning enough money to keep this family afloat. What do I get in return? Shit. That's what I get. Every time I come home it's the same bitching, *you're late, you didn't pick up the groceries.* You think I do this on purpose. No, I fucking don't. I have a job."

Marieke put on the bored expression of someone who's heard it all before. "Ah, of course, the job. Mister Rising-Star Prosecutor. The golden boy on his way to the top. Winning his cases, except the one that really matters, his family. If ignoring your family is a prerequisite for your job, you better quit it, or you'll find yourself alone."

Before he could return the last volley, a loud crash came from the living room. They both rushed to the door, the worry about Gaby momentarily trumping their anger. Gaby stood next to the sofa and looked down at the remains of a stoneware planter. Potting soil spilled all over the rug and the rubber fig that had once called the pot its home lay flat on the ground, several of its shiny green leaves broken off.

"What happened, Sweetie?" Marieke said.

"What do you think happened? I smashed the fucking pot. How else could I get your attention. The goddam rubber fig matters more than I do anyway."

It was true that the rubber fig was Marieke's prized houseplant. She'd gotten a cutting from her mother and raised it to its proud height of four feet.

Marieke stood with her mouth open. Vermeulen worked hard not to say, *You go girl.* He didn't have as strong of an aversion to the plant as Gaby, but he didn't mind seeing it demolished on the floor.

"How can you say that, Sweetie?" Marieke had to hold on the backrest of a chair.

"How can you say that, Sweetie?" Gaby's imitation was meant to cut deep and it did.

"Come on you two," Vermeulen said. "Let's settle down and discuss this like adults."

"What?" Gaby said loud enough to be heard outside. "Like you were yelling at each other in the kitchen? Is that how adults do it? Sure, let's all scream at each other, like adults."

The force of Gaby's anger was almost physical. Vermeulen took an involuntary step back.

"Has it ever occurred to you two that your constant fighting is making this like living in hell? It's supposed to be my home. Shit, living on the streets would be more peaceful than putting up with you two."

"Oh yeah?" Vermeulen said. "I hate to break it to you, but you have no idea of what it's like to live on the streets. Your mother and I have our disagreements. Big deal. Show me the family that doesn't."

Marieke straightened. "Don't you talk to my daughter that way. You've done enough to make her life miserable. Don't also drive her away."

"I've done enough? Oh, of course. You are entirely blameless. How could

I forget? I'm the one who argues at the drop of a hat. I'm the one who doesn't miss an opportunity to pick a fight. I'm usually too tired to rise to your bait and Gaby is old enough to see that."

The next thing he heard was the front door slamming shut with a loud bang. Gaby had left.

*　*　*

"DAD, ARE YOU OKAY?"

Gaby's voice pulled Vermeulen back to the present.

He blinked. "Oh, sorry," he said with a crooked smile. "I'm a bit preoccupied."

The moment he said it, he realized that he'd just given Marieke an opening wide enough not just for her wrecking ball, but also the crane to which it was attached. Being preoccupied had, of course, been her prime complaint back then. *You're never really here. Your mind is always elsewhere. You might as well not come home.* He almost ducked in anticipation of the inevitable.

It didn't come.

He held the door, let the women enter and followed them. He offered to pay for the buffet, but neither Marieke nor Gaby accepted. Fine. No obligations. Almost like a summit meeting.

The buffet was sumptuous, a broad array of cold cuts and cheeses, croissants and rolls, scrambled eggs, waffles, fruit and whipped cream. The filled their plates and settled at a table away from the windows where most patrons were sitting. A waiter had already poured coffee.

There was an awkward silence as each of them started their meal. It was exactly like a summit meeting. Nobody wanted to make the first move. The tension in the air made everything else seem pale. Vermeulen's eggs might as well have been cardboard.

Gaby broke down first. "What is the matter with you two? Is it too hard to be together and have a civil conversation?"

Vermeulen wasn't going to be the first to speak. Marieke had the same intention.

"What's it take?" Gaby said. "Do I need to get up and smash one of those flower pots?"

That brought a smile to Vermeulen's face. "It wouldn't work," he said. "They don't have one with a rubber fig."

Next thing he knew, he had water in his face. Not a glassful, just a few drops. Marieke had flicked her index finger across her water glass.

"You leave my rubber fig out of it," she said with a stern expression.

"Do you still have it?" he said.

"You better believe it. It's almost ten feet tall, I had to cut a hole in the ceiling. My neighbor upstairs gets to enjoy it too."

Vermeulen frowned and both women broke into laughter.

"Relax, Valentin," Marieke said. "That stupid plant is long dead. I never liked it all that much."

"You didn't?" Vermeulen said. "I think both of us thought it was the apple of your eye."

Gaby nodded rapidly.

"My mother gave me the cutting and every time she visited, she checked on it. I felt I had to take care of it."

"Grandma made you take care of it?" Gaby said.

"Not really, it was me. I thought that if I kept that thing thriving, it'd show her that I kept a proper house."

"Wow," Gaby said. "All those years, I thought that thing was like a fetish of yours. Did you know that, Dad?"

Vermeulen shook his head. Truth be told, he'd never paid much attention to the houseplants. But he remembered the rubber fig as special and not just because of Gaby destroyed it in such a spectacular fashion.

"What happened to it?" he said.

"I transplanted it, hoping to revive it. But by that time, it was clear that the divorce was coming. As far as my mother was concerned, that was a far more dramatic indicator of my failure as a wife than the rubber fig. I trashed it the moment you moved out."

Gaby had a puzzled look on her face.

"What's the matter, sweetheart? You can't imagine wanting to oblige your mother? I'm glad to hear that. At least I didn't lay that kind of guilt trip on you. I'm sure there were others," Marieke said.

"Come on, Mom, let's not get into blaming. All I wanted was having a meal with my parents."

Which they had for the next couple of hours. At the end they all hugged and decided that one meal together was enough for the day. The past wasn't erased, it just didn't matter quite as much anymore.

He was walking towards Groote Markt and the cathedral, feeling better than he'd expected, when his phone rang. It was Tessa.

"How'd it go?" she said.

"It was perfectly nice. We all learned a few things about each other that we didn't know at the time and we felt better about each other afterwards."

"What did Marieke and Gaby learn about you they didn't know?"

Leave it to Tessa to find the weak spot in his summary.

"Come on," he said. "You want me to replay the entire conversation?"

Tessa laughed. "I know you. But I'm very glad it went well."

"I think the gist of it was that Marieke and I thought we had to uphold images that others had of us. In my case, my boss, in Marieke's case her mother. Gaby got caught in the middle and hated both of us."

"You got all that out in one brunch? That's a lot. Congratulations. Lots of families never get past the blaming."

"Thanks," he said. "I know I dragged my feet even though I knew you're right. I guess, I move at my own pace."

"That's why I love you. You don't do things to please someone else, you do them because you've realized they are the right thing to do. It's also why you drive me crazy sometimes."

Chapter Eighteen

Bananas

———◆———

Back at the Kennel on Monday morning, Vermeulen worked his way through more irrelevant papers, updates and lists. The amount of paperwork they had accumulated was indeed astonishing. Most of it dealt with tracing the flow of cocaine, estimated arrivals of shipments and seizures. The task force's record was pretty good. They increased the quantities seized by almost fifty percent in a short period of time. At the same time, the street price seemed to remain stable, which meant that shipments also increased.

One report documented a particularly spectacular seizure. Almost a half-ton of cocaine was found in a container of bananas from Ecuador. The cartel had created special boxes that hid the shrink-wrapped drugs beneath a layer of bananas. Since the labels on the boxes were indistinguishable from the legitimate shipment, it stood to reason that the exporter itself was involved in the smuggling. The Colombian cartel clearly had diversified its routes so that shipments from most of northern Latin America were now suspect. The deluge of drugs coming back then seemed unstoppable. That made interrupting the flow of money even more important.

He came across the report he'd written about searching the paper shipments. Back in 2002, Frans Vinke had indeed texted the container numbers. Vermeulen had gotten a search warrant for both and they had descended on the port in force. But the search unfolded quite different from what he expected.

* * *

That afternoon in late June 2002, police cars and the VW Transporter carrying half of the task force descended on the Overseas Shipping Company at the *Delwaidedok*. The two containers in question had already been separated from the other cargo ready to be loaded. Port workers and OSC employees waited for the search warrant. Once Vermeulen presents it, a port worker clipped the seals on both containers and opened their doors. Vermeulen and Timmerman, hands gloved and wearing Tyvek booties, checked inside. Huge rolls of paper were stacked, two abreast for the twenty-foot length of each container. There wasn't enough space for a person between the rolls.

"We need a forklift to pull this stuff out," Timmerman said. He turned to the closest port worker and told him to get one.

Vermeulen shined his flashlight into the crevices he can see. There was no contraband visible.

They waited. Timmerman had serious difficulty containing his energy. He paced at high speed, mumbling things to himself.

"Hey, Alex," Vermeulen said. "Relax. We got this. Whatever's in there isn't going anywhere."

The forklift took its time. Timmerman kept pacing, the police officers lounged in their cars, the port employees looked bored.

Vermeulen eyed the space between the top of the stacked rolls and the ceiling of the container. There was enough of a gap to accommodate a person.

"Alex, make yourself useful and pull the VW over here," he said.

Timmerman was happy to be doing something. He drove the van close to the container door. Vermeulen opened the passenger's side door, stepped onto the seat and levered himself onto the roof of the van. The gap between the paper and the top was tight, but large enough to crawl inside. He stuck his head inside the container and pushed himself onto one of the paper rolls. Once inside, he wriggled his way forward.

The beam of his flashlight danced over the cargo. There was nothing, no shrink-wrapped packets of dollar or euro bills. He made it as far back as necessary to scout the last crevices. No money. That left the thick cardboard tubes at the core of each roll. As he scuttled backward, he peered down each tube. Nothing, until he got back at the door when he found what he's looking for. Something's been shoved down the tube on the last pallet.

"I found something," he said. "It's in the tube at the center of the roll."

As he got back to solid ground, Bastiaan Beukes arrived. "What are you doing with my cargo?" he said.

Vermeulen ignored the question and handed him the search warrant.

Beukes inspected the paper. He nodded. "Nobody is doing anything until my lawyer is here to witness this search."

They stood around another forty minutes. Even Timmerman, who never deviated from the legal path, was ready to ignore the rules and tell Beukes to go screw himself. Vermeulen saw this coming and took him aside.

"Relax, Alex. Whatever is in those tubes isn't going anywhere. If it's cash, we got him. Let's not screw this up."

Timmerman nodded.

When Vanderfeld finally showed up, he also had to inspect the search warrant. Since all the I's were dotted and the T's crossed, there was nothing he could do to stop the search. A dock worker drove the forklift to the door and lifted the two pallets onto the concrete.

"Can you lift the top rolls off each pallet?" Vermeulen said.

The forklift man nodded and started to push the tines between the rolls.

"Hey," Beukes yelled. "You're gonna ruin the paper."

Vanderfeld agreed and told Vermeulen that they'll sue for damages.

Vermeulen ignored him and waved for the operator to continue.

Beukes was right. The tines slid partway between the two rolls, but somehow got stuck. The driver stepped on the gas, the machine lurched backward and pulled the roll out. It crashed sideways onto the concrete with a dull thud. Vermeulen could feel the vibration in his feet.

He stuck his hand inside the tube. That shrink-wrapped package he'd seen was full of hundred-dollar bills. He stuck his hand in again but felt nothing. He frowned and checked again. There was nothing else in the tube. He checked the other roll. No packages there either.

The search of the second container yielded no more cash. Total haul of this operation? Fifty-thousand dollars. Vermeulen saw the look on Beukes's face and knew that he'd been set up.

* * *

VERMEULEN COULD STILL FEEL THE FRUSTRATION of that moment as if it had happened just yesterday. The fifty-thousand dollars weren't even the tip of the iceberg of cash that was sent back to Colombia. Beukes had flipped him off in what had felt like a prank. At least there hadn't been any other repercussions. Since they had found some contraband, Beukes couldn't sue them. They had nothing on Beukes, who simply claimed he had no clue how the money had gotten inside the container.

The next report was the summary of the interview with the boss of the paper factory in Zaventem. The man didn't know anything. He called in the two employees who had been in charge of loading. They were equally clueless. No, there was nothing with this delivery. The empty containers were dropped off, they loaded them like they always had, the full containers went to the dock. When the employees were gone again, Timmerman asked how long they had worked for the company. The first was the newbie. And he'd been there twelve years. The second one had spent double that with the company. Of course, they could have been bent. It was only a question of how much money was offered. But Timmerman had concluded that the paper factory was not part of the scheme.

Vermeulen got up from the desk and stretched. Back in 2002, he'd agreed with Timmerman. Maybe that had been the mistake. Maybe the whole idea was wrong in the first place. He closed the first binder and moved on to the second one.

"Any insights that might help the department defend itself against Theo Vinke's charges?" de Haas said.

Vermeulen shook his head. No surprise that de Haas was only worried about the department. Dekker hadn't been in all morning. He opened the next binder and saw that the first document was the transcript of an interview with Frans Vinke. Back in 2002, they had brought him in right away.

* * *

FRANS VINKE LOOKED HARRIED, out of sorts and out of breath after climbing the stairs at the Kennel.

"I can't just drop everything and show up here whenever you feel like it," he said. "I gotta have some lead time so I can come up with a good excuse."

"Give me a break," Vermeulen said. "You got a no-show-job. You can do whatever the hell you want."

"I wish. I told you before that Beukes makes me show up every weekday."

"Yeah? For how long? The whole eight hours?"

Vinke made a face and looked at the floor.

"Anyway, tell me what happened yesterday."

Vinke got big eyes. "What happened? I wasn't at the dock, I only heard about it afterwards. And let me tell you, I heard a lot about it. Beukes went on and on for hours."

"Tell me what was going on before."

"Nothing went on before."

"Were you even at work?"

Vinke rolled his eyes. "Yes, I was. I'm telling you nothing was going on."

"So Beukes didn't say anything about a change of plans, any indication that this shipment was going to be different from the others?"

"No. I told you. Beukes doesn't confide in me, but the office was calm. When something big is happening, I can tell. The whole office feels it. But that day? Nothing, really."

"Beukes say anything about playing a trick? Pulling the police's leg. Any sideways smile, like he'd planned something funny?"

Vinke shrugged.

"So how did the fifty-thousand dollars get into that shipment?" Vermeulen said.

"Beats me. Why would you even expect money in the paper shipments?"

"Because that's the only regular shipment and it always goes to the same recipient. It has money transfer written all over it."

Vinke frowned as if he was thinking hard. He got it after a minute. "Oh, I see. You think that's how Beukes sends the cash back to Colombia."

Either Vinke is really dense, Vermeulen thought, or he's good at playing the dummy.

"I don't think it's the paper shipments," Vinke said. "They go straight from the factory to the dock. Beukes doesn't have someone at that factory handling millions of dollars. I'd know that."

"So how do the millions get back to Colombia?"

Vinke gave him a wolfish smile. "If I knew that, I wouldn't be sitting here."

Vermeulen paced on the squishy carpet. His frustration was about to get the better of him. It didn't help that Vinke seemed way too smug for someone who was supposedly fearing for his life spying for the police. He felt a deep desire to smack Vinke. He could've, too. He was alone with him. He went to the window, grabbed the sill with both hands and took deep breaths.

"Let's try something else," Vermeulen said.

Vinke sat up.

"Those stolen cars you were caught with," Vermeulen said.

"I didn't know they were stolen. The sellers gave me the titles. How was I supposed to know they were forged?"

"Let's cut the crap, how would you even get the cash to buy twenty used cars, especially the makes you were caught with. But that's not what I'm interested in. Where were you going to ship them again?"

"Venezuela. Why do you want to know?"

"And Beukes was going to ship them for you, right?"

"We have an arrangement, yes."

"What was your cut from the whole thing going to be? What did you expect out of it?"

Vinke was flustered. He got up and walked to the window.

"Well," Vermeulen said. "You don't strike me as an altruist. There must've been something in it for you."

Vinke was still staring out of the window. He turned around, has a blank look. "Beukes pays me a commission."

"You don't actually steal these cars yourself, do you?"

"I'm not going to say anything else."

"I don't think you have a choice here."

"I'm not giving you what you need to lock me up."

"Trust me, Vinke. Being locked up is going to be the least of your problems. Besides, we have a deal."

"Yeah, but that deal involves me ratting out Beukes, not myself."

CHAPTER NINETEEN

CHICKENFEED

---◆---

THE PRESENT FELT AS FRUSTRATING AS THE PAST. The rest of Monday morning crawled past without any new insights. Vermeulen finished the second binder. It contained no more files related to Vinke. He put it back to the side of the desk.

De Haas looked at him. "Anything?"

Vermeulen shook his head. "I could've told you that at the beginning. The records don't include any evidence that I or anyone else on the task force leaked Frans Vinke's name. Have you asked Theo Vinke to produce the evidence he has? What if he's made that up, sending you and me on a pointless chase. I get that he's mad about his father having been killed, but directing unfounded accusations against me and the department isn't a way to get even."

De Haas shrugged. "No idea what evidence he has."

"Shouldn't you demand to see it?"

"I guess so. I could talk to Mesman, have him send a subpoena."

"And why hasn't Mesman done that already?"

"Mesman doesn't want to ruffle feathers. He thinks the public should be treated with respect."

"Come on, Theo Vinke isn't some poor citizen who's been wronged by a faceless bureaucracy. He's a criminal . . ."

"You have no evidence of that. He's never been convicted."

"That doesn't mean a damn thing. Beukes was never convicted either, but we knew he was a crook."

"It's up to the judge. But I'll ask him. In the meantime, keep looking for documents that can disprove Vinke's allegations."

Vermeulen sighed and opened the third binder. The first set of documents dealt with his analysis of the used car exports. It turned out that Beukes's company didn't ship those cars. That was handled by a different outfit, *Internationale Vortuighandel*. If the coated paper shipments occurred like clockwork, the car shipments varied in frequency and size of the consignments. And unlike the paper shipments, the cars weren't packed into containers, they were transported via roll-on-roll-off ships from a different dock. There was one constant. All of the cars exported were expensive makes.

* * *

BACK IN 2002, UNDERSTANDING THOSE SHIPMENTS had been his next strategy. He'd made a deal with the manager of the paper factory in Zaventem to let him know when the next order was being shipped. The search warrant was already written and only needed a signature. He was certain that at least some of the cash was being sent via these containers. The next time, he'd search them, just when they were being picked up at the factory. It was more an act of desperation than anything else.

He dug out the information about Frans Vinke's arrest. The stolen property rap on which he'd been arrested focused mainly on the cars, but not the fact that they were scheduled to be shipped to Venezuela, a neighbor of Colombia. Who was the exporter, *Internationale Vortuighandel.*

He consulted the usual business directories and registries and discovered rather little. The address of the company was in Saint Helier, on the island of Jersey. Further inquiries showed that the company was nothing more than a letterbox enterprise, housed with hundreds of others at a law firm with the bland name *Baker, Miller & Jones.* He checked the firm's website and found that Messrs. Baker and Miller were dead and that Beardsley Jones, Esq., looked like he had one foot in the grave himself. The website offered no listing of partners or associates, or much of anything else. Which made sense for a firm that capitalized on Jersey's status as Europe's tax haven and center of corporate secrecy. The one bit of information the site did include, presumably to show its global links, was a list of partner firms all over the world, including one in Antwerp, *Vos Partners.*

Vermeulen consulted the legal directories for more information on *Vos Partners* and found himself thwarted again. The usual sources listed only the name of the partnership and an address, but no partners. He called the Order of Flemish Bar Associations. A woman answered the phone. He told her a story about his looking for a job and that he was keen to see if there were any law school connections he could use. Could she tell him the names of the lawyers there?

The craven attempt at using connections didn't seem to faze the woman.

She asked him to wait a moment. He could hear the clicking of a keyboard. She sounded efficient and after a short while started listing names. Vermeulen asked her to slow down, pretending to be writing them down.

"That's all," she said after the ninth name. "Anyone you recognize?"

None of the names meant anything to Vermeulen. It is another dead end.

"Yup, a couple. Thanks for your help."

He was ready to hang up, when a thought struck him. The web of family relations that surrounded Frans Vinke includes at least one lawyer, Jordi Vanderfeld.

"There isn't by any chance a Jordi Vanderfeld listed as a partner?" he said.

"I don't see that name, oh, wait, there it is. But he isn't a partner anymore. He is listed as retired."

"Thanks," he said. "You've been very helpful."

He hung up and put the bits of information together. Vanderfeld, through his connections at *Vos Partners,* used *Baker, Miller & Jones* in Jersey to form *Internationale Vortuighandel.* The firm laundered drug cash by exporting stolen high-end cars and SUVs to Venezuela.

He called Jan Smits.

"Have you checked on the VINs of the cars that Frans Vinke was about to ship to Venezuela?"

"Hello Valentin. Long time no see. How are you?"

Vermeulen swallowed. Jan was right, he'd given him a big break and Vermeulen hadn't been in touch with him since that first meeting.

"Sorry Jan, things are crazy here. I'm just following up on a loose end. I'm fine, but frustrated, trying to get to the bottom of this thing and not able to do it. How are things with you?"

"The usual. Trying to keep ahead of the crooks and barely making it."

"About those VINs?"

"Yes, we checked. Most of the cars were stolen in Germany. Two came from France. I'm telling you, those open borders aren't making things any easier. The criminals adapt instantly, but the police bureaucracies continue as if nothing has changed. Checking in Belgium would've been easy. But none of the cars Vinke had stolen were registered here. When I contacted the *Bundeskriminalamt* about these thefts, it took them a while before they could confirm that these vehicles had indeed been stolen in Germany. France took even longer."

"Are these just random thefts and Vinke somehow gets to be the fence?" Vermeulen said.

"No, this is an organized activity. There are transnational gangs who manage the thefts. All you have to do is order a car, including options and color, and they'll steal it."

"These gangs aren't working for Beukes or Vinke, are they?"

"Of course not, organized car theft is a specialty. You order the cars, you pay the organization."

Beukes probably paid them with cocaine. No wonder, Antwerp was the largest cocaine transshipment point in Europe.

* * *

Back in the present—now in his sixth day in Antwerp—the clock was approaching lunch time and he was ready to get out of the Kennel. He flipped several more pages, none of them containing anything relevant, so they didn't warrant a pink flag. At twenty minutes to noon, he got up.

"Okay if I leave a little early for lunch?" he said.

De Haas looked up from whatever he'd been doing on his phone, checked his watch, looked at Vermeulen, his brows furled as if weighing a question of life or death. Finally, he said, "I guess so." He didn't sound certain.

"Relax, de Haas. Mesman isn't here, he won't know if you don't tell."

"That's not the point. We have a job to do."

"Yes, but it's an asinine job. I can tell you, there's nothing in these binders that would give credence to Vinke's allegation."

"You don't know that."

"As a matter of fact, I do, because I'm the one who put the documents into these binders."

Vermeulen got up and left the apartment. On the street, he took a deep breath. It was raining again, but at least the air was fresh. He opened his umbrella, walked to the next corner and turned left. Someone carrying a green umbrella fell into step with him. He lifted his umbrella and saw a dark-skinned face. It was Dekker. She was carrying a shopping bag.

"I've missed you this morning," he said. "I wondered what important task kept you from supervising me."

"I called in sick."

"Ah, and you aren't, are you?"

"No, I needed time to sort out things. Now I need to speak with you."

"Sure, I'm at your disposal, at least for the duration of the lunch break."

She took him to the end of the next block and steered him into a passage that lead to a narrow alley ending at a ten-foot brick wall. To the right stood an old apartment building three stories high, to the left was another wall with a single wooden door at its center. When they reached the door, Dekker pushed it open and he found himself in a square courtyard. A series of cafe tables stood there as if abandoned. The chairs had been stacked in a corner, right next to the rolled-up patio umbrellas.

Dekker unlocked a door and led him into a small room. All its tables were empty. It looked like a beach restaurant closed for the season and needing a new coat of paint before it could open again.

"What is this place?" Vermeulen said.

"Friends of mine just leased it. They're getting ready to do some renovation. The plan is to open a restaurant in the spring. I needed a place where we could speak without being observed. They gave me the key."

She put the shopping bag on a table and unpacked a couple of sandwiches and beers.

"You even brought lunch. To what do I owe this honor?" he said.

"Cut it out." She opened the bottles and pushed one to Vermeulen. "Don't get any ideas. I need to pick your brain."

Vermeulen suppressed a smile. "Don't worry, it didn't occur to me that this was anything but a business lunch. What do you want to know?"

She shifted in her seat, took a breath and pressed her lips together as if weighing the pros and cons of confiding in Vermeulen. "The reason why I'm stuck baby-sitting you rather than going to EUROPOL is connected to your case."

Vermeulen's skin tightened. "Why are you telling me now?"

"No particular reason. Or maybe all of them. When you came back to Antwerp after all these years, what was the first thing you noticed?"

Vermeulen hesitated. "I don't know, more traffic?"

She shook her head. "No, not that? Did you notice something about the people."

"More harried? More driven?"

"Man, don't you look at faces? There are lot more brown-skinned people in the city. And they aren't treated the same. That's not a surprise because there are very few people in the justice system who look like me. I became police officer because I care deeply about justice for all."

Vermeulen saw something in her eyes. It wasn't anger, more like impatience. "I see," he said. "Working with someone like Mesman and people from the New Flemish Alliance must be difficult."

She rolled her eyes. "Don't get me started. When Leopold colonized the Congo, he mandated French as the official language. And now we have this idiotic insistence on speaking Dutch only in a country where French is an official language. That excludes most of the African immigrants. So, yes, this judge is pretty much on the opposite side of every important issue we deal with. That's why I was looking forward to moving to EUROPOL. He nixed that with this bogus charge of mismanaging evidence."

Vermeulen saw her expression change from impatience to resignation.

"What's that piece of information that's gone missing?" he said.

"It's integral to this case. I've never seen it or held it in my hands, but it's a memo that proves you ratted out Vinke."

Vermeulen's mouth turned as dry as sand. He grabbed his beer and took a big gulp. "Do you have any idea what's in the memo?" he said.

"No. I swear. But you're here because of it. Judge Mesman had planned on arresting you the moment you arrived, but then the memo disappeared and he had no foundation for an arrest warrant. This whole thing, you reading the files and us watching you, is a last-minute improvisation. He needed a reason for having brought you here and keeping you from going home again. Basically, he's buying time while everyone in his office is searching for the memo."

Vermeulen sucked in his breath. That was a strange but not unexpected turn of events. A judge with a grudge. What had he ever done to Mesman? It was clear that this went well beyond cleaning up the image of the judiciary. There was something far more sinister going on.

"How did you end up with this case?" he said.

"I wish I could say I was next in the rotation. But there's more to it. Mesman is at work grooming a few inspectors he can depend on. De Haas is obviously one, but he's not too bright. He's had his eyes on me for some time."

"Has he made any inappropriate moves towards you?"

"No, it isn't that. He's very professional. But I feel like I'm being set up. I have the feeling he wants to do favors so he can call in those favors in the future."

Vermeulen took another gulp of beer. Dekker's revelation was a shock, but it also confirmed a suspicion he hadn't been able to verbalize. The sheer audacity of Mesman was enough to take his breath away. He couldn't even fathom why a judge who was still in law school when Vermeulen worked as a prosecutor had it out for him.

"What do you know about Mesman?" he said.

"He's a stickler for the rules, a pain in the neck, pedantic, what else do you want to hear?"

"No, not that. About his background."

Dekker shrugged. "He went to the University of Antwerp, had stellar grades, rose quickly."

"What about family? Is he related to influential people? Who's in his circle of acquaintances?"

She shook her head. "I don't know, I never had the urge or need to find out. Why do you want to know?"

"Because he's so eager to nail me to the wall. Why is that? Usually, judges give prosecutors the benefit of the doubt, but with him, I was guilty before the investigation even started. Your statement just confirmed that. There has to be something else going on."

Dekker raised her shoulders. "Sorry, can't help you there."

Vermeulen leaned forward. "I have to tell you something, too. On the day I arrived, someone shoved an envelope with a photograph under my hotel door.

It was a picture of me taken back in 2002 and showed me walking toward the Kennel. Then came a picture showing me at the door of the Kennel, and, finally a picture of me leaving. Each time, I also got a text."

Dekker leaned forward. "Any others?"

"Not so far."

"No idea who sent them?"

"Nope. I thought at first it was Theo Vinke, but now I don't think so."

"Why not?"

"Well, it didn't make sense. Also, Theo and his wife Nora have been following me. I finally confronted Nora on Saturday and ended up speaking to Theo on the phone. He says he wants to keep tabs on me so I don't skip out once the evidence of my guilt comes out."

Dekker pushed a sandwich to him and said, "*Bon appetit.*"

Vermeulen didn't feel much like eating but took a bite anyway. They ate in silence for a while.

"Here's what I'm thinking," Vermeulen said after swallowing a bite. "The photographs show that someone else knew about the Kennel. Our secret place wasn't so secret after all. Whoever took the pictures of me coming and going probably took pictures of everyone else too. They knew that Vinke was coming there, that he was cooperating with us."

Dekker nodded, but didn't say anything.

Vermeulen's heart skipped a beat. He slapped himself against the forehead. "Damn. How goddamn blind we all were back then. Beukes and Vanderfeld knew that we had turned Vinke and they used him against us. All the leads that didn't pan out, the seizures that were much smaller than we anticipated. Frans Vinke was like a double agent. We thought he was spying for us, all the while the syndicate gave him chickenfeed to keep us away from the real prize."

"But didn't you get the real prize in the end?"

"Not really, we didn't put Beukes out of business. The fact that we made any headway at all wasn't due to any information we got from Vinke."

And the personal cost had been terrible.

Chapter Twenty

Years To Come

———◆———

It was the first week in July 2002 and Vermeulen was talking to the judge about the subpoenas for any evidence that points to *Internationale Vortuighandel's* involvement in the money laundering. Cornelia Boogman signaled to Vermeulen and mouthed "Your wife." Vermeulen rolled his eyes. He held up his index finger, telling Cornelia to keep Marieke waiting.

He was sure that the stolen cars were payments for drugs, he just didn't know how to prove that. Searching their offices should help there. He needed this warrant. The judge wasn't persuaded and talked about a fishing operation. Vermeulen persisted. The judge said something about banking secrecy. Vermeulen countered that they weren't in Jersey, that the company operated on Belgian soil, and therefore was subject to Belgian law.

"Besides, we're not checking on their bank accounts, we've already got them. We're trying to figure out who the beneficial owners are, who actually benefit from the profits."

The judge hemmed and hawed. Cornelia was waving again. Vermeulen held up his finger once more. Cornelia shook her head. She put the receiver down. No problem, he'd just call Marieke back.

"Okay, I'll grant the warrant," the judge said. "You can pick it up first thing in the morning."

"Thank you, your honor."

He hung up and let out a loud, "Yeah, we're coming for you, Beukes."

The others clapped. He got up and walked to Cornelia's office.

"What was so urgent?"

"Your wife. Something with Gaby."

He called home. The phone rang and rang. The answering machine picked up. He called Marieke's mobile. The call immediately rolled over to voicemail. She'd probably turned it off again. She thought of her new Nokia as a precious instrument that shouldn't be overused. He'd tried to explain to her that the utility of a mobile phone depends on it being on. Turning it off to save the battery defeated the purpose. He left a message and went back to work.

It was hours later when Marieke finally called back.

"Gaby is gone," was all she said.

Vermeulen didn't understand. "Gone where?"

"Don't be an idiot. Gone, as in, run away."

"Why would she do that?" Yes, things had been tense at home. Yes, the word divorce had become part of the conversation. But those weren't reasons for Gaby to run away, were they?

"The fact that you even need to ask is probably a big part of the reason," Marieke said.

"Oh, give me a break. How do you know she ran away and isn't just staying over at a friend?"

"Do you even know her friends? Have you ever shown interest in her friends?"

Vermeulen was getting hot under the collar, was ready to let Marieke have it. But it's about Gaby. If she'd really run away . . . His gut felt hollow, he was getting scared. The idea that she could be out on the street, facing who knows which hoodlums rattled him.

"Sorry, I don't know her friends," he said.

"She doesn't have the stay-over kind. Anyway, she packed some clothes and took a bunch of money from my purse."

He did a quick calculation. Taking money means she was going somewhere. Still running away, but not to the slums of Antwerp. Maybe to France or Italy.

"How much?" he said.

"Why does it matter?"

"Just wondering how far she can travel."

"Oh Christ, you don't know the first thing about your daughter. She isn't going anywhere, she took the money to buy drugs, you idiot. She's been stealing money for a while now. I told you."

Vermeulen dimly remembered these conversations, remembered thinking that Marieke was over-protective. No daughter of his was stupid enough to get into drugs, he'd thought then. Now his gut told him that Marieke was right. Gaby was in trouble. Panic rose from his core. His heart pounded against his ribs. He was ready to run out the door and start the search immediately.

Saner thoughts pushed to the forefront. "How long has she been gone?" he said.

"A couple of days."

That was too long. "I'll get the police on it," he said.

Vermeulen started with the police, missing persons, and he went right to the top. He knew who was in charge and he wouldn't mess with some underling.

Commissar Janssen wasn't too keen to see Vermeulen. It was the end of the day and he wanted to go home. Vermeulen didn't care. He was a prosecutor, the police needed him to be on their side.

He explained that his daughter Gaby was missing. He couldn't bring himself to admit that she had fallen in with the junkies, crank heads and pushers. She's run away, took some money, was all he said.

"Any problems at home?" Janssen said.

Vermeulen shrugged. "Well, who doesn't?" He didn't want to hang out his family's dirty laundry out for Janssen to see.

Janssen's office looked spartan, not even a framed picture on the clean desk. "Big enough to drive Gaby away?" he said.

"I don't know. A bit of tension. I'm at work a lot. Like everybody else."

"Any drug use?"

"I don't think so."

The look on Janssen's face was bland, but Vermeulen sensed his disbelief. He felt his ire rising. Janssen was single, never married. What the hell did he know about family dynamics and bringing up kids.

"Look, Janssen. What do you want me to say? I don't know if she's into drugs. Maybe she is. My wife thinks so. But she dramatizes everything."

"How long has Gaby been gone?"

"A couple of days."

"My men can't do anything for another day anyway. Seventy-two hours is the minimum someone has to be gone. But I'd say, give it a couple of days. A few nights out in the rough and most runaways decide their bed is nicer, even if it comes with a mom and a dad and problems."

"So, you won't be looking for her?"

"Not until tomorrow. I know it's hard to just wait. But that's the best you can do now. Go home and be with your wife. She needs you."

Vermeulen got up and left without a word. A single cop giving marriage advice? What next?

Outside, he called the head of the narcotics unit, and asked for the addresses of the known drug squats. He scribbled as fast as he could. Most were in the Dam and Stuivenberg districts of north Antwerp, the poorest part of the city. Next, he asked about rehab places. The officer gave him the names of two clinics.

"But I'd go to the first one," he said. "They are strict, but they get results."

He jumped into his car and motored to Lange Stuivenberg Straat. It was almost dark and parking a car there wasn't safe, but he had bigger worries. He found a spot, hid everything that might entice a thief in the trunk and started his search.

The first stop was a derelict three-story fill-in covered in graffiti. Its owner had long abandoned any pretense of upkeep. A barely legible notice pasted to the door indicated that the place wasn't safe for human habitation. He entered. The street light outside was brighter than the bulb inside. He was confronted by a guy with stringy long hair and a vacant look in his eyes. Beneath the scabs and dirt, he was probably younger than he looked.

"Nothing here for you, gramps," the guy said, doing a tough-guy-routine.

"Out of my way, kid." Vermeulen pushed him aside as if he were a curtain.

He climbed the stairs to the second floor, avoiding the holes in the wooden steps. The railing was long gone. Another dim bulb lit the hallway. The walls were covered with badly done graffiti and candle smudges. There were three rooms on this floor. None of them had doors. In the first he could see three twin mattresses in the light of a single candle. They were occupied by three bodies. Two had passed out. The third, a girl, was staring at the candle stuck to the chipped linoleum.

Vermeulen's stomach lurched. These kids were too young to be so lost. What had happened to them? He thought of Gaby and his heartbeat picked up. Did he really treat her so shabbily? He couldn't accept that.

The girl looked at him and said, "Suck your dick? Ten euros."

Vermeulen stumbled backwards into the hallway as if hit by a bat. The scene in the next room was just as depressing. Here two of the occupants were awake.

"Any of you know Gaby Vermeulen? Sixteen, five foot eight, long blond hair?"

They looked at him as if he'd ask directions to Mars.

He went back into the hallway. The guard from downstairs had called in reinforcements. Two guys, mid-twenties, with upper bodies that showed they work out, each holding a knife.

"Get lost gramps," the guard said.

"Listen, I'm looking for my daughter, is all. I don't want trouble."

The two guys nodded and stepped aside so he could pass to the staircase. He wanted to go up a floor, but sensed the knives behind him and decided to go to the next address.

The scene on Handelsteeg was very much the same, except the guards at the door had their own knives and didn't need to call in reinforcements.

"Listen," he said. "I'm not a cop. Just a dad looking for his daughter. You know a Gaby Vermeulen, about five eight, blonde hair. She's run away and I have to find her."

"You a perv? You molest her, make her screw you?" the first tough said. "That's why girls usually run away."

"No, I didn't do any of that. I love her."

"If you're looking for her here, you ain't loved her enough."

Vermeulen nodded, although he didn't expect parenting advice from drug dealers. "Do you know her?"

"I've seen a Gaby," the second tough said. "But she got short hair. Like a buzz cut."

That wasn't his Gaby, but he's ready to grasp at any straw. "Where did you see her?"

"She was buying smack on Nikkelstraat last night."

He ran back to his car and drove to Nikkelstraat. The street was only a block long. He found a place to park and realized that he forgot to ask the guy where on the street he'd seen Gaby. He walked up one side of the street, where there were old buildings, working class housing, not as dilapidated as the last place, but shabby and worn. Young men loitered in several doorways, looking for customers. He approached the first.

"Coke, brown, hash, good prices," the guy said. His looks—dirty hair, disheveled clothes, blank stare—suggested he sold drugs to maintain his own habit.

"I'm looking for my daughter Gaby, about five feet eight, blonde. Did she buy from you?"

The guy slipped past him faster than Vermeulen could react. Next thing, he was running along the sidewalk, whistling. In a flash, the loitering men disappeared.

"Oh, fuck it all!" Vermeulen said.

He drove to the next address he got from narcotics enforcement. Another street, another row of public housing blocks, more people with empty stares, waiting for something, anything to happen that might give meaning to their lives. It was well past midnight.

The elevator was out of service and he walked up a dank concrete staircase with the sour smell of vomit and urine. He reached the fourth floor and was winded. How did anyone make it to the top? The corridor was a mess of kids' toys, refuse and syringes. He walked past the first door when it opened. An old woman looked at him, her mouth in a sneer.

"You oughta be ashamed of yourself. Get your stinking drugs elsewhere. I'd call the cops on you if they bothered to show up."

"I'm not here to buy drugs," he said.

"Sure. Why else would someone with nice clothes come here? This used to be a decent building, you know. But then pushers moved in and people like you support them."

"I'm looking for my daughter. She ran away."

The drawn face of the woman softened a bit. "If you're looking for her here, it's too late."

"I hope not. Her name is Gaby, have you seen her? She's sixteen, five foot eight and she's got blond hair."

The woman shook her head. "I see those poor girls come by my window. I'm a prisoner in my apartment, but at least I can bolt my door and keep the drug scum out. Those girls, they are prisoners too, and they can't bolt their doors."

She didn't say anything about Gaby. Vermeulen thanked her and moved on. He went to the apartment number specified by the narcotics guys. The same routine. A guard by the door, also armed, but not so tough looking.

"Whaddaya want?"

"You got coke?" Vermeulen said.

The guard gave him a smile that says, *You are new at this, aren't you?* He opened the door and Vermeulen stepped inside. A second guy, told him to go to the room at the end of the hallway. Vermeulen did no such thing. He locked the apartment door, grabbed the guy, twisted his arm behind his back and pushed his face into the wall. It was one of the skills he remembered from his army days. The guy grunted, but didn't seem too upset. Maybe he had experience with volatile customers.

"I'm not here to buy drugs, asshole. I'm looking for my daughter. I'm going to check every single room to see if she's inside. You can go outside and leave me to it, or I can break your arm. Your choice."

The guy opted for outside. Vermeulen opened the door, shoved him out, locking it again. Next, he went to the room at the end of the hallway. Inside, a third guy sat behind a table, small plastic bags lined up in front of him.

The guy cocked his head, "What's your pleasure?"

Vermeulen grabbed the table and threw it against the guy. His chair toppled over, the bagged heroin and coke went flying. Vermeulen pushed the table against the guy and looked around the room. The lock on the door looked solid, a necessity, since this is where the drugs were kept. He gave the guy one more kick, jumped back to the door, pulled the key, stepped outside and locked it. The bolt made a satisfying click.

In the first room to the left, a boy was holding a spoon over the flame of a candle. The liquid in the spoon was spattering. A girl—Vermeulen couldn't get over how young everybody was—had a syringe ready and drew the liquid inside. The girl was lanky and had her hair shorn to a half an inch.

The boy looked up. His face wasn't as blank as the others Vermeulen had seen that night. It was both anxious and full of anticipation. Ready for that hit that would take him away from all this. He had a soft face, almost feminine, were it not for the random hairs sprouting along his chin. He was *that* young. He had a belt around his bicep, ready to tighten it to make a vein pop out.

The girl looked at the boy first. What's the hold up? She turned to Vermeulen and her face was a punch to his stomach. Gaby. Unlike the boy's, her face looked hard, the buzz cut made the angles of her face stick out like ridges. Her eyes were red as if she'd been crying a lot. He knew it was the heroin. She saw Vermeulen, but her face only showed disgust. *You've had your chance*, it said. *It's too late now, so get lost.*

There was a part of Vermeulen that wanted to agree with her. He was guilty. Worse. He was a failure. He'd failed his only daughter. And now it was too late. A force from nowhere pulled him towards the door. *Get out, accept that you're a loser. Just go and hide.* He took a step back.

There was a different look on Gaby's face now. Something like recognition, as if she'd known all along that when it came down to it, her father would run. An expectation of abandonment fulfilled. That look made him take another step back. The sound of blood rushing in his ears drowned out the other voices in his head. He turned, he stopped. There was a small voice behind all the loud pulsing. He forced himself to listen to it. It told him with quiet urgency to take Gaby in his arms and hug her until they both run out of breath.

What eventually unfolded was a lot less romantic. He stepped forward and took the syringe from her hands. She got up and pushed him back. The boy was confused. What was happening to his shot? Gaby hissed something at Vermeulen. He didn't hear and didn't care. He took Gaby by her wrist and pulled her toward the hallway. She screamed and fought back. He yanked her out of the room, she held on to the door frame and called for the boy to help her. The boy didn't listen. He'd found the syringe and got ready to shoot up. Gaby yelled again. No use. The boy tightened the belt and looked for a vein. Gaby, desperation in her voice, asked him to help her. The needle sank into the vein. The boy pushed the plunger slowly, pulled out the needle and sank back. Gaby crumpled at the sight. She'd been ready for the next one.

Vermeulen managed to coax her to the door. She hissed again in a way that was almost feral. She told him she'll hate him forever. He unlocked the front door and muscled her past the two guys who'd been freezing outside. The woman in the first apartment stared from behind her curtains. Vermeulen half carried Gaby down the stinking stairwell and pushed her into the car.

He drove across the city to the rehab clinic his colleague had suggested. It was located well outside the city limits. Once there, he brought her inside and checked her in. The place was nothing if not prepared for emergency admittance. He handled the paperwork while they took Gaby away.

An hour later he sat in his car with tears in his eyes. He'd never treated Gaby this way before. Necessary roughness, he told himself and winced at the same time because deep in his bones he knew Gaby wouldn't speak to him for years to come.

CHAPTER TWENTY-ONE

SMALL AND MEAN

———◆———

AFTER HIS UNEXPECTED LUNCH WITH DEKKER, Vermeulen made his way back to the Kennel. The memory of the search for Gaby had left him shaken. He stopped to get a coffee. De Haas looked upset when Vermeulen finally returned.

"You sure took your time," he said. "There's still a lot to do. I wish you would take this as seriously as it is."

"How could I? There's nothing here."

Vermeulen went back to reading files. The last document in the binder summarized the information he'd gathered in response to the subpoenas sent to *Internationale Vortuighandel.* His hunch, back then, had only been partially correct. The company records showed a clear pattern. Regular shipments of vehicles to Venezuela. Always expensive brands, always used. There was no way to prove that they were all stolen, but it stood to reason they were. The inventory recovered after Frans Vinke's initial arrest was a pretty good indicator.

Where Vermeulen had been wrong back in 2002 was in his assumption that the stolen cars were payment for the drugs. If they were, there shouldn't have been any remittances. Since he didn't find any evidence of money deposited to Beukes's company, *Globaal Handelsbedrijf,* he thought he'd wrapped up the case. As it turned out, the company that shipped the cars, *Internationale Vortuighandel,* did get paid and the payments were in line with the approximate value of the cars shipped. Another dead end.

The frustration he'd felt back then was palpable. He'd thought he'd had a slam dunk. Instead, the ball rolled along the rim a couple of times and fell back to the floor. The memory was raw enough, he was tempted to hit the desk as he'd done thirteen years earlier.

They'd had no new leads and the old ones were disappearing like a freak rainfall in desert sand. He should've gone home, worked on his marriage, made sure his daughter didn't go off the rails again. But he couldn't let it go. After he'd gotten Gaby into rehab, he continued working deep into the night, checking any leads he might have overlooked. He was going to get Beukes, whatever it took. It took way more than he'd ever imagined.

His fury at the unsolved case became so poisonous that it became the last straw that broke his marriage. Marieke moved out because she didn't feel safe in their house anymore. Just thinking of her packing her things brought a deep sense of shame. Reading the case file, he felt himself tearing up. With the recognition that it'd been all his fault came a deep sadness and shame. All that talk about both of them having shared responsibility for their failed marriage? Nonsense. Yes, Marieke could be difficult. That was nothing compared to how he'd behaved back then. No wonder he'd been so reluctant to meet with her. Deep down he knew he had to atone for what he'd done, for how he'd been.

The memory made him feel small and mean.

With a deep sigh, he finished the third binder and began the fourth. It was the thinnest of the binders and it chronicled the end of his investigation. At the very top was the document that outlined the relationship between *Globaal Handelsbedrijf* and *Internationale Vortuighandel*. It was as opaque as he remembered.

* * *

It was still the first week of July 2002 and Vermeulen was back at his desk in Justitiestraat. There were teetering stacks of papers everywhere. He couldn't even find his telephone anymore. The biggest question, who owned *Internationale Vortuighandel,* was still unsolved. The authorities in Jersey had not responded to any official requests. Without that, he couldn't compel the law firm *Baker, Miller & Jones* to disclose anything. Therefore, he had no evidence that either Beukes or Vanderfeld controlled that company. The dream of putting Beukes behind bars was growing fainter and fainter. Through sheer tenacity, he accomplished the next best thing, shutting down the Belgian operations of *Internationale Vortuighandel.*

He started by combing through the Belgian bank records of the firm, the very records that show the receipt of payment for the shipments of stolen cars. This time, he focused not on the money coming in, but the money going out. At first, he hoped he could find payments that correlated with receipts of Beukes's business. No luck there. Beukes was smart enough not to leave a trail of deposit slips after he went to great length to hide the connection between the two firms.

He noticed fairly regular payments to several brokerage firms. The amounts were high enough to grab his attention. He contacted the brokerage, they demanded a warrant to reveal that information. He cajoled the judge into issuing one. The result was additional stacks of paper.

It turned out that *Internationale Vortuighandel* regularly bought shares of companies with cryptic names like *Alpha Partners, Ltd.* As he collated these trades, he realized that someone with little imagination had just followed the Greek alphabet. They had gotten as far as Lambda. All eleven of those companies were headquartered in The Turks and Caicos Islands.

He requested more warrants and more subpoenas. The piles of papers multiplied again. Van Dijk was commandeered to help him comb the materials. Boogman was concerned.

"You gotta take a break, Valentin," she said. "Go home, get some rest. There's not a lot of wax left between the two ends of the candle you are burning."

Van Dijk agreed, if only because he wasn't keen on overtime. He had a life at home.

Vermeulen wasn't having any of it. In the absence of seeing Beukes go to jail, he wanted some kind of victory. Anything that let him claim he won.

"It's not healthy," Boogman said.

Vermeulen kept pushing on.

Patterns emerged slowly. Number one: None of these companies seemed to be engaged in any active business. No matter which sources they consulted, the Greek alphabet firms weren't doing anything. No investments, no holdings, no real estate, nothing.

Number two: Nine of the eleven business closed their doors a few months after *Internationale Vortuighandel* bought their shares. Buying a company and then closing it down was a preferred way to get rid of competitors. Since none of them did anything remotely related to shipping automobiles, they couldn't have been competitors. Why buy the shares of a firm and then close it down? The answer to this question remains elusive.

Finally, a couple of days later, the last pieces of the puzzle fell into place after Vermeulen consulted the US Secret Service and EUROPOL. The Greek alphabet firms were all shell companies linked to Colombian drug cartels. Vermeulen had finally done it. He'd found the way by which the cash generated by cocaine sales in Europe was repatriated to Colombia. The cartels set up the shell companies. The profits earned from selling stolen luxury cars in Latin America were used to buy the same companies from the drug cartels in Colombia. On paper, each transaction looked like another boring financial deal. The funds came from a legitimate source, the sale of cars, and went to a legitimate purpose, the purchase of shares of another company. Except that these firms were created by the drug bosses in Colombia for the sole purpose of being sold to *Internationale Vortuighandel*, which eventually shut them down. Dirty money went in, sparkling clean money came out.

Vermeulen sat back in his chair and took a deep breath. He'd done it. The entire room broke into applause. His colleagues patted him on the back. *Good job, Valentin. You cracked the case.*

He didn't get Beukes, but he'd achieved his objective—interrupt the flow of cash back to the cartel. Within a month, *Internationale Vortuighandel* closed its doors. For the moment at least, the flow of cash stopped. The police noticed an uptick in the arrest of couriers with large amounts of cash in their luggage, a clear indication that their strategy had worked.

The victory was at best bittersweet. There was zero evidence linking Beukes to *Internationale Vortuighandel*. Without it, the man remained beyond the reach of the law. Vermeulen visited the judge personally.

"There's no need to come yourself," the judge said when Vermeulen pushed his way into the office.

"I came because it's crucial that we bring Beukes in," Vermeulen said, working hard on sounding calm and reasonable.

"You have nothing for an arrest warrant. I've told you that."

"We have a lot. We have Frans Vinke who handled the stolen cars. He's as close to Beukes as anyone."

"But can you prove that Vinke acted for Beukes? Has he testified to that? All you have him on is handling stolen cars. And why isn't he in lockup?"

Vermeulen swallowed. This wasn't the time to tell the judge about his deal with Vinke.

"But Vinke also works for Beukes. It's patently obvious."

The judge gave Vermeulen a look that says, *careful buddy.*

Vermeulen didn't get the message. "You got to be blind not to see that the two work hand in hand. That's plenty of reason for an arrest warrant. Once we have him in custody, we'll get him."

"Mr. Vermeulen, you better watch your words. I'm not blind. That's why I know you have no proof that Vinke acted on behalf of Beukes. And tell me why Vinke is not behind bars."

"That's immaterial. The real scandal is that you are giving Beukes a pass. We bring him and Vanderfeld in and sweat them a little and we'll get what we need."

"Out!" the judge shouted. "One more word and I'll have you arrested. You do not speak to me that way. I will not use my authority to make up for the lack of investigative work done by you or the police. You want a warrant, bring me the evidence. And now get out."

"There'd never be enough evidence for you," Vermeulen mumbled and slammed the door behind him. He was past caring. All he knew was this, Jordi

Vanderfeld had set up the perfect intermediary. Without knowing who owned and ran *Internationale Vortuighandel*, there was nothing anyone could do.

Vermeulen took the next week off, turning his overtime into vacation days. He went to an empty home. Marieke had filed for divorce. The papers were delivered early the second morning. He was too hungover to care. He checked with the rehab clinic. Gaby refused to see him. He went back home and filled his emptiness with more De Koninck and jenever. A couple of hangovers later he stood in front of the bathroom mirror and looked at a face that looked as bad as Gaby's when he found her. He showered, shaved, put on a clean shirt and suit. He sat down at the computer and wrote his resignation letter. An hour later, he walked into the crown prosecutor's office, dropped the letter on the desk and left without a word.

That afternoon, empty as the two bottles of booze lying on the floor, he sat down in front of the computer and started his job search. Any place but Belgium. France or Holland would be fine. He spoke both languages. Among the listings, one worse than the next, there was the link that lead him to the personnel website of the United Nations. Office of Internal Oversight Services.

* * *

VERMEULEN RUBBED HIS EYES. Sitting in the Kennel thirteen years later, the end of his career back then was the logical conclusion of his crusade. He looked at the final pages of the last binder. Copies of the warrants, subpoenas filed and amended, then refiled. They were boring papers that failed to capture the drama, the destructive climate of those last days. Seeing them now made the whole episode seem weirdly foreign, as if it had happened to someone else and Vermeulen was merely a voyeur, looking at someone else's life falling to pieces between the lines of legalese. He realized that he had been a fool back then. He'd sacrificed everything important to him for some stupid criminal case.

He took a deep breath. It had taken years to undo the damage. Yesterday's brunch with Marieke was part of that.

He flipped a couple more pages. Nothing.

"Well, I told you, it was a waste of time," he said to de Haas. "There's nothing in here that even hints at me or anyone else leaking Frans Vinke's name. A lot of money and time wasted for this nonsense."

De Haas was genuinely perturbed as if he'd been certain there would be such evidence. Vermeulen shook his head. If Dekker was right and the whole reading-the-files thing had been a last-minute diversion, cooked up to keep him busy while they were looking for the missing evidence, then de Haas didn't seem to know about it.

He flipped the next to last page in the binder and saw his name printed at the top of the last sheet. It was a memo. Next to his name were his handwritten initials. The recipient was Jan Smits. That was a red flag. He wouldn't have sent a memo to Smits. Except for having nabbed Frans Vinke, Smits had nothing to do with the investigation.

He started reading. In the first paragraph, he thanked Smits for having called him after the arrest of Vinke. Vermeulen scratched his chin. He didn't remember having sent this memo. The call about the VIN numbers had been the last contact with Smits in 2002. He hadn't seen the man until he picked Vermeulen up from the hotel last Wednesday.

He read the next paragraph and his heart skipped a beat. The first sentence started out explaining that Frans Vinke had served his purpose and that there was a serious danger that he would become a liability. The second sentence laid out that a couple scenarios how Vinke, shooting off his mouth, might compromise ongoing and future cases. But it was the last two sentences that made him break out in sweat. *The best way to prevent this is to let the syndicate take care of the matter. I'll drop his name to the right people.*

CHAPTER TWENTY-TWO

MENTAL DISCIPLINE

———◆———

IT TOOK ALL THE MENTAL DISCIPLINE Vermeulen could muster to idly flip a few of the previous pages back, and cover the incriminating memo. He felt flushed, his heart beating out a rapid pulse. Just one look at Vermeulen would tell De Haas that something was wrong. A second look, and he'd find the memo. And then all hell would break loose.

Vermeulen closed the binder. "Well," he said. "I guess that's it. Can I go and pack my suitcase? My job in New York is waiting for me."

De Haas looked at him. "You must be glad to be done with this," he said.

Vermeulen was waiting for that flash of recognition in de Haas's face, that expression that said something had changed, that the evidence had finally emerged. It didn't come. Vermeulen played it cool. "You better believe it. But I knew, of course, that there wasn't anything."

De Haas took out his phone and tapped a number. *Is he calling the police?* "It's Hendrik," he said when the other party answered. He turned toward the window. *Not the police, then.*

The memo was false. Someone had forged it. His initials were easily copied. He had to make it disappear. If it ever made it into the hands of Judge Mesman, he'd be stuck in Antwerp for foreseeable future. In the end he'd go free, but he had no intention of spending that time behind bars. He opened the binder again. He couldn't tear the memo out, that would make a suspicious noise. But snapping open the three metal rings that held everything inside was just as loud.

"Yes, sir," de Haas said. "He's done."

Vermeulen started tugging at the edge of the memo. Slowly, his arm making minute movements to avoid any sound.

"No, sir. There was nothing new related to the death of Frans Vinke."

Vermeulen could hear the voice on the other end getting louder. He pulled a little harder. The first tear sounded as loud as a jet engine. Vermeulen froze, ready to flip the binder shut again.

"Of course, sir. I supervised this carefully. Yes, he used the pink flags to mark documents related to Vinke."

Vermeulen decided to prize open the three rings instead. He pulled at the center ring and managed to get them apart far enough to slide the fake memo through the gap. That required letting go of one side. The rings snapped shut again.

"Yes, sir. I have checked all the flags on the previous three binders. No, not the last one. He only just finished it. Okay, I'll do that. Anything else, sir."

In desperation, Vermeulen tossed the binder on the squishy carpet. It made a dull thud. De Haas turned. Vermeulen shrugged apologetically and bent down to pick it up. De Haas looked at him, then turned to the window again, listening to instructions.

Vermeulen grabbed the binder, banged it against the desk and, in the process, tore out the last page. He folded it and stuck it in his jacket pocket.

De Haas came to the desk and took the binder and settled on the other side of the desk. "Gotta check the flagged documents," he said.

"I'm leaving then. Give my regards to the judge."

"Wait, you can't just leave. We have to meet for a debriefing. We'll let you know when that is. Probably tomorrow."

"As long as I get to my flight on Wednesday, I don't care."

"You already have a return flight booked?"

"Of course, it's cheaper that way and saves your department some money."

Vermeulen, standing now, grabbed his briefcase and turned to leave the Kennel.

"Why are you in such a hurry to leave?"

"Because this place stinks and you're not the most stimulating company." The words were out of his mouth before he could stop himself.

De Haas's face darkened. "What have I done to you?"

"Nothing, except pester me with this inane task. You expect me to be grateful?"

Apparently, de Haas did, because he stood up again and looked as if he was going to give Vermeulen a lecture on proper behavior. Before he opened his mouth, de Haas did a double take. "What's that in your pocket?"

Vermeulen's blood turned to ice. "What?"

"That paper. In your pocket. What is it?"

Vermeulen looked down, his skin tight as a drum. "That? Oh, it's a receipt."

"It wasn't there earlier."

"It's been in that pocket since last night. I bought a bottle of jenever."

"That's not a jenever receipt. That's a regular sheet of paper."

In a flash, de Haas was up and reached for the pocket. Vermeulen was too slow. De Haas got a hold of the paper. He unfolded it. Vermeulen lunged for it and grabbed the top. For a second, the two stood facing each other, Vermeulen holding the top and de Haas the bottom of the sheet. De Haas yanked at it, Vermeulen held fast. The sheet tore along the middle. De Haas held the half with the incriminating paragraph.

Decision time. Fight for the other piece or make a run for it?

Vermeulen ran.

* * *

OUTSIDE ON VERVERSRUI, Vermeulen turned toward *Centraal Station*. He couldn't go back to his hotel. Not now. Fortunately, he had his passport and credit cards on him. He hurried to the next intersection, dodged to the left, took a side road, took a right at the next corner, and wove his way through the narrow streets of the quarter. Although his general direction was east, he followed what would look like a random path to any outside observer.

The temptation to just take a train across the border to Holland or Germany and fly home was huge. He knew it wasn't an option, though. An EUROPOL notice would certainly be issued and they'd alert the authorities at Schiphol. No, he had to fight this here, prove that the memo was fake. And therefore, he had to disappear.

After fifteen minutes of random turns, he stopped at an ATM and withdrew as much cash as his two cards allowed. That'd be the last use of his cards. His next stop was a phone store where he bought a cheap phone and a short-term plan. He had to show his passport to get it, but figured by the time the authorities had caught up with that, this mess should be sorted out. Right now, he needed a couple of days to figure out how to prove his innocence. He couldn't do that in detention.

Outside, he took the SIM card out of his regular phone. No pinging off cell towers anymore. He hurried on. Near the main station, he caught a taxi to take him to the very neighborhood where he'd found Gaby so many years ago. If he knew anything about cities it was that the run-down quarters always stayed run down.

Halfway there, he changed his mind. He ask the driver to stop, paid his fare and got out. The run-down quarters always had a higher police presence. He stopped in a store entrance and used his new phone to search for an AirBnB. He found one very close to the old Justice Palace on Britselei. A perfect location. They wouldn't look for him right next to where his old job used to be. He was about to reserve it when he realized that he'd have to use his credit card. No AirBnB after all. He looked for low rent hotels and rooms for rent. The fewer questions asked, the better. He ended up taking a taxi to a B&B in the Old-Berchem district of Antwerp, located in a long building on the grounds of the former military hospital. A strange place to have a B&B, but the hosts were happy to accept cash and the room was comfortable. He explained that the airlines had lost his luggage, went to his room and stretched out on the bed.

The first call was to Tessa. It was morning in New York City and she was at their place. She rejected the call, so he had to text her first about his new number.

"I heard you had a civilized brunch with your ex," Tessa said once she answered his second try.

"I did indeed. Much better than I expected. Gaby must have filled you in."

"Uh-huh. You going to see her again?"

"Who? Marieke? I don't think so. Why?"

"Just wondering. When are you coming back?"

"Well, I thought I was done, but then all hell broke loose. The last document in the binder was a memo, which I supposedly wrote—I didn't—and in which I tell another cop that I'll rat out Frans Vinke to the syndicate."

"What? And you're sure you didn't write that?"

"Positive, it's to a cop who wasn't even involved in the case. Even if I had wanted to leak Vinke's name, I wouldn't have told *that* guy. But I didn't. It's a setup. I don't know why I'm being set up, but that's what it is."

There was a moment of silence. Tessa was thinking. He'd grown to appreciate her matter of fact approach to problems. While he was upset that things weren't the way he wanted them to be, she was already sorting out options.

"They know, right?"

"Yes, one of their minions was in the room and has half of the incriminating memo."

"You fought over it?"

"He tried to grab it from me and I didn't let go."

"Okay. But you got away, and bought a different phone. Good. Coming home is out of the question?"

"Yeah."

"You have to clear this up. Can you prove that the memo is forged?"

"I don't think so. It's a memo done on a computer. My handwritten initials are on it."

"Send me a picture of what you have. I'll see what I can do. Printers have changed, there may be a way of showing that the document was printed more recently than 2002. In the meantime, do you have any friends there?"

"Not sure. There is Maya Dekker. She's one of the cops and initially she struck me like a hard nut. But then we talked and it turns out she hates the judge because he's a bigot and blocked her from moving on to EUROPOL. I don't know if that qualifies as a friend."

"It might. Who are the enemies?"

"There's judge Mesman who clearly has it out for me. And there is Frans Vinke's son, Theo, who told me directly that he holds me responsible for his father's death. He and his wife followed me to make sure I don't run away."

"Wow, that doesn't look good," Tessa said. "A son with an ax to grind and an eager judge? A bad combination. If this is just a case of revenge, why's the judge behind this?"

"I don't really know. He's one of those new conservative nationalists. Wants to clean up the system, make it responsive to ordinary citizens."

"Hmm. There's got to be more. Well, you've got your work cut out. Send me a picture of that memo. You need anything?"

"A few clues would be nice, but, no, I think I'm set for now."

"Just be careful."

Vermeulen ended the call. He was tempted to call Gaby, but didn't want to drag her into this. Unlike Tessa, she lived too close.

Chapter Twenty-Three

Strange Radiance

———◆———

V ERMEULEN RESORTED TO HIS USUAL METHOD for sorting out complex cases, a few sheets of paper and a pen. He tore a couple of pages from his notebook and sat down at the tiny table.

Tessa's question about who were his friends was a good starting point. He didn't know if he could count on Dekker, but it was worth a try, later. The more pressing question was the origin of the photos that had been dropped at his hotel room. There was little doubt that whoever sent them meant to help him. He just couldn't imagine who that might be.

Theo Vinke could be eliminated right away. The man told him that he wanted revenge. He had no interest in helping Vermeulen. His wife, Nora, might be a possibility. She was at best halfhearted about her surveillance duties. She did what she was asked to do. Besides, how would she have gotten the photos in the first place?

That left two possible allies, someone in the prosecutor's office or the police, and someone in the underworld. Dekker didn't show any reaction when he mentioned the photographs. She might be helpful, but she wasn't the initiator. Who else was there? His old colleagues were gone, retired. They wouldn't still be lurking around the edges of a thirteen-year-old investigation. Boogman was on a sailboat somewhere in the Caribbean anyway. Maybe van Dijk could help. And there was Alex Timmerman. He might still be with the police. And Jan Smits.

The question of allies in the underworld was trickier. He could imagine a split between Theo Vinke and Bastiaan Beukes. Even though his stepmother was a Beukes, family relations have been torn apart over less than the murder of a father. After all, the trigger had been pulled by some contract killer. It stood to reason that the hit was ordered by Beukes for the same reasons the fake memo outlined. Frans Vinke was unreliable, lazy and compromised. Why keep someone like him on the payroll?

That didn't explain why Beukes would want to help Vermeulen now. Thirteen years ago, Vermeulen made a serious dent in Beukes's profits. If anything, the man should hold a grudge. Unless . . .

Vermeulen had assumed that the relationship between Beukes and the lawyer Vanderfeld was based on convenience. Every crook needed a lawyer who was not directly entangled in the everyday aspects of crime. Vanderfeld had to stay clean enough to manage the legal trouble of Beukes. But that relationship was further cemented by the family ties. Beukes's sister's stepson married Vanderfeld's daughter. In a crime syndicate context, it could be akin to the strategic marriages of European royal houses; it cements alliances.

The trouble with such alliances—both among royals and criminals—is that they merely paper over the sheer drive for power and control which each side harbors. European history was littered with the corpses of such alliances. What if the family alliance between Beukes and Vanderfeld had become such a corpse? Vanderfeld knew everything there was to know about Beukes's operation. As a good lawyer, he would have kept documentation of every minute detail, if only to clear himself of any wrongdoing should Beukes ever stand before a judge. After his death, his son-in-law would have access to that documentation. Why stick to an alliance if you have all the information necessary to take down your partner and take over his share?

Vermeulen sat back and, for the first time in a long while, felt the urge to smoke a cigarette. Being caught in a mob power struggle was really bad news. The term "collateral damage" didn't come close to describing what would happen to him. Either side would gladly sacrifice Vermeulen if that helped them achieve their goal. It reminded him of his mission in Turkey where he was caught between an aging mob boss and his niece, who was trying to take over the operation. He'd been the expendable pawn back then, just as he was now. He got as far as the door to his room before he stopped. Smoking was no solution.

He did put on his coat because he needed to buy some toiletries. He asked for directions to the closest department store. It ended up quite a ways from his B&B. There wasn't really anything he could do at this time of the evening, so he decided to walk the dark streets. Unlike the center of Antwerp, the cyclists here tended to the street rather than the sidewalks. The bright pinpoints of their headlights were enough warning for Vermeulen.

The store was about a half hour walk away. There he got himself a toothbrush and paste, a razor, and some underwear. Food was the next thing. There was a restaurant in the next wing over from his B&B, but that had two Michelin stars and he had to conserve his cash. He stopped at a nondescript eatery and forgot what he'd eaten the moment he left the place.

Back in his room, he went back to the pieces of paper. No matter what scenario he spun, he always ended up at the question "Why me?" The whole process of getting him to Antwerp was far too elaborate a scenario to scratch a revenge itch. Hell, if Theo Vinke wanted revenge, he could have ordered a hit in New York City. Nobody would ever have solved that crime. Sure, some people get a sick enjoyment from seeing their victims squirm before the kill. He shivered involuntarily. Nobody was talking about killing.

He had to do something. Sitting there just made his mind spin into ever weirder scenarios. He remembered that he had to send a photo of the piece of the incriminating memo to Tessa. He turned on all the lights in the room, placed the piece of paper on the bedspread and took the photo. There weren't a lot of camera settings on his cheap phone, but he tried them all and sent the images to Tessa.

Next, he searched for Kees van Dijk. He remembered that his former colleague lived in Linkeroever. Hopefully he hadn't moved after retiring. Van Dijk would be the kind of person who had a landline and an entry in the phone book. He checked the online directory assistance and, sure enough, there was a Kees van Dijk living at the address Vermeulen remembered. He dialed the number and waited. A woman answered and Vermeulen asked to speak to Kees van Dyke.

"Who's calling?" she said.

"Valentin Vermeulen. We used to work together a long time ago." He'd never met Kees's wife during the time at the prosecutor's office. "You must be Erma? I don't think we ever met."

"I am and you're right. Kees used to talk about you. You are the one who went to America, right?"

"Yes, I am."

"You haven't heard the news?"

"Yes, I heard about the stroke. That's why I'm calling. How bad was it?"

"It was pretty severe. He's in a wheelchair now."

Vermeulen swallowed hard. That was worse than he'd assumed. Van Dijk had been a good colleague.

"I'm so sorry to hear that. How is he doing?"

"He's managing as well as can be expected. He can talk some, very slowly, but he needs a lot of support."

"That must be really hard for you, too. Do you have help?"

"Yes, it is hard. We had all these plans to travel after his retirement. But I have a good support system in place. Are you in town? I'm sure he'd love a visit. Can you come tomorrow?"

Tomorrow would be too late. Vermeulen had to get to the bottom of things as fast as possible.

"Unfortunately, I'm a bit pressed for time. I know it's getting late, but could I come tonight?"

There was a moment of silence. He could hear the receiver being put down and some mumbling.

"I guess that's all right. Do you know where we live?"

"Yes, I have the address."

* * *

KEES VAN DIJK LOOKED ANCIENT IN HIS WHEELCHAIR. Gone was the portly man who'd always been the calming presence in the room. His skin seemed too large for his body. His hair was mostly gone except for a few wisps still wafting by his ears. The stroke had partially paralyzed his face so that one half looked permanently frozen while the other tried to make up for it with a strange radiance.

Vermeulen could tell that his mind was as keen as before. His good eye shone with that clarity that he remembered from the old days.

"Kees. It's good to see you. How are you holding up?"

Van Dijk responded with a half-smile. His right hand gestured as if to say, "Well, I am what you see."

"I'm sorry I haven't been in touch," Vermeulen said. "That time back in 2002 was just crazy and I couldn't put it behind me fast enough. It's no excuse, I know, but that's what it was."

"You . . . did . . . good, back then."

"Couldn't have done it without you. You know that. At the end you were the one holding everything together."

Another half-smile.

"We . . . were . . . something else. You, Cornelia . . . me . . . Best team."

Vermeulen heard the wistfulness in his voice.

"Why . . . you here?"

Vermeulen grimaced.

"The past came back to haunt me. That very case, to be specific. I'm being accused of having leaked Frans Vinke's name to the syndicate, thus condemning him to death."

Van Dijk made a squelched snort and shook his head. "Tell . . . me."

Vermeulen did so as briefly as he could. He was well aware that Erma watched them, ready to step in the moment she thought it would strain her husband too much.

"What . . . you . . . want . . . from me?"

Vermeulen couldn't help but smile. That was the old van Dijk, cutting through the bullshit, knowing full well that Vermeulen was here to ask for help.

"Can you remember any animosity, any infighting between Jordi Vanderfeld and Bastiaan Beukes? I'm trying to sort out who's on what side in this crazy affair."

Van Dijk leaned back in his wheelchair and closed his eyes. Erma took that as a sign that he was tired and said, "We better let him rest. It was nice of you to come. Only a few of his colleagues came by after the stroke. It was like they were afraid."

Before Vermeulen could answer, van Dijk made a grunt and raised his good hand.

"Not . . . tired . . . thinking . . . wait."

"You look tired, dear. You need rest."

"Got . . . goddam rest . . . all day long . . . wait."

Vermeulen smiled again. Inside the worn-out body was the mind and wit of the old van Dijk. Even if he didn't remember anything at all, the visit was worth it just to see him quip.

"After . . . you . . . left. Things got . . . tense."

The story van Dijk relayed was not really surprising. Once they had interrupted the money transfers back to the cartels, the alliance between Beukes and Vanderfeld began to unravel. Beukes blamed Vanderfeld for not keeping the banking transactions secret. Vanderfeld accused Beukes of having been careless with the stolen car scheme. After Frans's murder, the relationship between the two deteriorated fast. Eventually, Theo's need for revenge pushed Vanderfeld into retirement. The aging lawyer no longer had the energy to fight. When he died, Theo got his hands on the secret files his father-in-law had kept on Beukes.

"What about this judge, Mesman? How does he fit into the scheme? He seems rather partial to Theo Vinke."

After the long account of the fight between the criminals, van Dijk needed rest. He closed his eyes and Erma got up, ready to shoo Vermeulen out the door.

Van Dijk wasn't quite done yet. "Mesman . . . is . . . Vanderfeld's . . . bastard son," he said, not opening his eyes again.

Vermeulen sat up startled. *Why didn't he know this?*

Van Dijk rallied for the last time and managed to say, "Good . . . to . . . see . . ." before drifting off.

Vermeulen rose and thanked Erma.

"I'm glad you came," she said. "He hasn't talked this much in ages. I didn't like you dredging up the old stuff, but he was more alive than he's been in a long time. It was good to see him like he once was even for a few minutes."

"Can I do anything for him? Is there anything he likes?"

"He's beyond worldly pleasures. He can't chew properly anymore. I know he'd love a big pork chop, but he can't eat it. His food is mostly the consistency of *stoemp*. He does like a little nip of jenever once in a while."

"Good, I'll make sure he gets a very nice bottle. Thank you for letting me ask him all these questions."

CHAPTER TWENTY-FOUR

MEMOIRS

———◆———

VERMEULEN CALLED TESSA AGAIN and told her about Mesman being Vanderfeld's illegitimate son. She didn't say anything for a minute, then her question cut right to the core. "Is Mesman going after you because of some misguided sense of family loyalty or because he is part of a corrupt racket?"

"I wish I knew," Vermeulen said. "But it probably doesn't make a difference to me, in either case, I face an uphill fight."

"Well, there's a difference. If it's an imprudent sense of obligation, he could be convinced that he's been used for illicit purposes. If he's corrupt, you are right."

"I don't really know what to do next. Did you find anything on the photo I sent you?"

"Nope. As far as I can tell the paper you photographed doesn't have the yellow microdots that modern printers print. Maybe that's because I only saw a photo, or because it wasn't printed on a laser printer. Can you check the paper? Just rub a wet finger over a letter and see if it smudges."

Vermeulen had no idea what she was talking about, but he did what she asked. The print didn't smudge.

"Good. That means it wasn't printed on an inkjet printer. Put the piece under a light and check carefully if you can see tiny yellow dots."

"Sorry. Why am I doing this?"

"Since around 2005, pretty much all color laser printers also print an almost invisible pattern of yellow dots that identify the model of the printer and the date when the page was printed. It's an anti-counterfeiting measure. If those dots are there, the memo was printed after 2005."

Vermeulen shrugged and took his half of the torn memo to the lamp that stood on the nightstand. As much as he tried, he couldn't see any yellow dots. He told Tessa so.

"Hmm. Either it was printed on a black and white laser printer or it was printed before 2005. Sorry. I thought I had a quick way to show the memo was forged. I guess, you're on your own. If I were you, I'd contact the crime boss, what was his name again?"

"Beukes."

"Yeah, that guy. I know it's risky but if what your old colleague said is true, he'd be your best bet. Any idea how you could connect with Beukes?"

"I could always go to his business. I know that address by heart."

"The direct approach might not be the smartest. You don't want to surprise a dangerous man. If he wanted to be contacted, he would've given you a sign."

"Thanks, I know. Maybe those photographs under the door were the sign."

"Just be careful, is all I'm saying."

"I will."

He ended the call and sat wondering what to do next. Alex Timmerman would help, but he had no idea how to get a hold of him. He used to be at the headquarters of the Federal Police. It was a start. He found the number online and dialed it. A recorded message told him to choose one of too many options. He pressed zero in the hope he would get a human being, but that just started the litany from the beginning. Eventually, he got to an option that allowed him to type in the first five letters of the last name of the party he wanted to reach. He tried that, but the system told him that there was no one by that name. Timmerman must've quit his job or transferred elsewhere.

There was nothing left to do but to wait. He stretched out on the bed. Sleep when you can. The next two days were going to be crazy.

He woke up disoriented and groggy in the middle of the night. There had been a sound. That much his mushy brain remembered. What sound? He couldn't remember. Maybe the phone. He checked it, but there was no reminder or notification on the screen. He got up and turned on the light on the nightstand. Nothing was different, except his clothes now had that slept-in look. Stupid idea to lie down for a nap at seven-thirty in the evening.

He got up and went to the washroom alcove. On the way, he saw a piece of paper lying by the door. He rubbed his eyes and squinted. It was still there. At least it wasn't an envelope. Another photo from 2002 would have thrown him for a loop. Who'd be shoving a piece of paper under the door? Except for Tessa, nobody knew he was staying here.

The paper was just a regular size sheet folded in half. It couldn't be the bill, could it? Some hotels shoved it under the door the night before the scheduled check-out, except this wasn't a hotel and he wasn't checking out until Wednesday morning.

His brain had finally achieved regular operating conditions and he bent down to pick up the folded sheet. There was no writing on the outside. He unfolded the sheet. There were only three words, written in a hasty scrawl, *Get Out Now!*

How long had it been since he thought he heard a sound? Three minutes? A half hour? It might already be too late. Who cares? He put on his coat, grabbed his briefcase and phone and carefully opened the door.

The hallway was lit by night lighting in regular intervals. It ran the length of the building. There were nine rooms on this floor. His was the third, closer to the front staircase he'd used to come up from the reception. Before he could even decide which way to go, he heard a creak from that staircase. That was all the information he needed. He closed his door silently and headed toward the rear staircase. He sidled along the wall. The old boards were less likely to creak there than at the center of the hall.

At the rear, he turned the corner and leaned against the wall, letting out a slow breath. The echo of a door being pushed open reached him. Time to get out. He hurried down the stairs and pushed open the door to the outside.

The trouble with staying at a B&B on the grounds of a former military complex is a lack of options when it comes to making a quick getaway. The entire complex had only two exits. The one everyone used and one toward the rear. If whoever came after him was smart, they'd cover both. But his quick escape might have caught his pursuers by surprise. It stood to reason that they were improvising, too. He chose the rear exit.

There was commotion behind him. A car starting, then another one. Headlights raked the grounds of the former hospital. He ducked behind a colonnade that connected two other buildings on the grounds and waited until the cars had left.

The street was deserted. It was almost two in the morning and he stood in the cold drizzly night of Antwerp without any idea of where to go next. There was a gnawing hole in his stomach, a desperate sense of being all alone.

He didn't have a lot of time to feel sorry for himself because a large black car came racing toward him. Vermeulen managed to duck into a doorway, but it didn't provide much of a cover. Sure enough, the car skidded to a stop and a man jumped out. He motioned to Vermeulen and said, "Get in."

Vermeulen had never seen him and sure as hell wasn't going to do any such thing.

"*Get out now?*" the man said. "I knocked, you didn't answer, I pushed that note under your door. Now get in. We gotta get you off the street. There are bad people looking for you."

"What if you are the bad people?" Vermeulen said.

"You'd be dead already."

The logic was odd but it made sense. Vermeulen got into the car. The driver, another man Vermeulen had never seen, accelerated rapidly, but kept it just below burning rubber.

"Who are you?" Vermeulen said.

"We are the enemies of your enemies, or, for short, your lucky break."

"And here I thought I had some friends. Could you at least enlighten me as to who my enemies are?"

"If you haven't figured that out by now, you are as dumb as your enemies think you are."

"Theo Vinke thinks I'm dumb?"

"Theo doesn't think. And that's his major asset. But if he did, he would think you're dumb, too. I can't believe you put up with that charade of reading the files."

Vermeulen decided to ignore this slight. "Who's after Theo?"

The car shot around a corner and Vermeulen slammed against the door. The man had braced himself and stayed upright.

"Everybody and nobody. That's the rub. Theo has always been a waste of sperm. But he happens to sit on an archive that contains enough ammunition to blow everybody who's ever been on the other side of the law sky high."

"Ah. Jordi Vanderfeld's collected memories. I see. Is it safe to assume that you all feature in those accounts."

"That guy kept records of everything that happened in Antwerp for some thirty years. That's why he was untouchable while he was alive. But Jordi was smart. Theo is not."

The car swerved past another car on the road and turned into another cross street. This time Vermeulen was prepared and didn't fly against the man.

"It's nice to know you care enough to keep me alive, but I don't see why I'm involved in this or why someone wants me dead."

"Listen Vermeulen, I don't give a rat's ass about your life. It just so happens that your death would very inconvenient just now, so shut up."

CHAPTER TWENTY-FIVE

LIFE INSURANCE

———————◆———————

THE CAR CAME TO A STOP IN FRONT OF A BAR. All the lights were off and a sign in the door said, "Closed." The man unlocked the door and hustled Vermeulen into the bar none too gently. He stopped and locked the door again. His tense demeanor started seeping into Vermeulen's body too. He said, "Listen, man. Level with me. Who are you and who's out there coming for me?"

"Not my pay grade," was all the guy said and pushed Vermeulen forward.

The heat had been turned down inside the bar. It smelled of stale beer and used coffee grounds. The chairs had been inverted on the tables. Vermeulen's coat caught one of the legs and sent the chair clattering to the floor. Both men started at the sudden noise.

"Damn, I didn't know you were such a klutz," the man said. "Come on, we gotta get out of here."

"Out? We just got here?"

"You really are a babe in the woods, aren't you? I can't believe you're still alive."

The man shoved him into the back room and out a steel door, which he locked from the outside. The dark courtyard connected to a cobblestone alley. The man pushed Vermeulen along. Once in the alley, he turned left and hurried forward. Vermeulen couldn't see much more than the two brick walls on either side of them. It seemed a terrible place to be caught in. Only two exits, both easily blocked. Except there was a third option. The alley intersected with another one, and the man took Vermeulen into that.

About thirty yards further, they reached a door. The man unlocked it, pushed Vermeulen into another courtyard and locked the door again. Across the yard stood a four-story house. It's backdoor was open and dim light fell onto the patio.

Once inside, the man closed the door and breathed out. "You have no idea how close they were."

"I'm sure you are right, but unless someone explains to me what's going on, I'm not going to grasp how any of this applies to me."

The man just shook his head. The hallway was all lit up, and the man took him up two floors. There, he opened a door. "Here he is," he said to someone inside. Then he pushed Vermeulen inside and closed the door again.

The room was large and furnished in the manner of old Antwerp gentry. Dark wood paneling, parquet floor, floor-to-ceiling bookcases on one side, three windows on the other. The curtains were closed

In the back stood a massive oak desk and behind it sat Bastiaan Beukes. Vermeulen remembered him as a burly man who knew that his presence cowed most people enough to make verbal threats superfluous. The man sitting behind the desk had aged a lot more than the last thirteen years could account for. His shock of brown hair had turned thin and gray. His face no longer had that North Sea tan. Instead it had the sallow complexion of someone who hadn't been outside in a long time. His clothes hung off his frame like limp sails. The cuffs of Beukes's jacket reached just past his wrist, so it wasn't his size that had shrunk, just his weight.

"Ain't much to look at anymore," he said in a phlegmy voice.

"We all age at our own pace. Have you been ill?"

"Lung cancer. Twice they thought they'd gotten it. Twice the fucker came back. By the third treatment, I was ready to toss in the towel. But, hey, that time the docs got it and I'm still here."

"Congratulations."

Beukes gave him a grim smile and nodded. "Ah, just sit the hell down."

Vermeulen did so and said, "Could you tell me why I'm here and what's going on?"

Beukes sat back in his chair and shook his head. He leaned down, opened a door in his desk and pulled out a bottle of jenever and two small glasses. Vermeulen saw the label. It was *Filliers oude graanjenever*, aged for eight years.

"First we have a drink," Beukes said.

"That's a very fine bottle."

"Better than that crap you got at the night shop last week."

Beukes had been following him too. *What the hell?* But Vermeulen was past being upset. Beukes filled the two glasses with a surprisingly steady hand all the way to the brim and picked up his glass carefully. Vermeulen did the same and each sipped the first quarter of an inch off the top.

"This is excellent Jenever," Vermeulen said.

"Didn't think you'd be drinking with me back then, did 'ya?" Beukes said.

Vermeulen shook his head. "Nope. I wanted to see you behind bars."

"I bet you still do."

"Yes, but that train left the station a long time ago."

"You got close, closer than anyone ever had. You would've gotten me too. But Jordi had set up the perfect scheme. Best damn lawyer I ever had. They don't make 'em like that anymore."

All Vermeulen could do was nod. The absurdity of the situation was beyond description. It was like two players from opposing teams reminiscing about a long-ago match that had ended in a tie.

"You cost me a pretty penny," Beukes said. "Never really recovered from that. By the time I figured out new ways to get the cash back to Colombia, the vultures had settled in, waiting for me to roll over. I didn't, but the competition was there and cartels played us against each other. Your daughter doing okay?"

"What about my daughter?" That shift in topic caught him by surprise.

"You did the right thing back then. I'd have done the same. Cold turkey, it's the only way. She stay clean?"

Vermeulen said, "Yes."

"Good. She's in Düsseldorf, isn't she?"

"Why are you keeping track of my daughter?"

"No reason. Just making sure she wasn't following your footsteps. But she didn't, so I don't have to worry about her, do I?"

Vermeulen felt a chill running down his spine. That Beukes was even thinking about Gaby was scary. He realized that Beukes thought of everything as if it were a conflict between families. "Listen, I was doing my job back then. My daughter had nothing to do with it. Leave her alone. I mean it."

Beukes raised both his hands in mock surrender. "Ah, the old Vermeulen. Don't worry. I have no business in Düsseldorf or with your daughter."

"Good, can we talk about the situation at hand? Why have you brought me here?"

Beukes took another sip of jenever.

"You know that Jordi kept records of everything he was involved in. It was his life insurance."

Vermeulen agreed.

"It turns out, he kept track of a lot more than just his business. At least that's how I understand it."

"Yes, his memoirs, so to speak," Vermeulen said.

Beukes raised his eyebrows. "You know about them?"

Vermeulen nodded, as if that was common knowledge. It dawned on him that those memoirs were the key, not the forged memo.

"That wasn't a problem as long as Jordi was alive," Beukes said. "'Cuz I knew enough about his dealings. Kinda like the Americans and the Soviets, mutually assured destruction. Not that it would've come to that. We were mostly friends. And we had a deal. If he thought he'd be knocking at death's door soon, he'd give me the stack of papers that concerned me. I, of course, promised the same in return."

He sighed. "And, believe you me, I was ready to do it too. After the second round of chemo, I had my wife bundle up my records with the directive to send them to Jordi should I kick the bucket. Sadly, Jordi didn't have that chance. He had a stroke and was gone in twenty-four hours. I tried to get what would have been mine, but I couldn't get near it."

"Theo has them now? How did he even know about those records?" Vermeulen said.

"Beats me. All I know is that Theo ended up sitting on a pile of dynamite, ready to blow a big chunk of Antwerp's underworld to kingdom come. Since you knew about the papers, you wouldn't know where they are, would you?"

Vermeulen stroked his chin, waiting a few seconds longer than necessary before saying, "How would I?" The longer Beukes thought Vermeulen was of value to him, the longer he'd stay alive.

Beukes paused and took another sip of jenever. Vermeulen did the same.

"Did you send those pictures to my hotel room?" Vermeulen said.

"Yes, I did. Thought you would want to know that your apartment wasn't all that secret."

"Why three pictures and those texts?"

"Just making sure you get the message."

Beukes shifted in his chair behind the desk. He looked tired, not a surprise given that it was about three in the morning. Vermeulen's night had also been too short, but the adrenaline from the escape was still fueling his body.

"Did you leak Frans Vinke's name?" Vermeulen said.

"I didn't leak anything. It was no secret that you tried to turn him into an informant. He came to me right away and told me. We played you for a while. But in the end, I couldn't trust him anymore. Anyone who so easily betrays one side, is bound to betray the other side eventually. It was taken care of quietly."

"Why was there a document in the files that implicated me?"

"Theo Vinke musta forged it. He was convinced you wanted his dad dead. I don't know how he got so fixated on that. He wanted to pressure the judge to open an investigation. That way you'd come back to town and he could get his revenge. You know that Mesman is kinda his brother-in-law, don't you?"

Vermeulen nodded.

"Anyways," Beukes said. "I ain't just speaking for myself. There's a lot of men in Antwerp who'd love to see Theo get hit by a truck. It'll happen, too. He's being real careful, but, hell, he'll make a mistake and that's when he'll get it. In the meantime, though, everyone is sitting tight, hoping that Theo'll rat out someone else."

"Why isn't he dead yet?"

"I can't do that to Nora. I really care about her. Sure she fell in love with a dimwit, but there's no accounting for love, is there?"

"Has anyone tried to pay him off?"

"You kidding me? I'm the one doing the extorting, I ain't paying no blackmailer. Theo thinks if he drops the dime on a little guy, the rest of us will fall in line and pay him. Boy, has he got that wrong."

"Why are you helping me?"

"Because I'm a nice guy? Nah, who'm I kidding? You don't really matter all that much as long as you are alive. You'll beat that rap, no problem. Mesman will have egg on his face, and Theo might even get in trouble. Now, if you're dead, then it's a different story. Mesman will finger Theo for the murder and then all Theo can do to save his skin is trade Jordi's records."

"Oh. I thought Mesman was in league with Theo?"

"No, he's a damn judge. Why would he work with a bird brain like Theo? Mesman wants what we all want, Jordi's collected works. Can you imagine him dredging up the past, finding all those murders that were never even investigated, and closing all them cold cases? It'd be a national circus and it'd be his ticket to a seat on the highest court. And, after that, become minister of justice, who knows, maybe even prime minister. If he's anything, he's a careerist."

Vermeulen shook his head. It was bad enough to have the mob root for you. But to have a judge want you dead so he can move on in his career had to be the worst.

"What do we do?" Vermeulen said.

"We? You ain't doing nothing. We'll keep you locked up until we got Jordi's records."

"What? You'll keep me locked up until someone figures out how to steal Vanderfeld's memories from Theo Vinke?"

Beukes shrugged. "You got a better idea, that doesn't involve you getting killed?"

"Prove to the judge that the memo was forged."

"How you gonna do that?"

"There's got to be something."

"You don't get it, do you? All I want is getting my hands on Jordi's records. Having you alive might be helpful, but not really necessary. Think of me locking you away as a courtesy. You oughta thank me."

CHAPTER TWENTY-SIX

ODD ANGLE

———◆———

TWO MEN BROUGHT VERMEULEN TO A large bedroom on the third floor with an en-suite bathroom. The decor was similar to Beukes's office, dark walnut furniture and beige walls. There was one large glass door to a balcony half covered by heavy woolen curtains. On the bed lay a pair of pajamas. The men left.

He checked the door. It was solid wood and it was locked. He pull the curtains aside. The balcony door was also made of solid wood and double-paned glass. The balcony was small and had a metal railing. He tried the balcony door. It was looked too. He went to the bathroom. It was larger than the one in his hotel room. There were toiletries, towels and even a bathrobe made of Turkish cotton. It had a single stained glass window. It also faced the balcony.

There was a knock on the door. The lock turned and the two men entered. One carried a blazer and slacks and the other a couple of shirts still in the plastic wrapping and underwear. They put the items in the armoire and dresser and left again without saying a word.

Vermeulen sat on the edge of the bed. The one thing he knew for sure was that he'd have figure a way out. The threat posed by Theo Vinke was clear, but he wasn't at all sure that Beukes would keep him alive once he knew that Vermeulen didn't know anything about the memoirs. Why should Theo be the only one to hold a grudge? For the moment, it suited Beukes that he was alive. He'd better use that moment before it was too late.

So far, he'd assumed that Mesman was an overeager judge who'd get Interpol after him if he ever fled Belgium. Van Dijk's and Beukes's information shed a different light on Mesman's motive. There was a much larger prize to be had and Vermeulen's death was the easy way to get it. It wasn't just a forged memo anymore, it was a corrupt judge and the fact that he didn't finish his job thirteen years ago. That Beukes and Theo Vinke were even fighting about documents was only possible because he'd failed to put an end to Beukes's business back then.

Right about now, he could use Tessa's advice, but the men had taken both his phones. He still had his cash, passport and other papers, but they wouldn't do him much good being locked up in the mob boss's home. No matter what his strategy was going to be, he had to get away from Beukes. And that meant getting out of this house.

It was four in the morning. According to some rumor he'd heard back when he did his military service, that was the best time to plan an attack since the enemy was likely asleep. That would presume that the mobsters who'd hustled him to Beukes's house had gone to bed. Not very likely, given that Beukes was on high alert. Still, he had to get away from here.

He went back into the bathroom and examined the stained glass window. It displayed a stylized rural scene. Stained glass was much easier to beak. He wrapped a towel around his hand and pressed against one of the larger pieces of glass. The lead seams gave a little. He pushed harder. The glass cracked. The next step was the trickiest. If he kept pushing, glass would fall, shatter on the balcony and alert someone. They'd not taken his keychain and therefore he still had his penknife. He took it and gently pushed the blade into one of the cracks. One of the glass shards started to give way. He pushed it far enough to use the blade as a lever to push the adjacent shard toward the inside of the window. When it stuck inside far enough, he grabbed it and wiggled is back and forth until the lead seam gave way.

It took him another hour to create an opening large enough for him to climb out. The balcony extended just below the bathroom window, still, climbing out and sensing the patio of the courtyard three floors below made the hair on his neck stand up. He managed to tear his pants on a piece of glass that he hadn't bothered to remove. For a second, he thought of going back and exchanging them for the new pair, but it was better to move on.

The balcony was small, maybe a couple of square yards. He leaned over it and saw an identical balcony on the floor below. He climbed over the railing, lowered his right leg in the hope it could find a footing on the railing below. The idea of dangling in mid-air didn't sound very appealing. The plan didn't work. Those old Antwerp buildings had tall ceilings. He crouched as low as he could. With a deep breath, he clamped his hands around the railing posts and slid his feet out. His weight pulled him down until his hands got a hold of the cross bar at the bottom. He bounced to a stop. His fingers screamed not just because of his weight, but also because slivers of rust bit into his skin without mercy. Finally, his feet found a footing on the railing below.

He managed to lower himself onto the balcony below and stopped to catch his breath. There was a balcony door just like the one above. At least the curtains were closed. He couldn't afford to linger even though his palms were bloody from the cuts made by the metal slivers.

The only way to the ground was to repeat the procedure, except there'd be no railing to step on. He'd just have to let go and wish for the best. Worst case scenario, a broken ankle. He stared at the ground, willing his eyes to penetrate the dark. Had there been anything besides the pavers? He couldn't remember.

No time like the present. He repeated the climb over the railing and was again dangling in the air. At basic training, way back in his army days, they'd taught him how to break a fall by rolling to the side when jumping from a high spot. He let go. And hit the ground a second later with a thud. He didn't roll, but remembered to bend his knees enough to absorb the impact.

When the men had hustled him through the courtyard earlier, he hadn't paid much attention to its layout. The exit to the alley was opposite the backdoor of the house. He didn't know where he was in relation to the door, and he didn't want to make a racket by bumping into any garden furniture. He crouched and allowed his eyes to adjust to the dark.

The yard loomed dark. He turned his head and checked his surroundings. A dim sliver of light at ground level told him where the back door of the house was located. He stood up again and went to it. With his back turned toward that door, he strode out in the direction of the alley. He held his hands out in front. A couple dozen steps later he felt the wood of the alley door. He tried the handle, it was locked. The wall was at least eight feet tall. No way he could climb over it without a prop of some sort.

He leaned against the door and scanned the dark courtyard. As far as he could make out, there was no garden furniture near the center. He sidled along the wall to the left. After a couple of yards, he felt the leaves of some kind of vine growing up the wall. The branches were thin, he pulled one and it came away from the wall. Nothing to climb up on. He went back to the door and repeated the process on the right side. Again, he felt vines, the same kind he'd encountered on the other side. He was about to turn back when his foot nudged something hard. It was a wooden bench backed against the wall.

He stepped on the seat and his hands could feel the top of the wall. So far, so good, except there was no way he was going to pull himself up to the top. Thirty years ago, he might've been able to pull himself up, but those days were long gone. A couple of feet more and it might be manageable. The back of the bench was that much higher. He pulled the bench away from the wall. It was heavy, a solid piece meant to withstand the climate. He put one foot on the back rest, grabbed the top of the wall and stepped up. The bench teetered—his weight now off-center—and the back settled against the wall, almost pushing his feet off. He grabbed the outside edge of the wall and pulled as hard as he could, scrambling up the vines with his feet like a drunken spider.

It must have been a sad sight, but he didn't care. He lay on top of the wall, panting as if he'd just run a marathon. His fingers were scraped and sore and his knees skinned through his pants. For all he knew, the pants were torn too. And he was only half done. He had to get down.

The dismount as was clumsy as his ascent, but a whole lot faster. This time he didn't bend his knees upon impact and his right ankle complained bitterly when it hit a cobblestone at an odd angle. Just what he didn't need that moment.

CHAPTER TWENTY-SEVEN

PINEAPPLE JAM

———◆———

THE EMPTY ROOM WAS FIRST DISCOVERED BY A MAID who brought a breakfast tray at seven-thirty. She alerted the driver who had transported Vermeulen to the house in the night. The driver was loath to wake Beukes, who usually didn't rise before ten and probably even later that day, since he'd been up 'til three. Instead, he called Beukes's right-hand man who'd done all the talking during the night.

"Goddam idiot," the right-hand man said. "We rescue him and he runs away? How stupid is that guy?"

The driver didn't say anything, but wondered about the notion that they'd rescued Vermeulen. He thought of it more as an abduction. Whatever. He shrugged.

"You better wake the boss," the right-hand man said. "I'll come to the house."

The driver sighed and enlisted the support of the maid who brought a tray with a thermos of coffee and a cup and saucer. He knocked on Beukes's bedroom door. It took a while before a grunt came from the inside. The driver opened the door carefully. That old-man-smell he knew too well from his own father—God rest his soul—eddied around his nose. He peeked around the edge of the door and saw Beukes awake but still in bed, resting on his elbows.

"This better be good," Beukes said.

"It isn't. Vermeulen escaped."

The maid pushed past the driver, put the tray down, poured the coffee, added sugar and handed it to Beukes, who thanked her with a smile. After sipping a bit of coffee and letting the hot brew wake up his nervous system, Beukes put the saucer on his nightstand and slowly swung one leg and then the other over the edge of the mattress. With his feet near the floor, he pushed his upper body into a sitting position. The driver and the maid stood by and watched without saying a word.

Once sitting up, Beukes reached for the coffee again. This time he took a big gulp and sighed with pleasure. "You make good coffee," he said to the maid. He put the saucer back down and said, "Vermeulen has run away? How did he get out? I hope you locked the door." He looked at the driver, who nodded with emphasis.

Beukes pushed himself into a standing position and shuffled to the window. He pulled back the curtain. The balcony was empty as usual. "Idiot musta climbed right past me. Ain't no other way down."

The other two nodded.

"Did you call Fredi?"

The driver said that he had.

"Good. Well, at least Vermeulen didn't get any dumber since we last met." He turned to the driver and the maid. "Out, you two. You don't want to watch an old man dressing himself. It's too depressing for everyone involved."

* * *

Forty-five minutes later, Beukes sat at the table in his dining room and smeared butter on a roll. In front of him stood a jar of pineapple jam, a plate with slices of ham and Gouda and a soft-boiled egg. Across the table sat the right-hand man, Fredi Kuiper, who didn't have anything in front of him.

"What's his next move?" Beukes said.

"If I was him, I'd get on the next plane to America."

Beukes nodded and decapitated the egg.

"We could put men at Schiphol and Brussels," Kuiper said. "We'll spot him there, all flights to America leave from special terminals."

Beukes nodded again. "And if you wasn't him?" he said and spooned some egg into his mouth.

"I'd still go. It's a lot harder to get to him over there. The judge's gonna have to jump through a lot of extra hoops to get the cops there to do anything. That whole extradition thing is tricky."

"Where does that leave us?"

"We won't be using him as bait for Theo, that's for damn sure."

Beukes took a bite from his roll and drank more coffee. After he put the cup down, he shook his head.

"You're wrong, Fredi. You're thinking of it only from the perspective of someone running away. You gotta think of it from the perspective of a guy who's on a mission. You don't know Vermeulen the way I do. Once he gets his teeth into something, he won't let go."

"Sure boss, that's how he was when it was his job to be that way. But now? What the hell does he care about the dirt Theo has on everyone. It don't matter to him."

"You got a point. Ninety-nine-point-nine percent of people would think that. Not Vermeulen. If I know anything about him, it's that he'll want to clear his name. He'll try to prove that that memo was forged. Hell, he'll want to finish up what he didn't finish thirteen years ago. He's going to be trouble."

"That's pretty stupid."

Beukes had scooped out more egg, but stopped the spoon in midair.

"That it may be, but this is a guy on a mission. What's he going to do next?"

Fredi shrugged.

"The man needs his stuff," Beukes said. "Make sure you have someone watching his hotel. We want to know if he uses his credit card. We got two phones off him. One's obviously a burner, so he'll get another one. Get someone to crack the passcodes. I need to know who he phoned."

He swallowed the egg and bit into the roll.

"'kay, boss."

Beukes chewed on his bite and looked pensive. He swallowed and said, "I shoulda taken his cash and his passport. That woulda kept him here. Damn." He drank more coffee. "Ah, it don't matter. He's gonna confront Theo. I just know it. Keep an eye on Theo. I also want to know if Vermeulen has any current friends here where he can stay. The experience at the B&B last night will make him think twice about going to another place. It's too cold to sleep rough. He's gotta find a roof somewhere."

"I'll have our guys check."

"One more thing. Just in case you are right. He's got a ticket back home from Schiphol for Wednesday. I don't think he'll make it, but check out which airline he's flying on. And make sure he doesn't get on that plane."

"Got it. Anything else?"

"Nope, get it done. We got little more than twenty-four hours to find him."

After Fredi left, Beukes finished his breakfast. He'd always considered it the most important meal of the day and never let himself be hurried. When he was done, he leaned back and said, "Mr. Vermeulen. What are you up to? How're you gonna prove that Theo is lying?"

He picked up his phone and tapped on a contact. The phone rang a while until a male voice answered.

"Hullo Theo, Bastiaan here. Sorry to be foiling your little assassination plan last night, but I needed Vermeulen alive. Turns out the man didn't appreciate my intervention and flew the coop earlier. He is out in the wild again. And, consider this a friendly heads-up, he's coming for you."

Chapter Twenty-Eight

Biggest Error

———— ♦ ————

THE FIRST THING VERMEULEN DID AFTER HE ESCAPED from Beukes was find a shop to buy a new phone. That turned out to be difficult for two reasons. One, he was limping, which made exploring the tony Zurenborg neighborhood in Antwerp a lot more painful, and, two, most of the night shops had already closed and the regular shops were hours away from opening. He'd crossed Draagplaats with its massive railroad bridge, hurried across another square and finally was lucky on Plantin-en-Moretuslei, where he found a shop that hadn't closed yet. Some sixty euros later, he had a new phone. The first person he called was Maya Dekker.

"Who is this," Dekker said. There was some annoyance in her voice, as if seven-thirty in the morning was too early to call.

"This is Valentin. I got a different phone. Can you call in sick again? I have information that can help you and me."

"Are you nuts? Fighting with Hendrik about the memo and then running away? You might as well have signed a confession."

"I had no other option. I'd be in detention now and wouldn't be able to clear my name."

"Clear your name? What makes you think that is even an option anymore. Mesman issued a warrant for your arrest. The police are out looking for you. It's highest priority. Every cop in Antwerp has your photo."

"You know I didn't send that memo. Right now, the police are the least of my worry. I have Theo Vinke and Beukes hunting me. And they're not planning on arresting me."

"What happened?"

"I'll tell you later. Right now I need a place to hide. And if you still want the job at EUROPOL, I have the information that will get you that job. So where do you live?"

When Dekker finally spoke again, he could tell that she'd been wrestling with herself. She sounded tentative and unsettled. Not at all like the cool cop who'd interrogated him only a few days ago.

"I know I'm committing the biggest error of my life by saying this, but, okay, you can stay at my place. And I will call in sick."

She gave him her address and ended the call.

He took a taxi to *Het Eilandje.* The sun was finally up, although the clouds gave the morning light a shabby quality. Quite appropriate for his destination, he thought. When he last lived in Antwerp, that district was a rundown dockside neighborhood. He couldn't imagine a police officer choosing to live in those surroundings. When the cab got close, he saw how wrong he was. The streets weren't what he considered shabby anymore. There was a lot of construction and he saw brand new buildings fitted right next to older ones that would, no doubt, be renovated or torn down in the near future.

As the cab rounded a corner of the *Willemdok* he saw a building that hadn't been there before, a giant sandstone colored cube that towered over the water.

"What's that?" he said to the driver.

"The MAS."

"What?"

"*Museum an de Stroom.* The Museum on the River, Antwerp's newest museum."

"This area really looks different from what I remember," Vermeulen said.

"Yeah. The MAS did all that. I couldn't afford to live here. Everything's so expensive anymore. Kinda funny. Ten years ago, I wouldn't have wanted to live here and now that it's nice, I can't afford to."

"Yeah, if we could predict those things, we'd be rich."

"You got that right."

The cab stopped at Dekker's address. Vermeulen paid the driver and stepped onto the sidewalk. It was a new building, rather modern with glass and metal, but enough brick to make it fit into the streetscape. Cops must have received a raise since he left the service. He couldn't have afforded living in a place like this back then.

He found Dekker's name on the digital display and dialed the number next to it. Her voice came over the intercom and she told him to come to the third floor.

The interior had the same understated elegance, light wooden floors, tiled walls with wood inlays. He called the elevator and waited. When the car arrived a man and a woman exited. He took the it to the third floor. There were four doors. The second from the right stood ajar. He knocked on it and Dekker called for him to come inside.

* * *

HER APARTMENT HAD NONE OF THAT ELEGANT ATMOSPHERE he'd felt outside. The materials were similar, but that wasn't it. Dekker was—Vermeulen couldn't think of another word—messy. In the foyer, he saw a pair of balled up socks lying in a corner. Several boxes that probably hadn't been opened since she moved in stood jammed against a coat rack.

Dekker came around the corner wearing sweatpants that may have been green at one point and a black T-shirt, that sported the washed-out tour schedule of some band he'd never heard of. Her hair was flattened against one side of her head. She had the gritty look of someone who just woke up.

"Sorry," she said. "I was actually going to call in sick again, before I got your call. You got here faster than I thought you would."

"Don't worry about it, you should see my place." Which would have looked a whole lot better. He wasn't fastidious, but he did clean up after himself. According to Tessa, it was one of his appealing qualities.

The apartment had an open floor plan with the kitchen area off to the left, leading to a dining spot that connected to a living room/office space. The kitchen was a mess of dirty dishes and there were remains of breakfast on the dining table. The office looked like a windstorm had hit a paper factory. Under a pile of papers, he made out a sofa. Good, at least he didn't have to sleep on the floor.

"Have a seat," she said, clearing away more papers, a towel, a pair of socks and a bra.

He settled into a red-upholstered armchair that turned out way more comfortable than it looked.

"What happened," she said, still scurrying around trying to pick up random bits of stuff.

"I thought I was well hidden in a B&B, but in the middle of the night I received a warning to clear out immediately. A couple of Beukes's men scooped me up and brought me to his house. There he explained to me that this is all about Jordi Vanderfeld's memoirs—"

"His what?"

"Vanderfeld kept detailed records about everyone and everything in the underworld throughout his life. It was his insurance, so to speak. Now Theo has it and he's about to blackmail every crook in town. Beukes is worried about that, but he's even more worried that Theo's desire for revenge has gotten the better of him and that he's out to kill me. Which would give Mesman an excuse to arrest Theo and get his hands on those memoirs."

"That's baloney. Mesman could arrest Theo any time he wants to. With his *Frietkots*, tax evasion is always a solid reason. Why would he need to wait until he kills you?"

"Family. Mesman is related to Theo. Jordi Vanderfeld was their father. Theo's wife, Nora, is Mesman's sister."

"Wow. I did not know that. This is huge. No wonder Theo got off easy. That makes perfect sense. I can see Mesman eager to rid himself of that millstone around his neck and salivating at the chance to get those records. He'd solve every cold case of the last thirty years or so."

"Right, he'd be headed for a much brighter future. That's why I don't think he's all that eager to have me arrested. I worry about Theo a lot more. His goons were very close last night before Beukes's guys whisked me away. Or maybe Beukes just wants me to believe that."

"Did he tell you what he wants?"

"Not in so many words. He said he was going to hold me until he got those papers but I don't trust him. When it comes down to it, he's not above using me as bait to draw out Theo. My only way out is to prove that the memo is a forgery. Even the setup is ridiculous. Why would I send a memo to Smits? He had nothing to do with the investigation. I have no idea how that memo even got into the binder."

There was a pause, then Dekker said, "I wonder if Beukes had it stolen from the evidence locker and put in the binder. Remember how we both thought that someone had been at the Kennel? How the dust on the picture frame was disturbed? So he meant for you to find it."

"Yeah, that could be, except I screwed that up."

"You can say that again. Any other ideas?"

"My partner told me something about secret dots that appear on color laser printed pages. But I can't see anything on the piece of paper I salvaged. Maybe de Haas's piece has those dots."

"We don't have a color laser printer, just a black and white one. You won't find those dots, even if I could get the other piece. But it's a moot point. Nobody's allowed near it. And remember, I can't be seen as helping you or even speaking to you. My position in the office is iffy as it is. That's why staying here is a bad idea."

"Who would know? Nobody would be looking for me at your place. It's the perfect cover. I'm leaving tomorrow afternoon. It's just today and tonight. Tomorrow morning I'll be out of your life. I promise to be a courteous house guest and won't get in the way of you and your partner."

"I don't have a boyfriend. I live alone."

"Oh. Sorry. I shouldn't have made assumptions. I didn't mean to put you in this awkward situation. But we can help each other."

She sighed and said, "Okay, you can stay. What's your plan?"

"Besides proving that the memo is forged? I don't think I have a choice but to get those memoirs myself."

"How are you going to do that?"

"I haven't really thought about it. I'm thinking that his wife Nora might be a possibility. Last Saturday, she did a pretty lousy surveillance job and when I confronted her, she didn't really seem upset. She just called Theo and let him talk to me. I can imagine that she's not too happy about Theo's revenge dreams."

"Okay, that sounds like a way in, but it's not much."

"I don't even know what these memoirs consists of. Are they in a book, a binder, an archive?"

She gave him a cautious smile. "I have an inkling that it's not a book or a binder. The one thing that's changed in the legal profession over the past decade is digitization. Remember the reams and reams of paperwork you had to drag into court? We don't anymore. We sit in court with laptops, the judges have laptops. Vanderfeld's recollections of past crimes have probably been digitized too."

"How can you be so sure?"

"Well, like I said. I'm not a sure. But, remember, Vanderfeld's daughter Nora went to law school. It's not a secret that he expected her to take over his practice."

Vermeulen skepticism must've been palpable because Dekker became more animated. "Vanderfeld was central to organized crime in Antwerp. You knew that, and every prosecutor and judge who came after you knew that too. They kept close tabs on his operation and there was every indication that she would take over. He even filed the necessary paperwork to have her name added to the professional corporation."

"But she didn't."

"I know, but she worked in the office for several years, even while in law school. It stands to reason that she tried to bring the office up to modern standards."

"That's rather flimsy evidence. I sure wouldn't bet on it."

"I wouldn't either, but a couple of months ago, a truck from one of those professional shredding services stood outside their office for an entire day. That's a lot of shredding. Nora and Theo wouldn't have shredded anything without having made digital copies first."

"A shredding service? You know the mob runs them. Those two wouldn't have anything shredded they couldn't afford to have read."

"Yes, organized crime runs some of those, but the truck that disposed of Vanderfeld's files came from a company we know is clean. They shred our paperwork too."

Vermeulen leaned back in the chair and scratched his chin. He hadn't thought that the authorities would continue to keep an eye on the likes of Beukes and Vanderfeld. It made sense.

"You're saying that Jordi's memoirs could be on a flash drive?" It rather sounded like wishful thinking.

"Yes."

"And what if there are several flash drives?"

"It doesn't matter. You only need one."

Chapter Twenty-Nine

Blackmail

———— ◆ ————

When Theo Vinke heard that Vermeulen had escaped his men at the B&B, he hit the ceiling. The crew he'd put together at the last moment was pathetic. As much as he thought of himself as a player in the Antwerp underworld, he knew that his word only carried as much weight as the number of people he could field when it really mattered and that's where he fell short. The realization that he'd married into a family with deep criminal connections was quickly followed by the insight that his father-in-law's influence depended not on fielding muscle in the streets, but the ability to keep the authorities away from the underworld.

It had been a disappointment because the law wasn't something he understood. Nora, his wife, did, but that wasn't the same. He wanted to run things, do better than his father, and not depend on his wife for anything. So far, he hadn't gotten there. Sure, he ran a bunch of *frietkots* and used those sometimes to launder cash for some folks, but that was like riding your bike with training wheels.

Now that he'd finally found the key to open the door to the very top of the criminal hierarchy, he was foiled by an incompetent crew. To have Beukes call him and basically rub it in just added insult to the injury.

He paced in his office. It was across the hall from what used to be Vanderfeld's and now was Nora's office, at the ground floor of a spacious but not showy home in Zurenborg. His name wasn't even on the fucking deed. Nora was supportive of most of what he wanted, but she drew the line at letting him handle her father's assets. That he even got hold of Jordi Vanderfeld's stash of incriminating documents was sheer luck. They'd been sorting through Jordi's papers after his death and while Nora was busy with the mundane office stuff, he came across a wall safe hidden behind a cupboard in the basement. Vanderfeld had been an organized man who put all his codes and passwords into a secret notebook. Nora had it and he asked to check it. She was busy and handed it to him. He found the code to open the safe and realized right away that he had a trove of compromising materials that would guarantee him a seat at the table of Antwerp's criminal enterprises.

Nora was deeply unhappy about his plan. She'd never liked her father's associates and clients. Her plan was to use the money she inherited to open a legitimate law firm in her own name. That was just stupid. Why work hard when you had most of the crooks in the city over a barrel, ready to fork over cash to stay out of jail?

Theo's father, Frans, had never amounted to much, but Theo had been privy to the criminal milieu. He was grateful for that. He liked the swagger of people when they talked about their latest heist or fraud. It was camaraderie and competition at the same time—alliances were forged for a scam; the spoils were celebrated and then everyone went their own way again. He used to look up to men like Beukes, who ran a large organization as efficiently as any CEO of a legitimate corporation. He always saw himself as such a man, except he wasn't so stupid as to want to work his way up. That was for suckers. Vanderfeld's records were his shortcut to the top.

His father didn't have the wherewithal to get there. And after Vermeulen used him to get to Beukes, what little reputation Frans had was gone. His murder was only a question of time. Yes, Beukes was responsible for the murder—that's what Vanderfeld's files told him—but Vermeulen had set it up by exploiting him in the first place. It was payback time. He wanted to see that man disgraced and put behind bars. At first it seemed a sure thing; Mesman was on board, there was an investigation and they even got Vermeulen back to Antwerp. Then everything went to shit.

When he found out that the memo he'd given to Mesman had disappeared, he didn't agree with Mesman that it was a temporary setback or a clerical error. His gut told him that there was more to it, that someone had interfered. He'd wanted the police to arrest Vermeulen right then and there. Mesman patiently explained to him that there had to be a legal basis for an arrest. Theo grudgingly agreed to Mesman's scheme to occupy Vermeulen until they found the memo again.

Theo was intimidated by Mesman, something that bothered him to no end. At one point he thought of blackmailing his bastard brother-in-law. He figured that being the illegitimate son of the go-to lawyer of Antwerp's criminals would be a black eye for an up-and-coming judge, but Nora told him that it was a bad idea. The news would make the tabloids for a day and then die away. Mesman was brought up by his mother with some support from Vanderfeld. There was nothing in Mesman's past to suggest that he'd been anything else but an upright citizen, lawyer and judge. People might not like his politics, but that wasn't a reason for the judge to pay off a blackmailer. Theo dropped that plan and focused on Vermeulen instead.

The whole Vermeulen thing tested his patience more than he expected. He found himself unable to think of anything else and it dragged on. It felt like Vermeulen was mocking him. After Vermeulen confronted Nora last Saturday at the museum, Theo had made up his mind to just kill the man. It wasn't the public disgrace he'd wanted but at least he'd have the personal satisfaction of having his father avenged. This time he didn't tell Nora.

Once he learned that Beukes had Vermeulen, he called his men out to watch Beukes's house. And waited, pacing back and forth and mumbling to himself.

Finally, his phone rang.

"You got him?" he hollered.

"Uh, no boss. But there's a lot of commotion at Beukes's house. His men are coming and going. Something is going on."

"Can you find out what's going on?"

"I'll try."

Theo ended the call and resumed his pacing. The phone rang again. It was another of his men.

"Yes."

"Boss, I think Vermeulen has escaped from the house."

"What?"

"I've heard from a couple of sources that Beukes's men are looking for him."

Theo's heart jumped and he hit the desk. "Yes. That's great news. Follow his men. See what they see, and when they find Vermeulen, snatch him first."

"Yes, boss."

Theo ended the call and dialed the other crew and told them the news. Things were looking up again. He poured himself a shot of Scotch in celebration.

Nora came into the room.

"What's all that racket about? I'm trying to work in my office."

"Oh, nothing much. There's progress on the Vermeulen front. We—uh—they have a lead on him."

Nora shook her head. "I don't know why you are so obsessed with Vermeulen. If he did something wrong, Mesman will make sure he pays for it."

"Yes, dear, I know. I just want to make sure Mesman finds him again, that's all."

He tried to keep a bland expression, but Nora gave him one of her suspicious looks.

"You're leaving this to the police, you're not getting involved, right?"

"Bastiaan is after Vermeulen too. It's not just the police after him."

"I don't care what Bastiaan does. He's a crook and always will be one. You're better than that. I want you to stay away from him. Let the justice system deal with Vermeulen."

Theo couldn't care less about the justice system. The damn justice system hadn't done a thing for him, except keep him down. He raised his hand to tell Nora so, but thought better. He kept few secrets from her, but this was one. She just didn't understand how important this was to him.

He knew that Nora disdained the people he hung with, thinking herself better. She'd grown up protected from the business that made her father rich. When he told her once that she didn't have a problem using her dad's dirty money to go to law school and live in a nice house, she'd looked at him baffled, as if his point had nothing to do with her objection to his friends. He knew he'd scored a point when she refused to have sex for a week. By the end of the week, having scored a point seemed very irrelevant. He apologized for his comment. To which she said, "You know so little about me, sometimes I wonder about us." But the make-up sex was worth the wait.

CHAPTER THIRTY

GRACIOUS GUEST

———————◆———————

WITH LESS THAN A DAY AND A HALF LEFT BEFORE HIS FLIGHT TOOK OFF, Vermeulen couldn't afford to wait for things to happen. That ought to be a basic rule of life, don't wait for things to happen because then all you can do is react. If instead you took the initiative, your adversaries were forced to react, and that gave them as little time as possible to sort out their options.

Dekker had showered, dressed and gone out to shop for groceries. Eating out wasn't an option and she wasn't prepared for houseguests. Vermeulen sat on her sofa—she'd moved the stacks of paper to the floor—debating his next move. The logical thing was to contact Beukes and somehow enlist his support for stealing the memoirs from Theo.

Theo, Beukes, Mesman. What did each of those three men want? Theo wanted revenge and a seat at the table of Antwerp's criminal scene. Beukes wanted the memoirs destroyed to protect himself and his operations. Mesman wanted the memoirs to advance his career. As much as he turned that around in his head he couldn't come up with a solution that would satisfy all three. There could be a deal between Beukes and Theo, a deal between Mesman and Theo. Maybe even an arrangement between Beukes and Mesman. There was no scenario he could envision that would satisfy all of them.

He stood up and paced, if weaving your way past the piles of Dekker's stuff could be called pacing. He stopped. What the hell was he thinking? He didn't care one whit if any of his opponents got what they wanted. He had to clear his name and go back home. How could he achieve that? Beukes would let him go if he wasn't threatened anymore. Mesman might let him go if Vermeulen could prove that the memo was forged, or if Theo admitted to the forgery. Theo was the sole obstacle. To get him to change his story, he had to offer something that

Theo valued. That was the rub. He couldn't think of anything. That man wanted revenge and nothing he could offer would alter that. The fact that Theo went as far as forging a memo to implicate him showed how deep his hatred was.

Dekker was wrong when she said he needed only one flash drive. If Theo had multiple copies, losing one wouldn't change the threat he posed. Vermeulen could give the drive to Mesman to show that they didn't contain the incriminating memo. But Beukes would never let him do that. He'd be signing his own arrest warrant.

Dekker returned with two bags of groceries. Vermeulen wanted to help her, but she hefted the bags on the counter and let out a sigh. She turned to look at him. Her face was a mask

"You can't stay here," she said. "Sorry, I shouldn't have told you to come. Mesman will find out and I can kiss my job good-bye. And not just this job, but any job in the justice department. I've worked too hard to get where I am to just throw it away."

Vermeulen nodded. Her decision didn't surprise him.

"I understand," he said. "It was unfair of me to barge in here, only thinking of myself. You have a good career ahead of you once you make it past Mesman."

She looked at him, eyebrows raised as if she'd expected more resistance.

"I do have two requests," he said. "First, do you have Nora Vanderfeld's phone number?"

She shrugged. "Not on me, but I could call my office. We've got a file on her. What's the second request?"

"Could I eat something before I leave?"

Her tight face softened into a smile. "Sure. Help yourself. You sure are easy to throw out. I've had one-night stands who made more of a fuss."

"It's not my preferred option, but I'd rather you remember me as a gracious guest than a bully."

He went to the counter and rummaged through the bags. The package of whole rye bread, gouda and a red pepper looked just fine. He opened the rye package and looked around for a plate. There were plenty of dirty ones in the sink. Dekker saw this and pointed to one of the cupboards. "A knife?" She pointed to a drawer.

He went about fixing himself a sandwich. Dekker observed him cutting the pepper into strips. She continued to watch as he lopped off a chunk of cheese. He carried the plate to the dining table, and sat down, munching on his sandwich.

"You want some butter with it? Mustard?"

"Nah, I'm fine."

"Okay."

He chewed, very much aware that the atmosphere was unstable.

"What are you going to do next?" she said.

"If you can get me Nora's number, I'll call her and see if she's willing to help me keep her husband from doing something immensely stupid."

Dekker pulled up a chair and sat down. "You think she might be?"

"The one time I talked to her, she seemed both halfhearted in her surveillance efforts and pissed off that she even had to follow me."

"That's not a lot to go on."

"Yeah. I know. But it doesn't hurt to ask."

"Okay, let me call the office."

She took her phone to her bedroom and Vermeulen finished up the sandwich. He dug into the shopping bag and found an apple, washed it and cut it into slices. Too bad he couldn't stay here, but he knew he couldn't, even if Dekker was okay with it. The clock was ticking. Twenty-eight hours until his plane took off. There was no time to lose.

Dekker came back and gave him a piece of paper with a number. "It's the last known number. I hope it's still working."

"Okay if I call her now?"

Dekker nodded.

He tapped the number into his phone and waited for the call to connect.

"Hi, Nora. This is Valentin Vermeulen, your erstwhile surveillance target. I'm hoping you could spare a few moments of your time and meet with me."

For a few moments he only heard the static of the connection.

"What for?" she said finally.

"I think we both realize that your husband is embarking on a course of action that can only end poorly for him and, by extension, you. To the extent that he listens to you, we may be able to steer him in a different direction that's healthier for both of you."

More silence.

"Not sure he can be dissuaded from his goal. After all, you did throw his father to the wolves. I saw the memo."

"That memo is a forgery. I never wrote it, sent it, or otherwise caused his father to be killed. That responsibility lies elsewhere."

"You would say that, wouldn't you?"

"Because it's true. Why would I send a memo to a cop who wasn't even involved in the investigation? I spent the last few days reading every damn file related to that old case and there was absolutely no reason for me to send that memo. If I had indeed leaked his name, why would I send a memo about it?"

"Clean up loose ends? I don't know. For you, Frans was no longer useful, why not rat him out."

"I didn't. Beukes decided to have him killed on his own. He told me so last night."

"You spoke with Beukes?"

"Yes, after his men snatched me away from the killers your husband sent for me."

Vermeulen could hear a gasp.

"Theo did what?"

"Theo sent out people to kill me. Beukes's men warned me and took me to his house."

"Did you see those men who came to kill you?"

"No, but I heard them break into my room after I got the warning and cleared out."

"That could've been anyone," she said, her voice more hesitant.

"No, it couldn't. Who would even know I was staying there, except for Theo, who had promised me he'd keep tabs on me when we talked on your phone last Saturday."

"What do you want from me?"

"Your help to keep your husband from making a serious mistake."

"You mean killing you?"

"Yes. He may think it will get him revenge, but Judge Mesman is just waiting to arrest him for murder because the judge wants your father's memoirs like everyone else."

"My dad's what?"

"Don't play dumb, your father's records of the Antwerp organized crime scene. That's what everyone's after. Theo thinks those records are his way to the top, but the moment he kills me, they'll be his ticket to prison. Do Theo a favor and save him from himself."

Another long pause followed by a sigh.

"That may not be as easy as you think," she said. "He's fixated on you."

"I know, why else would he forge a memo to get me in trouble?"

"He didn't forge anything. He got that in the mail."

It was Vermeulen's moment to gasp. Dekker, who had been listening, must've noticed that something had changed and looked at him eyebrows raised. He waved her off and said to Nora, "Are you sure?"

"I am," Nora said. "I was there when he opened the envelope."

"No sender?"

"Of course not."

His mind had become a swirling mess. Nothing made sense anymore. If Theo hadn't forged the memo, who had?

"Listen, we still should meet," he said. "The mysterious origin of the forged memo doesn't change the fact that we have to keep Theo from making a big mistake."

"I agree. Where?"

"Some place where Theo's men won't be looking."

Dekker had raised her index finger, so he asked Nora to hold on and muted his phone.

"No crook I ever knew would venture into a museum," she said. "The MAS is close by and they have a special floor, the *Kijkdepot,* the visible storage, where they keep all the objects that aren't part of an exhibit. Some specimens are on display, but the rest is stored behind a wire fence. The light is low and few visitors go there."

"Great, thanks."

He unmuted his phone and said, "Lets meet at the *Kijkdepot* of the Museum an de Stroom—" He looked at his watch "—in an hour."

CHAPTER THIRTY-ONE

FRYING POTATOES

---◆---

NORA VANDERFELD HAD JUST ENDED HER CALL when Theo walked into the room.

"Who were you talking to?" he said.

"A friend. Why're you asking?"

"Can't your husband ask you questions?"

Nora rolled her eyes. "Really, Theo? You're gonna be like that? Jeez. Ever since you got onto that Vermeulen thing, you've been crazy."

Theo stuck his face an inch from hers.

"That man killed my father."

Nora turned away, shaking her head. "No, he didn't. It probably was one of Beukes's men."

"He might as well have. He leaked Dad's name."

"You have no proof of that. Just a shady memo that came in an unmarked envelope. Have you ever thought about who might have an interest in you going after Vermeulen?"

Theo stepped in front of her again. "Why d'you say that?"

"It's a logical question. Whoever sent that memo to you had a reason, otherwise they wouldn't have sent it."

"Maybe they wanted to see justice done."

"Theo, Theo, Theo. You know that's not it. Nobody in your circles gives a damn about justice. If anything, they work hard to keep that from happening."

"They're your circles, too."

"My dad's circles, not mine. The sooner you leave those, the better."

"And then what? You going to your boring law office all day and me twiddling my thumbs?"

"You have your *Frietkots*. You could expand beyond Antwerp, build a larger chain."

Theo sneered. "No way I'm gonna spend my life frying potatoes."

"You're not frying them right now. So don't gimme that. All I'm saying is, you're a successful entrepreneur, why not build on that and expand?"

"You don't know what you're talking about."

"Suit yourself, I've got to go. Meet a friend."

She went to the hall armoire and took out her purple raincoat.

"The friend you were talking to just now?"

She put on her coat. "The very same. Please think of what I said. I don't want to spend the rest of my life looking over my shoulder and worrying about you. Please."

* * *

THEO DIDN'T KNOW WHEN HE STOPPED TRUSTING HIS WIFE. For a long time, they'd just been in love. An unlikely couple. Nora, the law student, and Theo, the son of a small-time crook. They'd met at a Nine Inch Nails concert in Brussels and decided the odds of two kids from Antwerp standing next to each other in that large dark hall were astronomical. Of course, it meant they were destined to be together.

Neither knew much about the other, they just clicked over their love of music, and that feeling of finding someone who just felt right. He knew that she went to the university but didn't really care. Nora wasn't stuck up like some university girls he knew. He wasn't cut out for university education. Which didn't mean he wasn't smart. Hell, he was smarter than most guys he knew going to university. It's just that he had the bad luck to be settled with a father who didn't amount to much. If he'd had supportive parents, he'd be going places. After his mom Heidi took off, his dad was hardly ever there, either in prison or hustling. Only after Frans married Ingrid Beukes, did his life assume some normality.

By that time, lots of opportunities had passed by and he ended up hustling like his dad, but much more on the legal side because his father didn't want him to fall into a life of crime, which Theo would have embraced fully if he'd been given the chance. He ended up managing a *Frietkot*, then two and soon a whole chain. He hated the stink of frying oil laced with beef tallow.

He waited until Nora left the house before putting his coat on. She'd never been this furtive around him. She was up to something and it involved him. He left the house and saw her walking toward the end of the street. When she turned a corner he followed her. At Draaksplaats she waited. The supports of the rail bridge that bisected the square offered enough cover for Theo to catch up to her. The #11 tram arrived and Nora got on. He had to hustle to make it into the rear car, but he managed to get in before the doors closed. Theo took a seat in the middle of the car that gave him a view of the front car and its exits.

The more he thought about it, the more he realized that the changes began after her father's death. It was subtle at first, a quick "no" where she would have said, "yes," a decision made without asking him even though they used to consult each other on everything. When she froze him out of managing her father's estate, he knew that things were different. Just when he was ready to make his move and establish himself as a force to be reckoned with, she did what she could to keep him down. She gave him money and he bought himself a loaded Audi Q7, but she was in charge. All he ever wanted was respect from what he considered to be his peers. Instead he got the trappings of riches without any say. Until he found her father's secret files.

The tram wound its way toward the center of the city. When it stopped at the square fronting the Centraal Station, he stood up. Lots of riders were getting on or off and he wanted to make sure he didn't lose her in the rush. But she stayed on and continued toward the cathedral. It wasn't until the tram reached the Melkmarkt that Nora got off.

Theo almost missed her exit and had to put his arm between the closing doors to make them open again. He jumped out and thought he'd lost her. Then he saw a flash of purple at the end of Korte Niewstraat. He ran past St. Carolus Borrowmeus church. He stopped at the corner and he was almost hit by a cargo bike coming out of the alley. The rider gave him a dirty look. It took all his self-control to not yell at him, but he was on a mission.

He saw her purple coat disappear at the end of the alley. He ran again. At the next corner he lost her. She wasn't in the square near the church or in the narrow street to the left. It took him a moment to see that the alley dog-legged and continued north. By the time he got there, she was gone again. All he saw were the empty tables of a restaurant. He ran again, his heart now beating in his throat. It was obvious that he was terribly out of shape. Driving that Q7 all the time wasn't so smart.

The way she made him recognize his weakness made him livid. The person he wanted to be wouldn't be running through Antwerp, panting like an old dog. That's what she did, treat him like a dog. The anger gave him new energy and when he came to the next dog-leg, he didn't bother stopping. It didn't matter if she saw him. It was time to put his foot down. He was the man of the house.

By the time he hit Minderbroedersrui, he was ready to give up. But there she was, in her purple raincoat just a block ahead, weirdly enough, right in front of one of his *Frietkots*. Was she actually buying fries? She was. She left the shop with a tray of fries. She stopped and ate a few, continued munching until she got to the corner of Huikstraat, where she dumped the rest into a trashcan.

What was that all about? Was she dissing his fries? It told him all he needed to know about how she felt about him.

She sped up again and he tried to keep pace. How come she was in such good shape? He didn't think she went to a gym. Whatever, she set a pace that he struggled to keep. Where was she going in the first place? She was only a couple blocks away from the red-light district and the windows with the prostitutes. The only place nearby he could think of was that secret apartment where Vermeulen had met with his father.

While he was wondering about that, she disappeared again. First, she was there, hoofing it toward Falconplein, then she was gone. No purple raincoat. He ran forward, looked into shop windows, down the lanes that led left and right. When he reached Verversrui, he knew she had ditched him. No way he could have just missed her. She knew he was following her and she found a way to lose him. He was ready to smash the next store window.

* * *

NORA KNEW HE'D FOLLOW HER. Suspicion was at the core of Theo. It'd taken her a while to realize that deep down, Theo was nothing more than a bundle of insecurities, forever seeing slights and disrespect around him. She didn't know what happened to the man she fell in love with. Had he always been that way and she'd just ignored it?

For a long time, his aimlessness and vaguely articulated ideas for his life had been an important counterbalance to the meticulous plan she'd crafted for her life. He'd seemed so easygoing at first, taking life as it unfolded, muddling through, grabbing opportunities as they arose, and not worrying if they didn't. It was that very lack of worry that attracted her. She couldn't help but plan the future. Every step examined from every angle, fretting about forgetting something, and ever worried about the imponderables that might mess up everything.

This time, she was right to worry, she knew this was the moment she had to act and rescue him. He was headed for a world of hurt and it was up to her to prevent it. Despite his stupid obsession, she hadn't given up on him. Once he got the Vermeulen bug out of his system, they could sit down and discuss their future.

To allay his suspicions, she tried to make it easy for him to follow her. She even stopped at one of his snack kiosks and bought fries so he could catch up. They weren't very good and she dumped them. At first, she felt bad about it, but then she realized it made her appear oblivious to his following her. As she got closer to the museum, though, she started looking for ways to ditch him. He couldn't know that she was meeting with Vermeulen. It'd mean the end of their relationship.

There was a salon a couple of blocks ahead. Theo would never think of looking for her there. She saw a group of students dallying near the next intersection. They looked at her askance as she mingled with them and said "Hi," before skipping around the corner. She hurried around the block and made it to the salon before he could catch up. All chairs were occupied which suited her well. One of the stylists put her customer under a dryer and told her that it'd be at least another forty minutes before it was her turn.

"Can I make an appointment?" Nora said.

"Sure."

They agreed on a date and Nora called a cab.

"Okay if I wait here?" she said.

"No problem."

The cab came a few minutes later and she asked the driver to drop her at Napoleonkaai, the northern edge of the dock, across from the Museum. When she got there, she lingered behind the old lightship that was moored at the quay and checked the surroundings. No sign of Theo anywhere. She crossed the footbridge to the museum, took the escalator to the second level and entered the Visible Storage section.

Chapter Thirty-Two

Blind Pig

———◆———

Fredi Kuiper was following Theo Vinke. Since finding Vermeulen was the top priority, Kuiper had decided to handle that job himself. It took him only a few minutes before he realized that Theo was following his wife and it made following him easier. Theo was so wrapped up in following his wife, he was oblivious to even the notion that someone might be following him. Like Kuiper had told Vermeulen, dumber than a bag of hammers. Kuiper didn't make the same mistake. Keeping out of Vinke's sight was a given, but he also paid attention to what was happening behind him.

That Theo followed his wife bothered Kuiper. He must've thought Nora was up to something. Kuiper couldn't quite figure out what that might be. Was she having an affair? Even if she was, it felt odd that Theo, obsessed with Vermeulen, would spend his time following her. You'd hire a private dick for that.

Kuiper was as surprised as Theo when Nora disappeared. All along she appeared to be totally unaware that her husband was behind her and then she made a quick move and was gone. Kuiper ducked into a doorway and tried to sort this out. Ah, fuck it. As usual that was above his pay grade. He called Beukes.

"Hey Boss, I've been following Theo and, get this, he's following his wife like some cheap private dick. For a half hour, that was all, but just now, Nora disappears. She was there and then she's gone. Whaddya make of that?"

Beukes's breath sounded like an untuned whistle on the phone. It told Kuiper that the man was evaluating all the possibilities.

"You say Nora disappeared suddenly?"

"Yes, Boss."

"That tells me she knew Theo was following her. You think that's possible?"

"Sure, Boss. That man wouldn't know stealth if it bit him in the ass."

"Okay, so what does that tell us? She knows Theo is following her, she is okay with that for a while and then she makes her move."

"Like she don't want Theo to know where she's going."

"Did she know he was following her all along?"

"Hard to tell, Boss. I kinda think so, she bought some fries, ate a couple and tossed the rest. Like she was waiting for him to catch up."

"D'you think he noticed that?"

"I don't know, Boss, Theo don't operate on all registers, so, yeah, he might not have noticed."

Kuiper listened to that whistle again.

"Where are you?"

"At the end of Huikstraat, close to Falconplein."

"Isn't that close to where Vermeulen had his secret apartment back in the day?"

"It is, Boss. Verversrui is around the next corner."

More whistle breath.

"Nah, he couldn't."

"What do you mean, Boss?"

"Uh, nothing, just thinking aloud. Could Nora be meeting Vermeulen at that dank apartment?"

"You asking me, Boss?"

"Yeah."

"It'd be real stupid to choose that place. From what we know about Vermeulen, he's not."

"That's my thinking. He knows we know about the place. But here's the bigger question. Why would Nora be meeting with Vermeulen?"

"Do we even know that she's meeting him, Boss?"

Another pause. Kuiper had his own ideas, but knew better than to volunteer them without being asked.

"Who else would she be meeting?" Beukes said. "Who else would require that she ditch Theo first?"

"Maybe she's having someone on the side. Can't for the life of me figure out why she even married Theo. You know she's still hot. Why not, Boss?"

"Yeah, well, there's that. But my gut tells me she's after more than a little action in a cheap dive. Besides, it's a little early for that, no?"

Kuiper knew to never disagree with Beukes's gut. He kept his mouth shut.

"Tell you what," Beukes said. "Just keep following Theo. Who knows? Sometimes even a blind pig finds an acorn."

* * *

VERMEULEN FOUND THE VISIBLE STORAGE ON the second level of the MAS. He didn't even need a ticket. The entire floor was filled with objects stored behind white wire mesh fencing. A central area featured displays with artifacts and drawers full of printed materials. The rest of the floor plan was a grid, narrow paths leading to dead ends, each showing art and cultural objects stored up to the ceiling. A catwalk traversed the space with stairs at either end.

Since the museum had only just opened for the day, there were no visitors at this level. Vermeulen strolled through the narrow paths, waiting for Nora. Dekker had been right, this was a good place to meet someone. The wire mesh enclosures made it easy to see who was coming and going. Sure, they'd be just as visible, but pretending to be random visitors would be easy. A subtle change in the air pressure signaled that the entrance door had been opened. He remained engrossed in the sailing boat models in front of him. The door closed again. Out of the corner of his eye, he saw a woman walk into the central area. It was Nora Vanderfeld.

Vermeulen eased back into the darker recess of the path. It could be a trap and he had no reason to trust her. He waited for the door to open again. It didn't. He could hear the clicking of her heels on the tile floor. After a few steps, she stopped.

There was nobody else on this level. Vermeulen was about to step forward when the air pressure changed again. Someone had come in the door. He heard voices, so more than one person. The voices—two women— wandered toward the left side. As they passed his aisle, he heard snippets of their conversation. Apparently, their respective partners weren't living up to their expectations.

The door opened again. Vermeulen heard nothing. No voices or steps. Nora Vanderfeld hadn't moved either. Who'd come in this time? The quiet hum of the air conditioners and the voices of the two women were the only sounds in this large space. He started to feel warm. A layer of perspiration filmed his forehead. Coming here was a mistake. Nora wouldn't go behind Theo's back. Why would she? And he'd walked right into it, eager to believe that his reasoning was so logical, others would see it and agree. What did he know about their relationship?

The clicking of Nora Vanderfeld's heels started again. The steps sounded like they were going away from him. The air pressure changed again. She must've opened the door. Was she leaving? That wasn't good. His panic must've gotten the better of him.

"Nora, wait. I'm here."

The clicking stopped, then came closer again.

"Where?" she said.

He stepped into the main aisle.

"Listen," she said. "I don't have time for hide and seek. Theo is suspicious and followed me."

"He did?"

"Yeah, but don't worry, I ditched him."

They ambled to the opposite side of the two women with the less than stellar men in their lives. This part of the visible storage level contained a large collection of items that used to be exhibited in the old *Vleeshuis* or Butcher's Hall, after it had become a museum.

"How can we get Theo to stop this silly crusade?" Vermeulen said, not even looking the pieces that were supposed to highlight Antwerp's history.

Nora Vanderfeld shook her head. "It's not just you, there's more at stake."

"I know, Beukes told me all about your father's secret documents."

She arched her eyebrows.

"Yes," Vermeulen said. "He told about the pact between the two, about giving the incriminating evidence to the other in case of impending death."

"A pact?" Nora Vanderfeld frowned.

"Yes, both knew they had incriminating evidence against each other. Beukes called it 'mutually assured destruction.' But they'd also agreed to turn over that evidence once they felt death knocking at the door. Beukes said he'd bundled up what he had on your father after the second round of chemo."

She shook her head. "Beukes was pulling your leg. Whatever he might have on my dad is nothing compared to what my dad had on him. Remember, he was Beukes's lawyer. He knew every in and out of Beukes's operation. Sounds like Beukes was trying to enlist you in getting those documents away from Theo."

"Whatever, it doesn't change the fact that we have to make Theo stop this nonsense."

"That's what I mean. There's more at stake than revenge. He wants to replace Beukes and he thinks that my dad's documents will allow him to do that."

"I know that. But how does he think he can take over Beukes's operation? Beukes already told me that he's the one who's doing the extorting. He isn't going to be blackmailed. There's going to be all out war if Theo tries that and, excuse me, but Theo isn't a match for Beukes."

Nora Vanderfeld sneered.

"You're telling me. Underneath it all, Theo is a sweet man. But he's also lazy. I used to think it was cool. Not anymore. Theo doesn't see that Beukes, whatever else you might say about him, actually worked hard to get where he is. For Theo, achievements are only a question of luck. And he thinks he got lucky with my dad's documents. I wish I had been more careful. Should've just burned the whole lot."

Vermeulen frowned. "What happened to those files? Are they intact, or have you scanned them and shredded the originals?"

Nora Vanderfeld looked at him, her head cocked to the side. "Why would you say that?"

"You can't be naive enough to think that the authorities aren't interested in you. I heard that a commercial shredding truck stood outside your house for most of a day. It stands to reason that those documents exist only in electronic format now."

"Goddamn it. It'll take years for me to get out from under my dad's reputation."

"Did you shred the memoirs?"

"I wish. I should've searched for them before doing anything else. After my dad's funeral, there was just too much sorting. Believe it or not, quite a few of my dad's clients were not gangsters. I wanted to keep them for my practice. Determining who was and who wasn't a crook was a nightmare. Meanwhile, Theo just rummaged through the house. He must have found the stash hidden in a wall safe in the basement."

"How'd he know the combo?"

"My father had a book with all the codes and combinations. He took it when I was busy with other things. As I said, I should've been more careful."

"Can we steal them back? Where does he keep them?"

Nora shook her head. "I've racked my brain about this. I checked all the places I could think of. No luck."

"Do you think Theo would leave me alone if I could prove the memo was forged?"

Nora Vanderfeld grimaced. "I don't think so. Right now he's like a dog with a bone. He won't let go. I don't even know why he's so concerned about his father's death. Given that man's life, it was only a question of time before someone would kill him."

Vermeulen noticed that sinking feeling in his stomach coming back. He took a deep breath. What a mess. And just as he thought that, he knew the way out. Find those documents and get rid of them. It was the only way.

"You've wracked your brain for every possibility where they could be, right?" he said.

She nodded again and opened her mouth to say something, but didn't.

"Okay, so my job is to think of possibilities you didn't consider. What about his family, did they have a house?"

"Yeah, but they rented, and after divorcing Frans, his mum moved to a different place."

"Where does his mother live now?"

"She has dementia and is living in a home."

"Does Theo visit her there?"

Nora Vanderfeld shrugged.

"Well, does he?" Vermeulen said.

"Maybe a couple of times a year. But not this year."

"You go along?"

"No, I never had much to do with her."

"How do you know he didn't go this year?"

"Because he usually bellyaches for days before he goes. And he hasn't this year."

"Where else might he have put those files?"

Nora Vanderfeld shook her head. "Believe me, I've asked myself that question over and over. I don't know."

Vermeulen knew that pushing a witness too hard would be counterproductive. Instead of letting the mind roam freely, the pressure to come up with answers shut down the possibility of a random connection. He couldn't just stand there and hope for a flash of intuition in her mind.

"Does he have any other relatives?" he said.

Vanderfeld pursed her lips, then shrugged. "I'm sure he does, but I don't remember him talking about any uncles or aunts. His mum. That's about it."

"What was his relationship to his mother?"

"Lopsided."

"How so?"

"She adored him and he despised that."

"Tell me more."

"His dad didn't want Theo to follow him into the life of crime. He pushed him hard to do something else. His mum made up for that and then some. In her eyes, he could do no wrong. Theo didn't like that mothering, he always shushed her away. I don't think he liked her much. Either way I don't think he'd keep the files at somebody else's house."

"Why?"

"They are his treasure. Anyone who hoards a treasure loves to look at it from time to time, if only to imagine all the amazing things he's going to do with it."

"Do you think the files are in your house?"

"No, I've searched the place thoroughly. I know it better than he does. But I think they are close by."

"And his mother isn't close by?"

"No, her assisted living home is in Kapellen."

Kapellen was a small town, about a half hour drive from Antwerp. And Vermeulen knew why Nora was wrong about Theo.

Chapter Thirty-Three

Museum Guy

———◆———

THEO VINKE COULDN'T FIGURE OUT WHERE NORA HAD GONE. He stopped at the corner of Huikstraat and Falconplein, swearing under his breath. How could he have been so careless? Five streets came together at this corner and he scanned each of them. No sign of Nora. It didn't make sense to him. Nothing did. Why'd she come here? As far as he knew, she had no business this far from home, right near the red-light district. He ran through the shops he knew she liked. None of them in this neighborhood. He saw the salon on one of the streets and thought for a moment that she might have switched stylists, but this one was too far from home. He continued along Falconrui looking into each shop window and not seeing Nora anywhere. A taxi passed him and he thought he'd caught a glimpse of purple in the back of the cab. Nah. That couldn't be her. She'd taken the tram all this way, it made no sense to switch to a cab now. She could've taken one from home.

He kept wondering about this friend of hers. He knew all her friends and she'd seemed pretty cagey about this friend on the phone. A nasty thought crept into his mind. Was she having an affair? She couldn't, could she? He told himself that Nora was faithful, that he had no reason to think otherwise, but the nasty thought couldn't be unthought.

Stop. Focus. Vermeulen is the priority.

He pulled out his phone and dialed his guy. "Any sign of Vermeulen?"

"Nope. We're following Beukes's men and they are in the dark too."

"Where are you right now?"

"Near Centraal Station. Two of Beukes's men are there, but they're just looking as if they're hoping to see him on the street. That man's disappeared."

"And the others?"

"Two are on Plantin-en-Moretuslei, closer to Beukes's house. They are canvassing shops. The last one is near the Grote Markt."

"Is that all Beukes has?"

"Yup."

"Call me the moment there's something new."

Theo put his phone away and realized that he was far from where the action was, inexcusable to ignore his top priority and follow his wife. He turned around and hurried back until he reached Sint-Paulusstraat where he hailed a cab to take him back home.

He'd barely opened the door to his house when his phone rang.

"Boss, Beukes's men are acting as if they found Vermeulen."

"Where?"

"The two are standing outside a night shop on Plantin-en-Moretuslei and talking on the phone."

"Okay, get your ass over there. I want everyone on those guys. And be careful, communicate with each other, make sure to take turns for the close follow."

After he put the phone down, he almost wanted to join them. But that would have been bad form. The boss doesn't do the grunt work. All he could do was sit and wait.

* * *

BEUKES GOT NEWS OF THE BREAKTHROUGH when Fredi Kuiper came into his office.

"I've done some thinking," Kuiper said. "The first thing Vermeulen needed was a phone. Since he escaped sometime between three and seven-thirty, he couldn't just go anywhere to buy one. I checked all the night shops in the area and only the one on Plantin-en-Moretuslei was open during those hours. But that shop was closed by the time my men got there."

"So, call the owner," Beukes said.

"Way ahead of ya. The moment the owner heard your name, he got busy."

Beukes nodded. That's why he had Fredi. The man had a brain and he was loyal. The best of all worlds. "And . . ."

"The shop sold a phone around seven that morning."

"Did you get the number?"

"Not yet, I'm waiting for the call."

On cue, Kuiper's phone rang. He answered and listened. After a few moments, he said, "I need that number now! So make it happen. Send a cab, whatever. Mr. Beukes doesn't like waiting."

He ended the call and told Beukes that the receipt of the sale didn't include the number.

"But don't worry, Boss. They get these phones in packs of five and they are numbered sequentially. He told the night manager to go to the store and check the next phone on the rack. We'll have that number as soon as he gets there."

* * *

THEO VINKE'S GUY CALLED BACK THIRTY MINUTES LATER.

"They musta got the owner to open up the shop. They are going inside now."

"Any idea what they are doing in there?"

"One my guys is peering through the window. Hang on."

There was a click and a hiss, a moment later another click.

"They are looking at burner phones," his man said. "Maybe Vermeulen bought a phone there after he ran from Beukes."

"Yeah, that's it. Once they have the number, they can find him. Shit."

"You want we get that number, too?"

Vinke hesitated. The number would be no good to him. He had no connection at the phone companies, no way to find out which towers the phone pinged. But he didn't want to admit that.

"Nah," he said. "Just follow them when they leave."

* * *

BEUKES HAD VERMEULEN'S NEW NUMBER some twenty minutes later. He told Kuiper to locate Vermeulen's phone on Beukes's computer with an illegal copy of an app used by the police. The two men stared at the screen as a map of Antwerp appeared and eventually zoomed in on the *Willemdok*. The red dot pulsed over the water next to a quay.

"Is he on a boat?" Kuiper said.

"No, the triangulation isn't spot on. He's near there. What's in the area? Ah, the MAS. That Vermeulen, you gotta give it to him. He's meeting someone at the museum. You ever been to that museum?"

Kuiper shook his head. "Nope, not much of a museum guy."

"Me neither. That's why Vermeulen is meeting someone there. He knew none of you guys would be loitering near a museum. Well, we got him. Move your men there now. And get yourself over there. This has to be handled with care. I don't want some spectacle, some kidnapping that's recorded on every fucking phone in the vicinity. The last thing I need is a feature film on the internet. So, for God's sake, no guns."

"Sure, Boss. No trouble. You got it."

"I'll call you if anything changes."

* * *

THEO VINKE'S PHONE RANG and his man told him that everybody was leaving the store on Plantin-en-Moretuslei.

"Where are they headed?" Vinke said.

"Northwest, towards the Grote Markt."

"Okay, follow them."

"What do we do when we get where they're going?"

Vinke rolled his eyes.

"This is not rocket science. They got a lead on Vermeulen. That's where they're headed. You follow them and see what they got. If you see that they're ready to nab Vermeulen, you swoop in and snatch him."

There was a pause. Vinke waited. Why was he saddled with such incompetent people? Beukes's men wouldn't ask such questions. Just wait. Once Vermeulen was out of the picture, he'd go for Beukes, and before long those men would answer to him. In the meantime, he had to work with what he had.

"They're not gonna let us take him just like that," the guy said.

"Of course not. But you're not gonna ask their permission. You got guns, use them. How many are there anyway?"

"There's the two we're following. There's the three others we know about. But he's got more."

"You telling me you're scared of five guys? You got five guys and you got the advantage of surprise. Jeez, do I have to do it myself? Your three guys keep the five guys in check, two hustle Vermeulen out of there. Make sure you got a car ready."

"And what if they don't behave?"

"You plug 'em. Idiot."

"You're the boss. You want a massacre, you got it."

Vinke heard the sarcasm in the man's voice and felt the heat rising in his body.

"You better watch your mouth, buddy. Of course, I don't want a massacre, but if you need to use your guns, use them. That's what they're for."

There was no answer, but Vinke imagined his man thinking, "Riiight."

* * *

KUIPER ARRIVED AT THE MAS TWENTY MINUTES LATER. The ticket sales were at ground level, as was the restaurant. The exhibits were on the floors above and the only way up seemed to be an escalator. His men were already in position, covering the exits.

"Any of the guys go up yet?" He said to the man standing by the escalator.

The man shook his head.

"Why not?"

"The place got ten floors. Makes no sense to send five people up and search."

Kuiper nodded. "Let's find out what we can do."

He called Beukes to confirm that the phone location remained the same. The answer was affirmative. Next step was to consult the ticket counter. There he found out that one could go all the way to the top on the escalators for free, that the panorama on the tenth floor was open to all, and that the visible storage on the second level was also free.

Kuiper knew better than to make difficult choices on his own. He called Beukes once more.

"Your phone triangulation doesn't tell you what floor he's on, does it?"

"Nope."

"Well, there's ten floors, a couple are free, the rest require a ticket. I got five men. Bad odds. Besides, he could also be somewhere else."

"No, I checked with a contact at the service provider. That phone is definitely inside the MAS. Did you cover all the exits?"

"Yes. The only way down is via the escalator. The woman at the ticket booth told me that elevators are only for people in wheelchairs and they have to call to make arrangements."

"You wait. He'll have to leave sometime."

CHAPTER THIRTY-FOUR

SINNERS

———◆———

ONCE THE SOUND OF NORA VANDERFELD'S HEELS had stopped echoing through the Visible Storage, Vermeulen had to figure out how to get out of the museum. She may have believed that she ditched her husband Theo, but Vermeulen knew better. Theo wouldn't be the only one following her. Beukes was definitely somewhere near. The possibilities for trouble outnumbered the chances for a clean get away.

Fortunately, the MAS made surveillance difficult. It had been built on a quay jutting between the basins of *Bonapartedok* and *Willemdok*. With water on two sides, the only approaches were easily surveyed from the escalators that went from one floor to the next. The architects had designed the building so that all escalators were located along the outside of the building. They were protected from the elements by curved plexiglass walls that allowed him to see the ground level but made it difficult for someone below to identify anyone riding up or down.

All Vermeulen had to do was ride up four more floors to check every side of the museum. The only spot he couldn't see was the area straight down where the ticket booth was located.

By the time he'd gone up two floors, he'd already noticed a couple of men loitering outside the museum shop that was located adjacent the museum. He hadn't seen them before, and they didn't look like museum goers. Probably Theo's men. It was odd that they should wait that far from the museum's entrance. Either they had more guys stationed closer, or something else was up. Going up to the next floor, he saw two more men pretending to inspect the old lightship that was docked across from the museum. He thought he recognized one of the men as the driver from the night before. That explained the distance of Theo's men. Beukes's hoods were there too.

It complicated his situation quite a bit. As much as he'd thought the museum to be a great place to meet, it was also a trap. With only two ways off the quay, he'd have to figure out either something smart or something spectacular. Since smart would take more time than he had, he went for spectacular.

First, he let himself drop to the ground, grabbing his thigh, and hollering in pain. A museum employee came running and asked what happened.

"I've got peripheral artery disease and the pain in my leg just flared up worse than ever. I need to see a doctor. Is there anyone on staff?"

"No, we don't have doctors here. I'll call an ambulance."

"Oh, I don't want to make a big fuss. Can you just get me a wheelchair to get me downstairs. I'll call a friend for a ride."

"Sorry. In cases of medical emergency we have to call an ambulance. You can sort it out with them, but I can't just let you go. The museum would be liable."

Vermeulen did his best to look disappointed, but waited until the employee called an ambulance, got him a wheelchair, and called the elevator. By the time they reached the ground floor, Vermeulen could hear the sirens approaching. Museum staff crowded around him, curious visitors tried to get a glimpse of what was going on. At least three men, who didn't look like they'd enter a museum under any circumstances, stared at him.

When the yellow ambulance inched through the crowd toward Vermeulen, he saw the man who'd managed his rescue/kidnapping last night. Beukes's men were definitely here. He explained his new ailment to the EMTs, told them that dehydration wasn't a cause of the cramps and that he didn't need an IV. They put him on the stretcher, buckled him tight and less than five minutes after its arrival, the ambulance was leaving the quay again. Vermeulen could see the face of Beukes's man. It was a mixture of anger and admiration.

The ambulance hurried through the narrow streets of the city towards the hospital. Two EMTs were sitting up front, and the third one sat on a jump seat near the head of the stretcher. He was leaning forward and shooting the breeze with his colleagues. Vermeulen carefully unbuckled the belts that held him to the stretcher. He left them in place, in case the third EMT looked back. At the next intersection, he heard the driver say that this was the longest red light in the entire city. That was all Vermeulen needed to know. He jumped off the stretcher, opened the rear door and was on the asphalt before the third EMT even had a chance to leave his jump seat. If he were a betting man, Vermeulen would've put good money on the chance that none of them had ever seen a patient flee their ambulance.

The car behind the ambulance honked and the driver gave him a thumbs up. Vermeulen smiled and started running, not only because he didn't want the EMTs to come after him, but also because he was certain that the assorted goons were following the ambulance.

He reached Sint Paulusstraat and was tempted to wait for the tram, but he couldn't just stand there in the open. Running this far had pretty much exhausted the reservoir of energy he could call on. From now on, stealth had to take the place of speed. He ducked into a doorway and checked the street behind him. A couple of men loped around the corner he'd just rounded. They stopped and surveyed the street. On the other side of the intersection stood two others who looked just as out of place as the first duo. He couldn't tell if they were on the same team.

The doorway had become a problem. He couldn't get away without being seen by the pursuers. If he stayed they were bound to find him, and close quarter combat was the least of his abilities. He rang the topmost doorbell. The name next to the button was Meijer. The speaker above the panel of buttons made a scratchy sound.

"Yes?" The voice sounded like that of an older woman.

"Hi, Misses Meijer," Vermeulen said, improvising now, making the wildest stab in the dark. "It's Valentin, I have an AirBnB reservation for tonight and tomorrow. I hope I'm not too early."

"A what?"

"An AirBnB reservation?"

"What is that?"

"I rented a room for a couple of nights. On the internet."

"I don't go on the internet. And I don't rent rooms."

"But I have the reservation right here. It's at this address and got your name on it."

"It has Greta Meijer on it?"

"It does. Maybe you have a son or daughter who rented out their old room."

"I don't have a daughter and my son lives in Brussels."

"Well, I don't know what to say. I need a place to stay. I paid for it. Can I come in and at least call the company?"

"I'm not letting you in my apartment."

Under any other circumstances, he would've applauded the woman's common sense. But his circumstances required someone who wasn't as guarded. Well, no use fighting what was. He pulled out his phone and checked the map app. Now that he'd caught his breath again, he saw another way out.

He peered around the corner of the doorway. Back across the intersection, two men continued to linger as if they had no worry in the world. The first pair had ventured into the street, checking doorways and other potential hidden spots. It didn't matter if they were on the same team or not. They were after him and he had to get away. He dashed out of the doorway, ran past three more buildings and turned right into a grand portal that led to the *Sint Pauluskerk*.

The massive church occupied the center of the entire block. Since its construction and repeated renovations, the city had grown and surrounded the church and its adjoining monastery. Vermeulen vaguely remembered the seesaw history between the Dominican friars who'd first built this church and the Protestants who'd expelled them later.

He raced across the courtyard, scanning the length of the structure for a door. There was one near the transept. He entered a hall, climbed a few steps and found himself in the sanctuary. It was bright and soaring. He couldn't help but stop and marvel at the space. The dark oaken paneling provided a pleasing contrast to the light airy walls and ceiling.

To his left was the choir, leading to the apse and the high altar. There was no one in that section. To his right was the central altar and beyond that the nave flanked on both sides by aisles. Neatly aligned chairs stood in that part of the church. A smattering of people sat there, heads bowed. At the end of the nave was a massive organ on a balcony above the main entrance.

Vermeulen heard voices behind him and hurried past the altar toward the main doors, hoping not to alert the praying faithful to his predicament. After he'd passed the last of them, he stopped by the confessionals. If the men after him were smart, they'd split up so one could intercept him at the main entrance. He had no reason to assume they were stupid, so he had to hide to buy time.

Any other time, he would have paused to admire the masterworks of seventeenth century Dutch wood carving, like the life-size angel that guarded access to the confessional. But this time he needed a place to hide. A confessional seemed as good a place as there was in a church. Unfortunately, these confessionals shielded the sinner from the priest, but only partially from the rest of the church. The angels on either side provided some cover as long as his pursuers didn't walk right past him.

He heard steps on the tile floor. He peered past the angel and saw one of the men who'd searched the doorways. The man stood and scanned the sanctuary. None of the folks praying in the chairs could be mistaken for him.

Vermeulen heard the entrance door at the end of the nave creak open. He couldn't see the second man but had no doubt that the rest of the crew had arrived. He slid back as far as he could behind the wing of the angel.

They'd be searching the church next. And that would take a while. *Sint Pauluskerk* was laid out in the typical gothic plan. There were multiple altars, pillars everywhere, and statues on pedestals, all of which could be hiding spaces. And, if he knew anything about Antwerp gangsters, the two would make at least an attempt to respect the sacred space. Even if you didn't believe in God, it'd be better to hedge your bets by not starting a melee in His place.

He was so focused on making himself small, he froze in shock when he saw the second man standing right across from him on the other side of the nave. If the man turned his head just a bit, he'd be looking straight at him. The man stopped, pulled his phone from his pocket and held it to his ear. He spoke quietly. Vermeulen couldn't hear any words, just the sound of his voice. The man seemed calm, just phoning in a status update to his boss. Vermeulen pushed himself behind the angel as much as possible. It wasn't much of a cover.

The next minute felt interminable. Given his awkward position, he couldn't see the man anymore. Turning his head to get a better look might just be the movement to attract his attention. It wasn't until he heard more steps on the tile floor that he exhaled and dared to look. The man had moved toward the transept to meet up with his partner. They were talking to each other. Their attention seemed to focus on the room below the church spire. Sure enough, they disappeared into a passage.

Vermeulen used that opportunity to cross the nave. He planned to get to the exit and make a run for it. He only got as far as the opposite row of columns before he heard voices again. The men were back. Maybe there was no way up the tower. He looked for another hiding place. Besides the columns the only thing that offered any cover was the pulpit. It stood on a six-foot carved base between two columns. Wooden stairs led up to it. A red rope across the stairs told visitors that the pulpit was off limits. He removed the rope, stepped onto the stairs, replaced the rope and eased upward. He prayed that the stairs were solid. A single creak would echo through the church like a gunshot. The door at the end of the stairs was not locked. He opened it and ducked into the pulpit, pulling the door closed again.

Not a moment too soon. The steps grew louder.

"He's got to be in here," the first man said. "There's no other way out."

"We haven't checked by the high altar yet. I think there're a couple rooms behind the choir chairs."

"You sure?"

"Pretty much. When I was in school, we made a field trip here and I remember playing hide and seek back there. The teacher smacked me good for that."

"Would Vermeulen know about those?"

"Maybe. He grew up here."

"And do these rooms lead to the street?"

"Nope."

"Then Vermeulen wouldn't go there. He's hidden elsewhere."

"What about the pulpit?"

"A little too obvious, no?"

"Let's check anyway."

CHAPTER THIRTY-FIVE

HEAVEN AND HELL

———————◆———————

B EUKES LEARNED ABOUT VERMEULEN'S AMBULANCE STUNT bare minutes after
it happened. He shook his head. Everything he'd assumed about Vermeulen
turned out to be correct and then some. Not only had he spotted the men, he'd
managed to get out of the museum without them being able to do a thing about it.

Was it worth it to keep chasing him? Vermeulen wasn't all that important. Sure,
he would have been good bait to grab those documents from Theo, but this was
getting to be a little too much. The more he thought about it, the more the idea of
just putting a bullet through Theo's head appealed to him. Except, there was Nora.

Beukes didn't have children of his own, and as the daughter of his partner, Nora
became the apple of his eye. He spoiled her as much as he could and as much as her
parents would let him. He remembered playing with her when she was little, taking
her for walks in the pram, buying her ice-cream cones. The last thing he wanted
was to upset her life or cause her trouble. He had an inkling that her relationship
with Theo had cooled since Jordi's death. But killing him was out of the question.
He couldn't do that to Nora. He had to figure out another way to get those files.

His phone rang again.

It was Fredi. "He's run from the ambulance and is now inside Sint
Pauluskerk," he said.

"Inside the church?"

"Yes. I have two men inside."

"Two men inside? Are you nuts? They cause any trouble inside that church
and I'll never hear the end of it. What were you thinking?"

"There are too many exits and I don't have enough men here. Theo's guys
are following us and I gotta keep two of mine to keep track of them in case they
make a move."

"Then get more men."

"I tried, but it's kinda short notice. That Vermeulen is sure a pain in the ass."

"That he is, indeed. I'm starting to think we should just let him go. He isn't worth the aggravation."

"How are we going to get Theo's files then?"

"We should just grab Theo and put the screws on him. He's weak and won't last long."

"Yeah, but won't that get Mesman on your case?" Fredi said. "If anything happens to Theo, Mesman knows who's behind it."

"Well, it could've been a lot of people. Besides, I'm not planning on killing him. Couldn't do that to Nora."

"So what do you want me to do?"

"Get those men out of the church. Pull the other men away from Theo's men and have them watch the doors. Follow Vermeulen and wait for the right opportunity. And if Theo's men interfere, get them out of the picture."

* * *

THEO VINKE SAT IN HIS HOUSE and waited for updates. If he'd been in a better state of mind, he might have thought himself to be a general conducting the battle from behind the lines, marshaling his troops, sending them to the right spot, initiating all the appropriate maneuvers.

Except, he wasn't. He had no troops, just five men who couldn't find their own dicks with their trousers down. He wasn't directing the battle, he was reacting to random calls that kept him in the dark as much as they revealed.

Vermeulen's latest trick—escaping in an ambulance—was another painful reminder that the man had outwitted him at every turn. And that only deepened his fury. He wanted Vermeulen dead so much, his whole nervous system was vibrating as if he'd touched a high voltage wire.

Finally, the phone rang and Theo almost dropped it as he grabbed it from his desk.

"Yeah, you better got some good news," he said.

"Kinda."

"Whaddya mean, kinda?"

"He ran into the Sint Pauluskerk."

"Run after him."

"Beukes's men are already in there."

"How come they got there first?"

"Because they were closest to him. You told us to stay back and watch for the right moment."

"Vermeulen's getting into the ambulance was the right moment."

"You wanted us to yank him off the stretcher with the EMTs right there?" The disbelief in the man's voice was thick as fog.

"Well, it's too late now. Go into the church."

"And do what?"

"Grab him. If Beukes's men get in the way, ice 'em."

"In the church?"

"What? You worried about the devil? Trust me, you ain't got no chance of getting into heaven, might as well make hell worthwhile."

"Tell you what, Boss. Why don't you come down and do it yourself? I'm quitting."

"What?" Theo swallowed too fast and his saliva went down the wrong tube. That made things worse. After a coughing fit that took his breath away, he managed to croak, "What did you say to me?"

"I said I'm not going to kill anyone inside a church. If you're so eager to do it, go ahead. But, think about it, Boss. It's going to come back to bite you. Do you really want the federal police after you for ordering a hit inside a church?"

The man was right, but his insolence couldn't go unpunished.

"If I wanted advice, I'd ask someone who could give it, not some numbskull like you," Theo said. "You think you're the only hired gun on the market? I can get loads more and they're smarter than you and your lot."

"Sure you can, but they ain't here. I am. I'll go inside and observe, but I won't pull a gun inside a church. You don't like it, get one of those guys you're bragging about."

That asshole was smarter than Theo had expected. Must've been a union man at one point. He knew when he had his boss over a barrel. Theo gritted his teeth, but he took a bite from the sour apple he'd been handed.

"Okay, sorry, my temper got the better of me. Yeah. Go inside and keep an eye on things. Once they move, keep up. And let me know if anything happens."

* * *

ONE OF BEUKES'S MEN had started climbing the stairs to the pulpit when the other man's phone buzzed. He answered. It was Fredi Kuiper

"Get out of the church, now," Fredi said. "Two of Theo's men are moving in. I don't want a confrontation inside the church. Hurry."

The man told his buddy to come down.

"Theo's men are closing in. Fredi wants us to meet these yahoos outside the main entrance."

"What about Vermeulen?"

The man shrugged, "Beats me. Not for me to worry about. The boss calls the shots."

The two men hurried through the nave to the massive doors under the organ balcony. They each opened one and stood face to face with Theo's guys. For a long moment they stared at each other without saying a word. When the tension had gotten palpable, Beukes's man said, "Let's take this outside. No reason to have a fight inside the church."

Theo's guys nodded and stepped aside to let the other two pass. Once they'd closed the doors, the four looked at each other.

"Where's Vermeulen?" one of Theo's men said.

"Still inside," Beukes's man said.

"Are you sure?"

"Pretty sure."

"You see him?"

"Not really."

"How can you be sure?"

"Did you see him leave?"

Theo's man shook his head.

"Neither did we, so he's got to be inside," Beukes's man said

They stood, unsure what to do next. A few pedestrians walked past. A delivery van inched by, the driver looking for an address on the other side of the street. Fredi came jogging past the van.

"Everything cool here?" he said.

The four men nodded.

"Good, let's keep it that way. What are your orders?"

"Kill Vermeulen," Theo's man said.

"Isn't that a little over the top?"

"You're telling me."

"Are you going to?"

"Not if I can help it. Theo is nuts."

"Let's make a deal. We all make sure Vermeulen doesn't get away. Whoever sees him calls the others and we detain him. My boss wants to talk to him."

"How does that help me with Theo?"

"Why don't we let my boss handle that? Once we have Vermeulen, Beukes is going to get together with Theo and they can sort out their beef. No use us putting the crosshairs of the police on our backs for Theo's vendetta."

The two Theo men looked at each other, obviously liking the idea, but hesitating.

"Tell you what," Fredi said. "We'll say you all put up a good fight but you were outmanned. I got three more men waiting? You?"

"Two more, but I don't know where they are."

"It's not like you got a lot of choice."

* * *

VERMEULEN HEARD THE TWO MEN DISCUSSING their new orders and exhaled in relief. His assumption had been right. There were two teams after him and they weren't cooperating. Good to know. Now he needed to get out of that church and find a way to get to Kapellen and see Theo's mother.

Nora had told him that Theo despised his mother. She couldn't be more wrong. Everything he'd learned about Theo told him that, deep down, he was a momma's boy. His father had been distant, stern and didn't approve of his direction, his mother was the opposite. Vermeulen could imagine how he craved that attention. As he grew up, the macho culture of the crime world meant he had to pretend he didn't want it, but that didn't change the nature of their relationship.

The regular visits were an obvious clue. He was complaining, but anyone who despised their mother wouldn't bother visiting. There was also no reason to stop visiting her. Vermeulen was sure he went to see his mum, but didn't want Nora to know about it. The reason? Jordi Vanderfeld's secret files.

First, he had to get out of Sint Pauluskerk. He peered over the edge of the pulpit. The faithful on the chairs were looking down or forward. It was as good a moment as any. He exited the pulpit carefully and hurried towards the organ and the exit doors. His pursuers would be watching all exits, so he had to figure out a diversion that would keep them occupied long enough to get outside.

One idea was calling the police and claiming there was a man with a gun in the church. That'd be one hell of a diversion, but it would be difficult escaping from the church once the police had set up their perimeter.

Fortunately, he didn't have to call in the cavalry. Just to the left of the exit and three steps down was a tiled passage. He followed the passage and ended up in a small church garden. The south and west side were delimited by the backs of houses. To the north stood the church and a stone path lined with elaborate stone figures of angels let back to an artificial grotto with a statue of the Virgin Mary attached to the transept. It was blocked by an iron gate. Not the way out. That left the east. There, a simple stone wall separated the garden from whatever lay beyond. It was the only possibility.

Climbing up the wall wasn't too hard. The rough stone offered enough footholds. Once on top, he saw that the other half of the church bordered a paved area, like a small-town square. On it stood a few cars. That meant there had to be an exit. The only obstacle were the brambles right below him. The last thing he wanted was showing up at the care facility in Kapellen with torn and dirty clothes.

He found the best spot, climbed down and made his way to the square and stopped near one of the cars to brush himself off. He looked a bit worse for wear, but not disheveled. Now for the exit. The obvious path led around the back to the very passage he'd used to get into the church in the first place. That's where they'd be waiting for him. The path was too narrow for the cars. There was another passage under one of the houses lining the square. He ran to it, peered around the corner and saw that nobody was waiting for him there.

A couple of corners later, he stopped to call Dekker. He needed her car. She didn't answer the phone. He turned back to see if anyone was following him and he saw two men a block away. They started running. Damn. He hurried to the end of the block, turned left and then back to Sint Paulusstraat, the closest thoroughfare. There'd better be a taxi.

There wasn't, but the next best thing. A tram had just arrived. He climbed on and started walking forward. If the tram didn't leave before his pursuers had a chance to get on, he wanted to be able to get off again. But the tram left right after he got on. He caught his breath and settled into a seat. Closer to the city center, he saw a taxi stand and got off.

The cab driver didn't know of any assisted living facility in Kapellen but Vermeulen told him to start driving anyway. He settled in the rear seat and used his phone to search for the facility's address. It turned out there were two. He called each and inquired about visiting hours. The first receptionist told him he was welcome to come before six in the evening and asked who he was planning on visiting. He gave them the name of Theo's mother, Heidi Vinke. She told him that no one by that name lived there. The second told him that Mrs. Vinke would be available, but that visiting hours ended at five-thirty. That gave him an hour and a half, plenty of time to find what he was looking for. He gave that address to the cab driver and a half hour later he got out in front of a villa not too far from the train station. It was four-thirty.

CHAPTER THIRTY-SIX

A GOOD BOY

————◆————

VERMEULEN DIDN'T KNOW WHAT TO EXPECT, but it wasn't the once stately mansion that had been converted into a care home by amateurs. The outside looked like a weekend projects that had been abandoned halfway through. The plywood ramp that was supposed to make the stairs to the grand entrance handicap accessible looked too fragile to be a professional conversion. Its handrail didn't look strong enough to support a child, never mind an adult with dementia.

The structure was longer than it was tall. The roof was a low-slung affair of red tiles that were covered with moss. The second floor jutted through the roof, dormer style. The walls were covered with stucco and featured large windows. At one point it could have been the estate of some minor gentry. Vermeulen climbed up to the landing, noticing that the aluminum rails didn't match the style of the house at all. He opened the door and saw right away that the conversion was worse than the ramp indicated. The inside of what had once been a grand entry hall had been subdivided with wallboard that made a feeble attempt to match the angles of the ceiling. The reception desk stood so close to the door that the woman behind it would be permanently freezing from the winter draft.

"Good morning, may I help you?" she said with a smile. She had blonde hair, blue eyes and a fresh face. Her white coat sent the unmistakable signal that this was a medical facility. Her name tag read, "Lore Jansen." Given the shoddy construction, Vermeulen knew he had entered a low-cost facility and half expected the type of grumpy employees one usually found there.

"Yes, you may," he said. "I'm here to visit Heidi Vinke."

"Are you family?"

"Uh, yes. I'm a nephew of hers."

"Your name?"

"Valentin Vermeulen."

The woman opened a book, turned a few pages and slid her index finger past the lines until she found what she was looking for. She looked up, a frown on her face.

"You're not on the visitors' list."

"Oh, I didn't know there was one."

"Of course, we are a facility for dementia patients. If we don't control access, all kinds of swindlers will try to exploit these poor folks."

Like me, Vermeulen thought. But he said, "Can you check again? Theo told me I could come and visit."

"Sorry. The list is very short. Just one name."

Vermeulen rubbed his chin. "I don't understand, I called Theo and, like I said, he told me it was okay for me to come. He must've forgotten to put my name on the list. He hasn't called, has he?"

"I wouldn't know, the receptionist is out sick. I do know he usually visits in person."

"What a devoted son. I wonder if you could make an exception. I'm visiting from New York and I won't be able to come back. It's been years since I saw Aunt Heidi."

"New York, eh? What's that like?" the woman said, newly interested in the stranger standing before her.

"It's wonderful. I mean there are problems like in all cities, but I love living there."

"Sounds great," she said with a dreamy look in her eyes. "I've always wanted to go to America, but I've never managed. Time and money, you know how it is."

Vermeulen agreed. "Yeah. Sometimes you just have to say, 'I'm going.' There are always reasons not to go. Just decide to go. You'll love it." He handed her his private card. "If you ever manage to come across, you can stay with us. We have a nice guest room on the upper westside. It's a great base for exploring the city."

"Really?"

"Why not. From one *Antwerpenaar* to another. Besides, you're taking care of Aunt Heidi. It's one way I can repay your kindness just a little."

She took the card and inspected it. It only contained his name, his email address and his phone number. No chance she could show up at the door unannounced.

"That's so nice of you."

"Don't mention it. Well, do you think I could at least sneak inside the room and squeeze her hand?"

She made a face.

"We're short staffed today. The receptionist and one of the orderlies are out sick. I'm a nurse but had to staff the desk, so the other nurses are extra busy."

"Oh my. That must make your job even harder," he said. "You can't leave the desk just for a minute?"

"No, I can't. Let me see if one of the nurses can help."

She picked up the phone and dialed a short number.

"Yeah, hi Lia, it's Lore at the front desk. There's a visitor for Mrs. Vinke, can you escort him to her room? It's just to say hello."

There was some back and forth, but in the end, Lore Jansen frowned and said to him, "She's busy."

"What about an orderly? It'll just be for a moment."

She sighed, but said, "It's not procedure, but since you came from so far . . ."

She took him past several partitioned offices to a broad stone staircase with carved marble newel posts. After all that slipshod remodeling, Vermeulen saw what the original mansion must have been like. The second floor showed the same signs of subdivisions. New doors were cut through the wall that didn't match the original ones. A young man with a ponytail, wearing green scrubs was mopping the floors near the middle of the hallway.

"Hey Leon," Jansen said. "This is Mr. Vermeulen, he's here to visit Heidi Vinke, can you accompany him? Nobody else is available and it's just to say hello."

Leon didn't look very happy but nodded anyway. "Come on, then," he said and pointed to a door down the hall.

"Don't stay too long," Jansen said.

Leon opened a door at the middle of the corridor and let Vermeulen enter.

An old woman was sitting in a chair by a window. Strands of limp white hair framed a pale face. Her blue eyes focused on something far, far away. She wore a cotton dress that seemed thin for the time of year, but the room was overly hot.

Although a new wall basically cut the once grand window in half, the room on the whole looked comfortable enough.

"Good afternoon, Heidi," Leon said "We have a visitor for you."

Heidi Vinke looked at them, confusion in her eyes.

"Is that you Frans?" she said. "You're looking nice."

"No Aunt Heidi, it's Valentin, your nephew."

"I don't know any Valentin."

"Of course you do. You remember, Frans's sister's son."

The confusion in her face got more pronounced. She looked at the orderly, then back to Vermeulen. "Frans has a sister?"

"Yes, don't you remember," Valentin said. "I'm visiting from America and wanted to stop and say hello."

"America." Her face lit up. "Frans always dreamed of America. When we were first married, he always talked about taking me, but he never did."

"Ah, that's too bad. Mind if I sit a moment?" Vermeulen said.

"Who are you again?"

"I'm Valentin, Aunt Heidi. Your nephew."

Heidi Vinke nodded.

That must've been enough for Leon because he said he'd be right outside, mopping.

"Thank you very much. I won't be long," Vermeulen said.

Leon left the door open and Vermeulen sat down in the other chair.

The room was small and there weren't a lot of places a stack of documents could be hidden.

"Theo comes to visit often?" he said.

Heidi looked at him with suspicious eyes.

"Theo is a good boy," she said.

"I know he is, swell guy, all around. How often does he come?"

She pursed her lips. "He's a good boy."

Vermeulen smiled. "I know. Does he visit you?"

"Yes, he visits."

"Oh what a good son he is."

"Yes. He visits. A good son."

"When did he come the last time?"

She wrinkled her forehead. "He comes sometimes."

"Did he come last month? In September?"

Her eyes lit up, "Yes, Theo comes in September."

"Good, did he bring you a present?"

"Theo comes in September. Theo comes in August. Theo is a good boy."

"Did he bring you a present."

Her face darkened again. "A present?"

"Yes," Vermeulen said.

She thought for a while, then shook her head.

"Maybe you forgot?"

"Yes, I forgot. I often forget."

"Are you cold, Aunt Heidi? Let me get you a sweater."

Vermeulen got up and looked into the hallway. Leon had moved on with his mop.

Vermeulen pulled the door closer and opened the wardrobe. It didn't contain much. On the right side a few changes of underwear, a few tops and sweaters and a gray cardigan. On the left side three skirts, a coat, two pairs of shoes at the bottom. But no box or bag that might contain Jordi's files. Nora Vanderfeld was right. And he had just waisted precious hours.

"What are you doing in my closet?" she said.

"Oh aunty, just looking for a sweater to keep you warm. It's cold."

"I'm fine. Who are you?"

She sounded different and Vermeulen turned to look at her, the cardigan in his hand.

"I don't know you," she said. "And I don't have a nephew because Frans didn't have a sister. Unless you tell me who you are and what you are doing here, I'm going to scream."

Her brain must have decided to switch to lucidity, because Heidi Vinke was completely present.

"Aunt Heidi, how can you say that? Of course Frans had a sister, and she had a son, and that's me."

His attempt to sow confusion didn't work.

"You can talk all day long, but that doesn't make it real. What are you after? I don't have any money and Theo manages my affairs. Get out of here."

"Do you know that Theo isn't a good son, but a gangster?"

"Of course, the apple doesn't fall far from the tree."

"Did he bring anything on his last visit?"

"That's none of your business."

"I'm afraid it is. Your son is trying to kill me. And I'm not too keen to help him with that. So where is it?"

"I'm not going to tell you."

Her eyes did. He closed the wardrobe and went to the bed. Sure enough, between the bed and the night stand stood a portable file box, half hidden behind the photo frames that stood on the shelves of the night stand.

Vermeulen grabbed the box. Heidi Vinke became very agitated. He put down the box and draped the cardigan over her shoulders.

"It's okay aunty. I just have to make sure that this gets to the right person."

This wasn't the right way to treat her, but he saw no other way to get the files. He took her hand. "It's nothing to worry about. I'm doing Theo a huge favor." He squeezed her hand gently. She responded to the touch by sighing. As she breathed out, the vacant look returned to her eyes. "Theo is a good boy," she said.

"He is. And I'm making sure it stays that way."

A car came to a sharp stop outside, sending gravel skittering. He looked out the window and saw a black Mercedes and two men getting out. They were the men who'd taken him to Beukes the night before. How'd they even know he was here? They couldn't have followed him. Had Theo paid the staff to alert him when someone came to visit his mother? Nah, it was Beukes's men who showed up. He grabbed the file box and looked out the door.

There was another staircase at the other end of the corridor. Beukes's men would come up both ways. Loud voices came from downstairs. He could hear Lore yelling at the men. Near the end of the corridor, Leon was still mopping. He heard the noise and went downstairs. Vermeulen ran after him. When he heard steps on the stairs, he opened a door that didn't have a name next to the room number. It opened into a dark room that smelled of disinfectant. He didn't sense any human presence. Maybe an empty room waiting for a new occupant. He closed the door.

Leon yelled. Someone hurried past the door, followed by another person. Outside another car stopped. He looked out of the window and saw a green Peugeot right behind the Mercedes. He hadn't seen those men before, but there was no doubt in his mind that they were Theo's minions.

He waited another beat and pushed the door open. Using the cover of the open door, he took long steps to the staircase and hurried downstairs. Lore was talking to the two men. Since there was no yelling, Vermeulen figured Theo had indeed made a deal with the staff. He made a dash for the door, but she saw him and yelled, "There he is."

The men came after him. One of them was fast, faster than Vermeulen. No way he could make it outside. He waited until the man was right behind him and spun around, swinging the file box like a roundhouse punch. It hit the man in the chest. He fell backward to the floor. The handle ripped off the box and it flew to the ground. The second man stumbled over the prone figure on the floor. That gave Vermeulen time to step sideways and pick up the file box. Without a handle he had to clutch it to his chest. With the first man still trying to catch his breath, the second one came toward him swinging his right fist. Vermeulen used the box to deflect the blow. The impact of the strike cracked the plastic of the file box. Vermeulen couldn't wait for another hit. It would shatter the file box and the files would be all over the floor. A swift kick to the man's kneecap stopped him in his tracks.

Vermeulen ran out the front door and got outside before his pursuers could regroup. He jumped into the green Peugeot that was parked behind the black Mercedes. They'd left the key, ready for a fast getaway. That suited Vermeulen just fine. He locked the doors, started the engine and shot out of the parking lot. The file box sat on the passenger seat. The fact that they found him was still a puzzle to him. His phone was the logical answer, but he couldn't conceive of any way Beukes could have gotten his new number, and that didn't account for Theo Vinke's goons.

CHAPTER THIRTY-SEVEN

BAD REPUTATION

———————◆———————

VERMEULEN IGNORED THE PROHIBITION of using his phone while driving and dialed Nora Vanderfeld's number. She answered on the second ring.

"I have your father's documents," he said.

"You do?" There was surprise in her voice. "Where did you find them?"

"In Theo's mother's room."

"In Kapellen?"

"Yeah."

"I want them."

It was Vermeulen's turn to be surprised. "Didn't we agree that getting rid of the files was the best choice? An incinerator sounds like the best place for them."

"I don't remember ever having agreed with you. You might want to rethink your plan. Those files would be better used for leverage."

"Leverage for what?"

"Your life?"

Vermeulen almost veered into the oncoming lane. "Are you threatening me?"

"What makes you think that? I do want my property back. A simple exchange, you know, supply and demand. I demand the files and you supply them. Nobody gets hurt."

"I thought you wanted to protect Theo."

"I do, from himself. But that doesn't mean I don't want my insurance back."

"What are you planning to do with those files?"

"Wouldn't you like to know. Let's meet at my house. Theo isn't here at the moment."

"I don't think so. Besides, you'll have to find me first."

"That's going to be easier than you think."

Vermeulen ended the call. Near the interchange with the A1 freeway, he pulled into a gas station and stopped at the far corner of the lot. This was it, then. He had no allies, no friends. Instead he had what everybody wanted. Not a good spot to be in. He dialed Tessa's number. She didn't answer. Of course, he had a new phone number. He sent her an SMS to that effect. A moment later, his phone rang.

"Where the hell have you been? I've called you over and over. And why do you have a new number?"

"Sorry, sweetheart. Since we last talked, everything has gone sideways. They came for me at the B&B and I made a run for it. Once outside, Beukes's men scooped me up and brought me to his house. I got away from him and have been on the run for the past twelve hours. Then I managed to get my hands on those files everybody wants, and now they all are after me. The last person I thought was on my side just let me know that I better turn that stash over to her or be killed."

"What's your plan?"

"I don't have one."

"Good that you called me."

"I didn't have time to call you earlier. I was always on the move. I haven't slept since the night before last."

"Listen, I have some really good news for you. You can prove that the memo is forged."

"Oh, yes? How?"

"The memo was written with the Calibri font."

"So what?"

"That's the default font for Microsoft Word."

"Sorry to be repeating myself, but so what?"

"It only became the default font for Word in 2007. It wasn't available before then. The memo is dated 2002. So it has to be a forgery. It couldn't have been written until after you'd already left Belgium for the UN."

Vermeulen took a deep breath and exhaled. Indeed, the first bit of good news in a week.

"You should contact that cop you thought was on your side," Tessa said. "She might be able to help you strategize."

"That's the best thing I've heard today. Let me do that."

"Are you still planning on coming home tomorrow?"

"I sure am, but that doesn't mean I'll actually make it. At least three different parties are busy devising alternate plans for me, and I don't quite know how to dissuade them from executing them. Let me call Dekker. Maybe she can help. Thanks for the good work on that font. When I get home, I'll properly thank you."

"You better."

He ended the call and dialed Dekker.

"I have proof that the memo was forged," he said when she answered.

"Okay, let me hear it."

"The font used in the memo wasn't released to the public until 2007. But the memo is dated 2002. So it was written after I had already left Antwerp."

There was a pause on the other end. Then, "Hang on."

A minute or so later, she came back and said, "You're right. That's great news."

"Should I call Mesman?" he said.

"Let me talk to him. You're not high on his list of trustworthy witnesses."

"We also don't know who sent the memo to Theo. It would help to sort that out."

"Do you have any ideas?"

"None."

"Well, find a place to have a cup of coffee and wait until I call you back."

"I can't do that. I have pretty much every faction of Antwerp's underworld on my heels."

"Why?"

"Because I have Jordi Vanderfeld's documents."

"You do? How'd you get those?"

"Long story. I'm thinking of destroying them. That way nobody gets them."

"Don't tell me. I can't be party to obstruction of justice."

"Okay, forget what I said. But please make Mesman see that the memo was forged."

"I'll try my best. In the meantime, good luck staying alive," she said.

At that moment the black Mercedes pulled behind him.

"Thanks, I'll need it. The bad guys just arrived."

He put the car in gear and shot back onto the road. He could hear the squeal of the other car following him back into the traffic and the cacophony of car horns registering everyone's complaints against the blatant violation of traffic rules. Vermeulen merged onto the A1, the four-lane freeway toward Antwerp. Traffic was dense and moved slowly. Vermeulen sought cover in the endless line of trucks that plied the right lane. It was no use. The Mercedes squeezed behind him. In the rearview mirror he recognized Beukes's driver behind the wheel of the other car. The man in the passenger seat had brought him to Beukes the night before. He needed a plan but his mind was preoccupied with managing way in the busy traffic.

His pursuers made no effort to pass him. They just followed him like a bad reputation. On his left, a bumper-to-bumper stream of cars passed. He'd figured traffic would be coming out of Antwerp at rush hour, not heading back into the city. Whatever the cause was, he was pretty much stuck between Beukes's men and a trailer carrying a forty-foot baby-blue container.

As they reached the city limits, a white Audi Q7 inched past Vermeulen. He looked over and saw a man who looked very much like Theo Vinke might look, thirteen years older. Vermeulen quickly looked away, but it was too late. Theo had recognized him and slowed to drive next to him. The driver behind Theo was clearly upset. He flashed his brights to get him to move out of the way or speed up. Theo was having none of it. The driver honked, impatient. In response, Theo slowed down.

Vermeulen thanked whoever was in charge of the universe that Theo was being his annoying self because the slowdown opened a gap in the stream of traffic on the left lane. Vermeulen saw his chance, floored the accelerator and swooped into the left lane with only inches to spare between the trailer and his bumper. His glee lasted only seconds because he reached the next car and had to slow down again. Rush hour didn't permit a high-speed pursuit. The white Audi caught up and hung on his bumper with the same persistence the Mercedes had. Vermeulen, copying Theo's move, tapped his brake. The Audi fell back a few yards. Vermeulen sped up again. It made no difference. There was no way out. All he could do was follow the road.

Finally a sign indicated an exit. Anything had to be better than this slow-motion car chase. He braked, forcing Theo to slow down as well. Then he floored it again, shot past the baby blue container and the tractor pulling it and squeezed into the gap in front of the truck. Its driver didn't like that move at all and honked. It sounded like a tugboat had joined the traffic.

Vermeulen stayed in the right lane until he was three-hundred meters from the exit. He steered to the break down lane and accelerated. Passing the next truck on the right, he saw a car blinking its turn signal to take the exit. Not expecting someone racing along the breakdown lane, the driver eased into the exit lane. Vermeulen blew his horn and flashed his brights. The other driver didn't notice in time. Vermeulen steered to the right. With a terrible screech, the Peugeot scraped along the rail, but he got past the other car.

Theo's Audi flashed past him, still in the left lane. At least one pursuer less. Beukes's driver, on the other hand, had no trouble taking the exit ramp. At least there was one car between Vermeulen and the gangsters. He found himself on a street he didn't know. Not having a plan meant that he just followed the street. Getting to the old port was probably a good idea. There were lots of small streets where he could try to lose his tail.

The street made a sweeping turn to the left. Vermeulen saw water again. It was one of the older docks, but he still didn't know where he was. He crossed a bridge over a short canal between the docks. On the other side, the street curved to the right and headed straight for a large building partially encased in scaffolding. Vermeulen finally knew where he was. He'd reached the Port of Antwerp headquarters.

Beukes's men were still behind him, but weren't making any attempt to stop him. He turned left onto Mexicostraat at the next intersection. It led to a double bridge across another canal, one for each lane of the road. They were massive steel behemoths, rolling lift bridges that were built a century earlier, with heavy machinery to raise the bridges. Vermeulen didn't care much how it functioned, but he did care that the structures blocked his view of the other end. Had they not, he might have seen Theo Vinke's white Audi before he entered the bridge on the right side. When he did see the car, it was too late. The Audi pulled into the single lane at the far end. He stepped on the brake and the battered Peugeot slid to a stop in the middle of the bridge. He looked back, Beukes's men already had blocked the other end. He was trapped.

Chapter Thirty-Eight

Wimbledon

———◆———

There weren't a lot of options. He slid down in the seat and called Dekker. She answered almost immediately.

"Did you persuade Mesman that the memo was forged?" he said.

"I told him. He nodded and told me he'd get back to me. I think he's on the fence."

"Is the arrest warrant still active?"

"As far as I know."

"Okay, good to know. It's decision time. I'm standing on a bridge at the end of Mexicostraat. Theo is waiting for me at one end and Beukes's men have blocked the other end. I don't know if either one will use force, but I'm not getting out of here without handing over these documents."

"Call the police."

"Yeah. That thought has crossed my mind. I'll sort it out. If I get arrested, I'll call on you for help."

He ended the call. The standoff hadn't changed. Theo stood next to his Audi's open door, speaking on his phone. He was probably talking to his wife. The last conversation with Nora Vanderfeld told him the two were back on the same team. He looked back and saw that Beukes's men had gotten out of their car too. One of them was on the phone.

* * *

Bastiaan Beukes wasn't happy with the way his men had handled the matter. He prided himself on selecting the best men in town. But Vermeulen had outfoxed them at every turn. The escape from the museum was one thing. Fredi was right not to mess with the emergency services. It would create bad blood for a long time. But being outsmarted at the old people's home in Kapellen? There was no excuse for that. He'd told Fredi not to underestimate Vermeulen, but that's exactly what happened.

When the phone rang again, he was prepared for more bad news. To his surprise, it wasn't as bad as he'd expected. Vermeulen on a bridge, Theo on one end and Fredi on the other. A standoff, for sure, but everything was still in play. He decided to call Vermeulen.

When the man answered, he said, "What is it you want?"

Vermeulen sounded angry when he asked how he'd gotten his new phone number.

"Come on, man. It didn't take long to find the place where you bought the phone, and those burners are issued with consecutive numbers. So, piece of cake. But let's talk. You're stuck on a bridge. I'm your only ticket out of there. Tell me what you want."

"I'm not negotiating with you."

"I don't think that's an option. Theo wants to blow your brains out. He isn't going to make you a deal. And the judge? He wants to lock you up. I'm all that's left."

"Mesman isn't going to lock me up because I can prove that the memo was forged."

"Well, how about that? But it doesn't change the situation you're in right now."

"And what are you going to do for me?"

"In exchange for those papers? I'll get you out of the country and back home to New York."

"I don't believe you."

"Listen Valentin. I could've had you killed a hundred times in the last week. I didn't. That should tell you something. All I want is those documents . . ."

"Hang on, I got another call."

Beukes stood in his office, his mouth open. Had Vermeulen really just hung up on him? He dialed Fredi.

"Go over to him and get those documents. Your guy will keep an eye on Theo. Shoot the fucker if you need to."

"Who? Vermeulen?"

"No, Theo. But, yeah, Vermeulen, too, if he behaves like an idiot."

* * *

THE NEXT PERSON CALLING WAS NORA VANDERFELD.

"I don't know what you're aiming at," she said. "But those papers are mine and I want them back. So, quit playing around and give them to Theo."

"Why would you want Theo to have them? Didn't we agree that this was a mistake?"

"Because I talked to him and told him he had a choice. Either I'm in charge of everything, or I'll tell the police about his little money laundering operation and divorce him. It didn't take very long for him to choose the right thing. If there's one thing I know about Theo, it's that he doesn't like to work. He chose ease over pride."

"What do I get out of the deal?"

"You get to stay alive."

"That doesn't sound very convincing. The papers are my only insurance. Besides, Beukes has made me a far better offer."

"I wouldn't trust Beukes farther than I could throw him."

"Ah. But you expect me to trust you? Sorry. No deal."

"What are you going to do?"

"Well, you'll find out."

Vermeulen ended the call and dialed Tessa's number. The phone rang for a while, then rolled over to her voicemail. He left a message telling her that he loved her, then dialed the emergency number. The emergency operator answered. He quickly explained the situation on the bridge and added that there was an arrest warrant out for him. The operator was thoroughly professional and told him that police were on their way.

He looked up and saw Beukes's righthand man coming toward him. He turned and, sure enough, Theo was on the move too. This prize was too important for him. Except, Theo was alone. His minions were still looking for their car. The second Beukes man had already positioned himself behind some steel girders. It gave him a clean shot at Vermeulen and Theo while being well protected. Good team work, Vermeulen thought in the second before the severity of the situation fully sank in.

Beukes's man was about fifteen feet away when he shouted, "Get back in your yuppie mobile, Theo. There's nothing here for you."

Theo pulled a pistol from his pocket. "You aren't telling me what to do, Fredi. I'm my own man, not someone's lackey."

"Yeah, and you're gonna be your own dead man. My pal has got you covered."

"But not fast enough that I couldn't put a bullet through you first."

"Come on Theo, we both know you're not gonna do that. Get back into your car."

"The hell I will."

They sound like a B-movie, Vermeulen thought, watching the exchange between the two like a spectator at Wimbledon.

"Hand me the case, Vermeulen," Fredi said.

"No, hand it to me," Theo said.

Vermeulen had no intention of doing either. He didn't talk about it. He opened the lid of the file box. In it, were tightly packed folders full of papers, some of them yellowed with age. Between the two bridges he could see a narrow strip of water. He stepped toward the railing.

"What are you doing?" Fredi shouted.

A shot rang out. The bulled hit one of the steel girders and whined into the canal.

"The next one is gonna hit you," Fredi said to Vermeulen.

Theo ran forward and rushed Vermeulen, who sidestepped the obvious maneuver. Theo crashed into the railing. The commotion made the trigger finger of the man with the gun even itchier and another shot shattered the window of the Peugeot. Theo had gathered himself again and lunged once more at Vermeulen. This time Fredi got into the game and grabbed Theo. The two struggled, but Fredi clearly had the better skills. The gunman moved closer, but the melee was too tight for a shot at Theo.

Vermeulen knew this was the only chance he'd get and he upended the file box to dump all the papers into the canal. The tightly packed folders didn't slide out as he expected. He pulled one of them. The thin cardboard tore. He grabbed another one. Same result. He shook the damn box. Nothing.

The two men realized what he was up to. Fredi let go of Theo to stop Vermeulen. Theo used his chance and hit Fredi hard in the neck. Fredi slumped onto the street. The gunman finally got a clear shot and fired. The bullet hit Theo in the left arm. He screamed. Stumbled for a moment but lunged again at Vermeulen. Theo was slow on the uptake and Vermeulen simply sidestepped the assault again. Theo tumbled onto the bridge deck.

Fredi had gotten up, his eyes speaking murder as he pulled a pistol from his pocket and went after Theo. That suited Vermeulen just fine. His fingers finally got some purchase on the slippery cardboard of a folder. He pulled it out and dumped it into the canal. As it unfolded, the pages fluttered in the wind and scattered over the water like a flock of terns. The rest of the papers in the file box gave way too and the entire memoirs of Jordi Vanderfeld slid into the canal. The heavier folders sank. Individual pages floated on the water. Vermeulen dropped the file box last.

Nobody moved. Fredi looked at the paper scattered over the dark green surface below him, his face more in wonder than anger. Theo held his arm, his face distorted in a mixture of rage and disbelief. He charged Vermeulen one more time, but stopped in his track when he heard the wail of approaching sirens.

Fredi heard it too and stepped back. His accomplice raced back to the Mercedes, but Fredi lingered near the steel girder of the bridge.

Theo looked at Vermeulen with a vicious sneer, raised the gun and aimed it at Vermeulen's chest.

"I've been waiting for this moment for a long time," he said. "Finally, you pay for what you did."

"You do that and you'll go in prison for a long time. Is that really worth it?"

"I don't care."

"You should care. The memo was forged. I have proof for that. You will be killing me for no reason at all."

"You forced my father to become a rat. Even if you didn't leak his name, he would've gotten killed because he was a rat. It is your fault."

"You don't know the whole story. Beukes knew all about it and made Frans give us false information. Why you are lionizing your father? The man didn't care much about you, did he? You didn't get any support from him. It was your mum who kept you going. Don't try to be like him, Theo."

Theo stood there chewing his lip, his eyes dull, his face blank as if he hadn't expected that question. The gun no longer pointed at Vermeulen's heart.

"Your father never amounted to much," Vermeulen said. "Not as a crook and certainly not as a father. But he knew that."

"Don't talk shit about my father." Theo's hand with the gun rose again.

"I'm not. I'm just stating what everybody knew at the time. But he did one good thing. He tried hard to keep you away from his life of crime. That's why he was so distant. He knew it wasn't a good future for you. So rather than trying to be like your father, you should be grateful to him."

Theo chewed his lip some more. His eyes darted from Vermeulen to the gun and back.

"You have an opportunity here," Vermeulen said. "You can turn over a new leaf, go back to your wife and help her with her business. Despite everything, she loves you."

The screech of the sirens was getting louder. Theo pointed the gun at the deck of the bridge.

"It's your choice, Theo. Throw that gun over the railing and start over. Not many people get that chance. Use it."

Theo didn't follow Vermeulen's advice. Instead he raised his gun again. "You can talk all you want. I don't care anymore," Theo said. "Nora is better off without me anyway. I only know that I owe it to my father."

He aimed at Vermeulen's heart.

Vermeulen didn't move. This was it. He was out of words, out of options. He'd tried to talk sense into Theo and he'd failed. Theo was a lost soul, who would take Vermeulen down with him. He closed his eyes

A shot rang out.

Vermeulen didn't feel anything.

Is this want dying is like? It can't be. I'm still thinking.

A gun clattered onto the bridge. Vermeulen opened his eyes.

Theo grasped his chest with a surprised look on his face. He stared past Vermeulen. His face froze and he dropped on the deck.

Fredi said, "Next time don't wait for someone else to save your bacon."

Vermeulen heard the squealing tires of the Mercedes as it raced away.

Moments later, two police cars skidded to a stop near the white Audi.

Two officers raced toward him, guns drawn. One yelled, "Get on the ground, now." Vermeulen was more than happy to comply. When one of the cops finally cuffed his wrists, he said, more to himself, "What took you so long?"

CHAPTER THIRTY-NINE

PENSION FUND

---◆---

V ERMEULEN WAS A LAWYER AND HE KNEW when to speak and when to keep mum during the police interrogation. He asked to see Dekker instead of a lawyer. Better to have someone official on his side. They brought him to the holding cell. It was eleven that night when she finally came to see him in prison. She could only shake her head when they sat in an interview room.

"Man, of all the stunts you could've pulled, dumping those files into the canal has got to take the cake. Why would you do that?"

"It was the only way. The situation was tense, guns drawn on both sides. I prefer being alive in a jail cell to being dead on a bridge."

"From what I heard, you were only moments away from being dead. What do you want me to do?"

"Get me out of here, for one. Remember, I have a plane to catch."

"And what makes you think I can do that?"

"Because you are outstanding and can make things happen."

She said, "Yeah, like you."

"Of course not, I was better."

"You were not. You bent the rules. I don't."

"I'm not going to argue my merits. I do need to get out of here, though. My plane leaves in fourteen hours and I would like a shower before I get on it."

"You better make peace with the possibility that you won't be on that plane."

"Why? I haven't done anything to warrant an arrest. The worst they can charge me with is littering and I'm happy to pay that fine. Everything else was the responsibility of others. You can call Mesman and tell him I'll sue him to kingdom come for issuing a false arrest warrant, for forcing me to come to Antwerp under false pretenses, for being in league with criminals and for forging that memo."

"You sure you want me to tell him that? You can prove that memo was forged but not that he forged it. Why would he?"

"I don't care if I can make that part stick or not, but I want him to know that his career path will be seriously compromised."

"Okay, I'll relay that message. I'll try my hardest to not gloat during that call."

The rest of the night was tedious. Since it wasn't a weekend, the number of drunks were mercifully limited. A couple of toughs joined the holding cell around two in the morning. They kept arguing over who'd have won the knife fight had the police not interrupted them. Since knife crimes now carried a significant penalty, their argument was simply idiotic. Vermeulen found a spot next to a stinky drunk and dozed on and off. At five in the morning, a cop came and called Vermeulen's name. After he approached the door, the cop told him he was free to go and opened the door.

That was it. No explanation, no statement. He got his phone, his cash and his passport back and found himself standing across from the *Stadspark*. He called Tessa to let her know that he was okay. She didn't answer, so he left a message. Next, he trolled for a taxi to take him back to the hotel where he'd left his suitcase after he fled from the Kennel. When he finally found one, it was already six.

Devahu was at the concierge desk. He never slept.

"Ah, there you are. I wondered if you'd skipped without paying the bill."

"I wouldn't do that. Besides, I think the prosecutor's office is paying for the room."

"They are? That's news to me. Anyway, someone left an envelope for you."

He handed it over to Vermeulen, who took it to his room. Inside he ripped open the envelop and found a single sheet.

I'm sorry. Jan.

Was that Smits apologizing for not giving him a ride back to the train station? That didn't make sense. Vermeulen shrugged, stripped off his clothes and spent the next twenty minutes in the shower. Afterwards he was tempted to take a nap, but was afraid he'd oversleep and miss the train to Schiphol. He put on fresh clothes, packed his suitcase, settled the bill—he was going to ask for a refund once he was back home—and took a taxi to *Centraal Station*.

After booking a ticket on the next Thalys to Schiphol, he decided to get some breakfast at a waffle stand in the station. It wasn't much, but his stomach was grateful for the calories. After all the turmoil of the last week, waiting for the train was a bit of a letdown. *I got chased all over Antwerp and I didn't even get a T-shirt.*

He was about to call Tessa with the good news when he saw Fredi approach. He got up, ready to make another run for it, but the man raised his hands, "Relax, Vermeulen, this is a friendly visit."

The man pulled up a chair. "I wasn't around thirteen years ago, but last week showed me that you could've beat Mr. Beukes back then, and you sure did this time around. He rarely admits defeat, but this morning, he told me so. Anyway, he asked me to bring you your phones."

Fredi handed over Vermeulen's regular phone and the first burner.

"Thanks for saving my life yesterday," Vermeulen said.

"Think nothing of it. I kinda knew Theo wasn't going to see reason. His brain's not wired that way."

"How does your boss feel about you killing Theo."

"He's fine with it. Always thought the guy held Nora back. He loves Nora as if she were his own daughter."

"Nora would not agree."

"It is what it is. Are you going home?" Fredi said.

"You better believe it. Antwerp just doesn't suit me."

"Ah, don't blame the city. It doesn't change. It's the people."

"You are right. Say, d'you know cop by the name of Jan Smits?"

"Sure do. Not my kinda guy, though. I like straight shooters, that guy's bent."

"How so?"

"Far as I know, he was in Jordi Vanderfeld's pocket from the get go."

"You mean he leaked police business to Vanderfeld?"

"Yeah."

"Even thirteen years ago?"

"As I said, from the get go."

"What happened after Vanderfeld died?"

'I don't know. Probably found someone else to sell his info too. Anyways, Bon voyage."

Fredi got up and headed for the exit.

Vermeulen used his own phone to call Dekker and thank her. She sounded no different from how she'd sounded twenty-four hours ago.

"Do you always call people at such early hours?" she said.

"It's not that early. Hey, I got out of jail."

"I know, that's why I only got two hours of sleep before you woke me. Mesman wasn't very happy when I called him in the middle of the night. But, as you requested, I made it clear that you were going to take legal steps for false imprisonment and forgery of evidence. He did a little huffing and puffing, but made the call to order the release."

"How did he react to the forgery claim?"

"Not nearly as emphatically as I had expected. He might have written it after all. I guess we'll never find out."

"Thank you for all you did. You went out of your way for me and for that I'm grateful. If you ever come to New York City, you'll have a place to stay."

"That better not be an empty promise, because I will take you up on it."

"Nope. I mean it."

"Are you on your way home?"

"Yup. Sitting at the station waiting for the train to Schiphol. Listen, something strange happened. First, I get a note at my hotel from Jan Smits, just saying, "I'm sorry." And then Fredi, Beukes's man tells me that Smits was on Vanderfeld's payroll for a long time. He must have been the leak that Timmerman always complained about. Do you know who's paying him now?"

"I didn't even know he was on the take. I'll tell internal affairs to check him out."

"Okay. Well, thanks again. And do come and visit."

"I will."

He'd barely ended the call when the second burner rang. Tessa was calling back.

"You are in the clear?" she said.

"I am. They released me from jail at five and told me I was free to go. I got a good shower and am on my way to the airport. No word from the judge, but Beukes sent his man to return my regular phone. A nice gesture, for what it's worth."

He could hear Tessa exhale.

"When are you going to pursue a less hazardous line of work?" she said.

"When my pension fund is large enough to support me when I get old."

"Don't gimme that. There are plenty of ways to pay into your pension fund that don't involve getting between two mob factions."

"Is that your way of telling me you were worried about me?"

"Yes, you idiot."

"Aww. Thanks, love. You know I don't do this on purpose."

"I'm not so sure. You end up in trouble all the time. That can't be an accident. I vote for a less hazardous way to build up your pension."

"I'll tell you when I find it. See you at home."

* * *

HE HAD JUST TAKEN HIS SEAT on the airplane when his phone rang again.

"It's me," Dekker said after he answered. "About Smits? I dug around a little. Turns out that earlier this year, Mesman must've heard that he took money from Vanderfeld. Mesman demanded an explanation. His voice was so loud, the secretaries heard it and, of course gossiped about it. But then everything went quiet again. I couldn't find any record of any investigation.

"I wonder if Mesman made a deal with Smits."

"I guess that will remain a mystery."

"Thanks for the info, though. See you soon in New York City, okay?"

"Sure. Safe journey."

Vermeulen ended the call and leaned back in his seat. He knew why Smits had send that apology. Mesman had made him write that memo. Smits may have traded information for cash, but forging a memo to implicate a former colleague was too much even for a bent cop.

The last call he made was to Gaby.

"Hi Dad, where are you?"

"I'm in the plane at Schiphol, on my way back home. The case is all sorted out and I'm in the clear. But that's not why I'm calling. I wanted to thank you. You are your father's daughter, at least when it comes to being stubborn, and I'm glad you were. Getting your mom and me in the same room was the sweetest thing you could have done."

"Thanks for saying that, Dad. Beating you in stubbornness is an impossible feat but I managed it, and having you admit to it, is like the whipped cream on top of the cake. I'm glad to have you two as my parents. Be safe, and give Tessa a big hug from me."

* * *

MICHAEL NIEMANN GREW UP IN A SMALL TOWN in Germany near the Dutch border. Crossing that border often instilled in him a curiosity about the larger world. He turned that curiosity into an academic career in International and African studies. Writing international thrillers has become another way to satisfy that curiosity. For more information, visit: www.michael-niemann.com.

Additional Valentin Vermeulen Thrillers

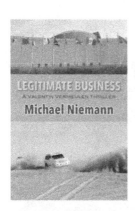

Vermeulen Stories by Michael Niemann

Big Dreams Cost Too Much

Africa Always Needs Guns

Some Kind of Justice